Stuart Courtman

Stuart moved to the Peak District in 2002 to live in a hamlet established in the eighteenth century industrial revolution. In 1865, the hamlet was described as "a small row of cottages, standing on a bleak and wild looking moor-like prominence, as if the buildings had been lifted out of the adjoining valley to look about them." That valley is dominated by Litton and Cressbrook cotton mills and Stuart was drawn into the fascinating history of the area. The research threw up many interesting facts but also left unanswered questions. Stuart's first novel *Blincoe's Progress* fills those gaps with a fiction set in the eighteenth century centred around local characters and events.

BLINCOE'S PROGRESS

Stuart Courtman

An imprint of Peak Platform
New Bridge, Calver
Hope Valley
Derbyshire
S32 3XT

First published by Jumping Fish 2011

Cover Design

Printed in India

A CIP catalogue record for this book is available from the British Library

This is a work of fiction based on real events and real people.

ISBN: 978-1-907219-25-5
www.peakplatform.com

ACKNOWLEDGEMENTS

I would like to thank those who have had the foresight to preserve the documents that I have had the opportunity of studying, especially the diaries of Parson Brown and two large boxes of research by Miss MacKenzie (both in Sheffield Archives). Complementing this are the fiery exchanges between Miss Mackenzie and Doctor Chapman regarding relative working conditions at Cressbrook and Litton mills, *Derbyshire Archaeological Journal,* which were especially interesting. Blincoe's main narrative, *A Memoir of Robert Blincoe* provides an insight into life and work in a cotton mill, although the reliability of this document has been questioned as it may not have been sanctioned by Blincoe, and it may not have been an accurate report of his situation.

I also want to thank my wife, Sandra, for her patience, her invaluable support, and the many hours of help that she gave as both reader and critic.

INTRODUCTION

In 2002, we bought a small terraced cottage at Littonslack: a hamlet comprising a row of ten terraced cottages near to Litton mill. The cottages were occupied in the late eighteenth century, although their precise age remains unknown. I began to research the history of the cottages, and this led me to its connections with Litton mill and the larger than life characters of Robert Blincoe, Parson Brown, Ellis Needham and William Newton, who were all living, and working, in the immediate area at the turn of the eighteenth century. Researching any history from this period is difficult and naturally there will always be gaps in the information. This novel fills those gaps and connects disparate pieces of information with a fictional tale.

The novel is set in North Derbyshire and covers the years 1796 to 1799 with Robert Blincoe, a cotton mill apprentice, as the main character. Many of the events in this novel are based on evidence from Blincoe's life. His childhood was spent in the workhouse at St. Pancras and later as an apprentice at Litton cotton mill. Whilst at Litton mill he was interviewed by John Brown, a journalist from Bolton for an article on child labour, and this was published in 1828 as weekly episodes in *The Lion,* a radical newspaper. It was then printed in 1832 as a book, *A Memoir of Robert Blincoe*. In 1833, Blincoe was interviewed by a Royal Commission that was central in reducing the working hours of children. There are some parallels between Blincoe's story and that of Oliver Twist; John Waller in his 2005 non-fiction work *The Real Oliver Twist*, (Icon Books, 2005) argues that Blincoe was Dickens' inspiration for Oliver Twist.

Other important characters in the novel, living and working in the immediate area at that time are: Parson Brown, Rector of Tideswell; Ellis Needham, owner of Litton mill, and William Newton, owner of Cressbrook mill. These people and the significant events that occur to them are consistent with historical documents. By the age of 24, Parson Brown was rector of Tideswell. He kept diaries for fifteen years all of which are now in Sheffield Archives. The mills owners, Ellis Needham and William Newton have been written about extensively, and in many popular commentaries of today, Needham emerges as a tyrant, whereas Newton is represented as a model employer.

The novel follows Blincoe during his working years at Litton mill, Parson Brown in his early years as Rector of Tideswell and the two mill owners, in particular Needham as he battles to create a success of his cotton spinning business at Litton mill.

Blincoe's Progress, is constructed around those fragments of historical facts that have survived, and mostly the novel is faithful to those facts. But *Blincoe's Progress* is neither a documentary, nor is it a history book: it is a work of fiction; one merely inspired by the events and characters of the local mills and villages.

There are some areas where the novel deviates from the facts, and in making the fiction, conversations have been imagined, minor characters, such as Nancy, Sam Slater and Nathan Booker, have been invented, and there has been some manipulation of dates so that the real stories of the cotton mills, and the people connected to them, can be compressed into a few years: essentially the period encompassing Blincoe's journey to, and from, Litton mill.

All of the social, political, and historical issues included in the novel, mirror what was happening at the end of the eighteenth century. For example: the struggle of most mills on the river Wye for water power and labour; the anti-slavery movement, which includes the frustration felt by many that we were ignoring the problems 'at home' and favouring the problems of the black slaves; illness and death; accidents and injuries in factories; the abuse of child labour; the move to steam power; the introduction of the first factory legislation; primitive abortion methods. Most of these subjects permeate the whole society and single events from the recorded local history do not always adequately cover these matters. But many significant events in the novel are based on historical facts, such as: Needham's struggle with Litton mill, Newton's leanings towards the literary world, Cressbrook mill being burnt down, and Litton mill being idle for some time when the mill's water wheel failed. Similarly, there are many minor events in the novel that are based in fact, for example: Blincoe being hung over the machinery, Blincoe becoming involved in a cotton waste business, the rebuilding of the apprentice house on the Taddington side of the river Wye, the party at Litton mill, entries in Parson Brown's diary.

Above are some discrete facts that are either included from the history, or invented, but there are many greyer areas. For example, the first apprentice house at Litton mill was rebuilt on the Taddington (rather than Litton) side of the river, and there are hints that this was deliberate to remove any legal responsibility from the Litton parish. However, how that came about is unknown, but the fiction that I have provided, may well be true. Parson Brown, according to most accounts was an unpopular vicar, yet he survived 57 years in the Parish. Again I have provided a fictional explanation for this.

The recorded history itself brings its own set of problems; events of the time were often recorded for political reasons and with a political bias, and this already unreliable history has, over time, become shaped and simplified. With this in mind, it is difficult to be certain that documentation from any period is reliable in representing the 'truth.' But this confusion over what may or may not be true or accurate, makes any burden of shaping and adjusting past events much more bearable.

Finally, one omission from the novel is that the abuse the children suffered was much worse than recorded here: Other punishments used by the overlookers included: spitting into the children's' mouths; putting pitch on their heads and then tearing it off to scalp them; filing their teeth. Then there was the sexual abuse that the children, mainly girls, suffered from their overlookers and masters. This was only occasionally documented; presumably, a difficult matter for people to speak out about, and with all the commissioners being men, also difficult to investigate. Such events are hinted at in the novel.

John Brown, author of Blincoe's memoir, claimed to be a radical journalist and abolitionist, but he too skirts carefully around any detailed enquiry, describing John Needham as follows:

'To boys, he was a tyrant and an oppressor. To the girls the same, with the additional odium of treating them with an indecency as disgusting as his cruelty was terrific. Those unhappy creatures were at once the victims of his ferocity and his lust'.

Printed at the same time as this text, also by Stuart Courtman, is *Robert Blincoe and the Cotton Trade.* This contains longer historical notes, placing Blincoe's memoir in its local and global context. In addition, the original 1828 text of *A memoir of Robert Blincoe* is included. It is hoped that *Robert Blincoe and the Cotton Trade* will complement this novel.

One

TUESDAY 4TH SEPTEMBER 1798
LITTON MILL, DERBYSHIRE

The boy stood in a corner of the coal-shed; cold, trembling, nervous, excited. A splinter of moonlight shone through a gap in the door, falling on the upper half of his grubby face. Looking out, the boy could see that it was a clear night; that was good.

Litton mill had just finished working for the day; the machinery had stopped, and all the workers had gone. In the silence, the boy waited. He wanted to move around, to pace about a little, but there was no space, and so after a while he sat down on the coal heap. Around an hour later, he heard footsteps approaching. They stopped. He heard the lock being removed and the chain loosened. The footsteps went away. Again, he waited. It was too soon to go now, and so he tried counting minutes, but with his mind full of what he was about to do, his counting soon became muddled. He occupied himself by checking the two tinderboxes he would take, and he took them down from the roof timbers where they had been hidden all day. The tinderbox cloths were well charred and dry, and they both gave good sparks. He took down from the same place a long bar that he might also use. He was as prepared as he could be and excited about tonight's adventure. He stood up again, as he was afraid that he could fall asleep, and again he waited.

When he thought sufficient time had passed, he slowly opened the door. It was a dry night with a light breeze. There were a few stars shining through gaps in some patchy clouds; there was plenty of light to see by. He carefully closed the door, draped the chain so that it appeared to be locked, picked up the tinderboxes and the bar, which he had wrapped in a cloth, and he set off.

There were many routes to Cressbrook, but the track alongside the river passed no houses, led straight to the other mill and there was unlikely to be anyone on the track at this time. There was now no one about at Litton mill, and as he turned the corner at the end of the buildings, he came to the track and the crashing noise of the river where it echoed off the sheer stone on the other side. As he followed the river downstream, it became calmer, and there was then no noise.

From Sunday outings with his friends, the only free time they had, he had often walked as far as Cressbrook mill, and although he had never been inside the mill, he knew the layout. With his chin resting on a cold stone wall, his grubby face peered into the mill yard, and he could see clearly where he needed to be: the cotton bale store room. He listened; again, there was silence, and so he climbed over the wall. Slowly, and silently, he walked around the building, looking for ways he might break in. There were a dozen windows where he might enter, and although two of them were open, they were just a foot or so out of his reach. He tried pushing and pulling on the main door, but that was secure. He needed something to stand on to reach a window, and he crept around the yard until he found something he could use. He found a ladder.

In no time at all, he was perched on the inside of the window cill. With ample starlight, he immediately saw that he was in exactly the right place: the room was full of new bales of raw cotton and untidy piles of waste cotton. His mind was sharp tonight, and as he knew he could not make his escape the same way he had entered, he dropped down from the window cill and first set about finding his exit. The main door was bolted from the inside, but there was no other lock, and so he slipped the bolts. That would be his escape route. He had planned to start two fires, but in the event, he changed his mind and lit three. From his tinderboxes, he started small fires made of piles of oily waste cotton; he knew these would light and take hold quicker than the raw cotton. Each fire was started next to a bale of cotton, the bales chosen, not too close together. He remained calm, although his movements were now swift. The small fires caught easily casting occasional bright flashes and sharp shadows around the store, and in no time the large bales caught and they burned brighter still; the fires were established. He slipped carefully out of the main door, pushing it to behind him, and then he moved swiftly back to the river track. From behind the relative safety of the stone wall, he watched as the fire began to crack and shatter the windows. After only a couple of minutes, he could see from the broken windows, flames escaping to the outside of the building, and from the eaves of the single story building, he could see thick swirling grey smoke lit by the flames below. The fire had really taken hold, and for the first time he felt scared that he had done the wrong thing. Had he made the wrong choice? Might he be caught and punished? This was not the time for such doubts, and there was nothing to be gained by standing there. He knew he needed to be back in the safety of the coal-shed, and even though he had not heard any voices or shouting, as he had expected he might, he began to run. He ran back along the same path that had brought him to Cressbrook mill, but the running did not last, as he was too weak from his imprisonment in the coal-shed. Some of the cuts on his back, which had been healing, had now cracked and started weeping and stinging, and less than halfway back, he slowed to a walk. The distance between the mills was short, and a few minutes later, he slipped unnoticed into the yard at Litton mill.

Before he closed the coal-shed door, he looked at the sky. There was no doubt that he had been successful as there was a bright orange glow over Cressbrook.

He sat down in the coal-shed, for the first time reflecting on what he had done. Up until he started the fire, he had been in no doubt that he was doing the right thing, but now he was not so sure. He wondered how he had come to be living in a coal-shed in this bleak place in the far north of the country, and he reflected on the chain of events that led to the events of tonight. He found himself looking back fondly to his time in the workhouse in London; a place where he had been safe, comfortable and cared for. He knelt, closed his eyes, put his hands together and prayed, just as Parson Brown had taught him.

'Please forgive me if I have done wrong,' he said.

He lay down on his sacks, and as he fell asleep, his doubts turned into nightmares. Suddenly, the masters of Litton mill and Parson Brown were leaning over him, waving fingers in his face.

'What have you done Blincoe?' Parson Brown asked. 'What have you done?'

Blincoe heard nothing when the lock was replaced. He was sound asleep on his sacks.

Two

SUNDAY 18TH DECEMBER 1796
TIDESWELL CHURCH

Two and a half years before the fire at Cressbrook mill, Robert Blincoe was twelve years old and still in the workhouse at Saint Giles in London. He was yet to meet the owner of Litton mill and his overlookers. He was yet to meet Parson Brown. In the coming years, they would all loom large in his life.

Parson Brown was conducting the evening service at Tideswell Church.

'I propose to direct your attention at the present time, to the subject of oppression. I do not suppose, my beloved hearers, that any of us, even those who have thought most and prayed most in reference to this subject, have any adequate conceptions of the extent to which it involves the destinies of this nation, but it is a subject in which this nation, and every individual of this nation, ought to feel a deep and trembling interest.'

Parson Brown delivered his sermon from the pulpit, which was high above the congregation. He was dressed in his Sunday attire of cassock, knee breeches and silk stockings, but this costume did little to keep out the cold, and he was in no doubt, this was the coldest he had ever felt whilst delivering a sermon. Brown was so cold that he felt nothing for the words he was speaking, and tonight he had no *trembling interest* in oppression. What he did have was trembling knees, a significant self-interest in survival and a dream that after the service, he would be provided with a hot Sunday roast.

On his way to church, he had trampled through a good six inches of snow, and he reached the porch at the same moment as Abel Walker and Elizabeth, Abel's wife.

'Twenty degrees of frost,' Abel muttered, and on seeing he had attracted Brown's attention continued, 'and it's been the same since Wednesday. The sheep don't like it, the cattle don't like it and I don't like it.' The farmer disappeared through the inner porch door and into the church, but he turned and called back to Brown, 'And I dare say you don't like it either!'

Brown, as always, had prepared well for the service, although the preparations for tonight centred largely on how fast he could get through the entire event. Obviously, there were limits on what he could do, and there were expectations that he would follow the usual order of service, which he did, more or less. So Brown had looked for other shortcuts: he had chosen the shortest prayers, the shortest hymns and from his collection of sermons, selected one of the shortest.

Under other circumstances, Brown might have had to sit down and write this evening's sermon, but he had been lucky, as the previous rector had left the parish in a hurry, leaving behind all of his sermons. He had been fortunate to come by that pile of sermons, but his next move was much more calculating: He borrowed sermons from the neighbouring rectors of Eyam and Buxton, and whilst the papers were in his possession, he copied them all.

Brown had never understood why other rectors would spend hours writing sermons each week, when all that the problem needed was some organisation in recording and cataloguing. This was exactly what Brown did. His collection of sermons was now quite comprehensive, and he had catalogued them in order of the church year, so that when, for example, Whitsuntide came, he could easily pick out a relevant sermon.

It was as a nine-year-old child that Brown became aware of the cycle of the church calendar. Initially he was confused how Jesus, born in December, was a grown man and being crucified by the following Easter, and if that was not strange enough, it happened every year! Now as a grown man, he used this observation to his advantage, believing that most congregations were quite happy to hear the same story again, which of course they did every year, and if that story happened to be one of his sermons, then so be it. As far as sermons went, he was now set up for life.

Today, though, they were not getting the *same story again*. Brown has selected a sermon from the section at the back of his catalogue, the section that did not relate to any part of the church year. He selected it partly because it was short and partly as it was a subject that interested him, but the bitter cold in the Church had removed any last remnants of interest.

So it was, that with his misty breath floating and freezing in the air in front of him, that he continued his sermon.

'Slavery is sin. The testimony of the scriptures in reference to this point is sufficiently clear and decisive. They condemn every species of oppression. Unjust men and extortioners are by the law of the Eternal excluded from heaven. For it is written. "the hope of unjust men perisheth."'

Parson Brown, now just twenty-five, had been in charge at Tideswell for eighteen months. He had begun as curate, covering the duties of the rector, but just before the last Christmas, he had been ordained as the rector. Tonight the rector looked out over a tiny congregation, made all the more insignificant by the enormous church in which they sat. The church's wide aisles were lined with stout cold pillars, above which were balanced high pointed arches. Huge painted glass windows lifted high towards the even higher timbered ceilings, which tonight were hidden in the blackness. Back at the congregation's level, there were rows of long and mostly empty pews.

Brown quickly counted the heads in the congregation; there were precisely nine. If he counted Nathan Booker, who sat at the organ and doubled as both the organist and the churchwarden, then this reached a pitiable ten. This was not spectacularly fewer than normal; twenty or twenty-five was as good as it got, although previous incumbents reportedly attracted double that figure. The congregation tonight were all local to the town, and those from further away had sensibly not tackled the difficult journeys and would probably, by now, be enjoying their Sunday roasts, or if not, sitting in front of a roaring fire, their bellies already full.

It was the custom, on a Sunday, for the parson to be invited to dinner by someone from the congregation. This week there had been no prior invitation, but not all was lost as hospitality was sometimes offered at the end of the service. Brown examined each of the nine members of the congregation as to the possibility of a free Sunday roast. There was Abel Walker, farmer and weather expert and his wife Elizabeth, but they had never yet invited him. Thomas and Sarah Walker, who were Abel's son and daughter-in-law, lived with Abel, and so there was nothing more to be gained there. William and Nancy Bennet owned the pork butcher's shop in Tideswell and had invited him on three previous occasions to dinner. However, he had been there just two Sundays ago, so would they invite him this week? That was a possibility. The remaining three in the congregation were Grace Ball, a teacher and spinster; Mrs Hibbert, a widow; and Mrs Redfern, another widow, and whilst nothing was written in ecclesiastical law to say that a single woman could not invite the rector to dinner, it was unheard of.

Grace Ball looked up at the parson, his tall strong figure, his blue eyes and his uncombed long blonde hair. She had never missed one of his Sunday services and if it were possible, would have had him to dinner every night. Their paths crossed occasionally at the school; she had made sure of that, but he had not flattered her with any look or invitation. She was not yet passed the time of child bearing and although she was twelve years his senior, she still nursed a faint glimmer of hope.

For completeness, Brown considered the likelihood of Nathan Booker offering an invitation, but having been in Nathan's cottage once, Brown did not want a return visit. It was filthy and untidy beyond belief, and in any case there would be no invitation. He concluded that his best hope was a return to the Bennets' with an outside prospect of an invitation to the Walkers'.

Brown continued to read the short sermon, but he paid little attention to what he was saying: he just read the words. He had developed a technique of raising and lowering his voice – which he thought gave the sermon the effect of showing his commitment to the sentiment, whatever that sentiment might be. His second technique was his *pause*. He paused every now and then for two or three seconds his eyes gazing to the heavens. This was to give the impression that he was thinking what he might say next, and he hoped that this would trick the congregation into believing that his fine words were from the heart, the mind and his thorough understanding of all things theological and not from the prepared document he had placed on top of the Bible. The pauses could be anywhere and in fact were best in the middle of sentences. He had learned that pauses at the end of sentences confused the congregation into thinking that he might have finished. His techniques certainly worked with Grace Ball who sat captivated, her mouth slightly open, gazing up at him.

'Let us humbly pray for its extirpation from our land and from the world; and instead of—' Here Brown paused and then resumed on a much firmer note, '—contributing in any way to encourage a further traffic in the souls of the much injured blacks, unite our exertions with those of—' Again he paused, but on this occasion replaced the heavenly gaze with a earthly and shivering nod towards Nathan, to allow Nathan time to prepare himself for the final hymn, '—the benevolent and pious, to send them the blessings of civilization and religion. Amen.'

Brown launched, without delay, into his final prayer; this time he just read the words, in his rector's sing-song voice with no pauses as it was understood by the congregation that he was reading from the prayer book.

'O Lord our heavenly Father, high and mighty, King of kings, Lord of lords, the only Ruler of princes, we beseech thee with thy favour to behold our most gracious Sovereign Lord, King George.'

At this point, it came to Brown that he could miss out the next four lines, and the prayer would still make sense. It was a split-second decision shortening the service by a few precious seconds.

'And finally, after this life, he may attain everlasting joy and felicity; through Jesus Christ our Lord. Amen.'

Brown felt as though he was in a race now. He was sprinting through the service, and the end was close. But would there be a roast dinner prize at the end? He announced the final hymn.

'We shall sing the hymn "Thy name, almighty Lord! Shall sound through distant lands," It is the very last hymn printed in your prayer books.'

The seventy-year-old Nathan shuffled around on his seat having done nothing to prepare for the hymn since Brown's nod. Nathan was an accomplished musician and had spent his early twenties as a travelling entertainer playing almost any musical instrument. He was now part retired, having spent his recent years as a stonemason, although most of his stone-masonry was patching up the church and engraving headstones. He and Brown got on as business colleagues rather than friends, and although there was a mutual distrust, each needed the other. A few moments later, the organ groaned into life, and the congregation stood. Brown gathered up his papers, and as this was only a two-verse hymn, the shortest he could find that shared a vague accordance with his sermon; he stepped immediately down from the pulpit and made his way through the congregation to the door at the South porch. This was the only open door to the church that night and was where he had left his overcoat that he now badly needed. In addition, it would give him an advantageous position in impeding the departure of his congregation in the hope of finding a kind face who would provide his dinner.

Brown only slightly impeded the congregation as the bitter cold gave them a strong desire to be in their homes as soon as possible. As he shook hands and thanked them for their attendance, the talk was mainly of the weather. Those who agreed with the sentiments of his sermon, thanked him. Those who disagreed were either too polite to say, or too cold to risk any further delay. Grace Ball slipped by without a speaking and then regretted not speaking for the rest of that night.

Brown walked home alone.

Three

SUNDAY 18TH DECEMBER 1796
TIDESWELL SCHOOLHOUSE

The weather was no kinder after the service than it had been before. The snow tried to fall, but the wind tossed it around, and all the roads and pathways vanished from view. Brown had no lantern, although tonight a lantern would have been no use; those that left the church with them, only saw more snow. Brown's home, the schoolhouse, was just a short walk around the back of the church, and on reaching there, and relieved from his temporary blindness, he mopped his face and hurried inside.

Tonight it was a very bleak and lonely house; although Brown employed a seventeen-year-old maid, Kezia, she was not at the schoolhouse tonight but at one of her very few relatives: her grandmother's house. The arrangement with Parson Brown was that she lived in, cooked for him and looked after all of the domestic chores. Each week she had time off with her grandmother from Sunday afternoon, returning at noon the following day. This arrangement suited Brown as she had to have some time off, and he was usually out on Sunday evenings, and he could easily fend for himself on a Monday morning.

This Sunday evening, Brown returned home to a cold dark house with no meal prepared and no fire lit. He had left one low oil lamp burning in the hallway, and from this, he lit another. He then lit the fire that Kezia had left laid for him, and to busy himself whilst the room grew warm, he prepared to fill in his diary for the past week. Brown recorded just a few lines for each day describing the main events. He sat down and began writing:

'Monday. Took a ride this morning to see my cow at Litton. I called at Mr J Baker's and had breakfast there. Went to Peak Forest this afternoon to inter the body of Adam Minter. I bought a sack of potatoes for setting later. Saw Sam Slater and he agreed to forward dig two graves – the weather is bitter and we will need them soon enough.'

His entries recorded the day-to-day events. Had there been room on the page, he might have separated his different activities, but there was little space, and so side-by-side were the mundane, the mysterious and a record of his pastoral work; the mix was a true reflection of how his life was. On another page, he kept an account of his incomings and outgoings. For this week, he had already recorded outgoings of

'One sack of potatoes, one shilling; Sam Slater, digging of two graves, one shilling and sixpence; Tobacco, two pence; Ale, five pence.' His incomings were, 'Churching Mrs Wild, six pence; Funerals, two shillings and sixpence; Won betting with cards, three pence.'

Brown was well aware that the income he could make from being a rector was not enough to live on, and so he supplemented this in whatever way he could. His repertoire included, sign writing, measuring land, estimating quantities of hay, farming, school teaching and on occasion, money lending. Many of his parishioners disapproved of these additional activities; they expected someone more committed, in both time and attitude, to the church and *their* needs, and they saw many possible conflicts between his church work and these other occupations. Brown though, at just twenty-five, could see no conflicts, and he gently added more coal to the fire before fetching from the pantry a bottle of currant wine. The room was beginning to warm, and Brown planned to finish his week's diary with an accompanying glass of wine.

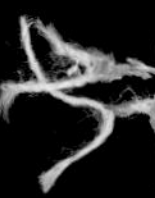

Then he would see what he could find for his dinner. But as his pen hovered over where he was to write 'Tuesday', he became preoccupied with another matter, and his diary, for the moment, was abandoned. He moved to the floor nearer to the fire that now coming to life and giving occasional bursts of brightness from the flames. He was thinking of Tuesday night the previous week when he had last sat in this room drinking wine.

He had eaten at home that night, and after his meal, he went into the scullery to make sure that Kezia knew that he would be out all the following day. Kezia should have been washing the pans and crockery from his dinner, but he caught her wrapping a bottle of currant wine and a block of butter in some brown paper that she had laid out ready. She was stealing from him, and when he confronted her, she admitted taking it for her grandmother.

Brown was furious, and whilst still in the scullery he hit her twice in the face. He then chased her into the hall screaming at her to get to her room. After she had gone upstairs, he went to the kitchen, quickly opened the same bottle of wine, poured himself a large glass and drank half of it in one mouthful. Although he was still angry, his mind was confused with a multitude of other thoughts. Should he dismiss her? Could he cope without her? Had he hurt her? Had he behaved inappropriately? What should he do now? What *should* he do now? His glass was empty, and he sat down, poured a second glass and decided to turn to his religion for guidance in this matter.

They were both in the parlour, Kezia sitting near the fire, Brown standing a respectable distance away. Kezia had been crying, and her eyes were full. Her head was bowed, and her red curls now fell forward covering her face. When she looked up at him, he could see a redness contrasted against her pale skin, but there was nothing more, thankfully.

'Kezia,' Brown began, 'you have done wrong and you know you have done wrong. I have done wrong also. I over reacted to the situation and I am sorry.'

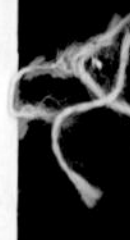

Kezia began sobbing again and in a gargling and meek voice said, 'Please don't throw me out, please don't.' She again looked up at him, and Brown, now feeling guilty and feeling genuine compassion for her suffering moved towards her and took both of her hands.

'Kizzie,' he said, 'we are both sorry for what we have done. Shall we forgive each other?'

Kezia nodded. Brown's face suddenly lit up, not just at her nodding or at the agreed reconciliation, but an idea to properly consolidate this agreement came to him.

'You will join me in a glass of wine!' he announced, and he was pouring a third glass for himself and a glass for her.

They sat on the armchairs, either side of the fire, and they were warm, merry and enjoying a second bottle of wine. Kezia was quite unused to wine, and Brown, as he later acknowledged, had drunk far too much.

Until that point, all had gone well, and their relationship was, if not better than before, certainly back to where it was before. Precisely what happened next was still a mystery to Brown. He remembered them both sitting on the floor by the fire, but he didn't know how they came to be in such an informal position. He remembered his head in Kezia's lap, though he had no memory of how they came to be like that either. He remembered her stroking his face. He remembered them kissing, though who kissed who first was equally unclear, and with some anguish, he remembered them on the hearth rug in front of the fire. Afterwards she more or less passed out, and he carried her to her bed and laid her there. Before going to his own bed, he tried to make her comfortable and awkwardly pulled her skirt down over her knees in an ill-timed act of good manners.

That was Tuesday, and the following day he was awake before her and had gone out before she was downstairs. He regretted what had happened and worried that she might be awkward with him. Might she expect him to visit her again? Or, and worst of all, could there be a consequence? When he came in that evening he wanted to say something but he had no idea what he might say, or what he should say, so he said nothing. He thought there would be a better time, but there never was, and as the week moved towards the weekend, the difficulty in then saying, whatever it was he might say, became nigh on impossible.

Kezia said nothing either, and although she was firm in her belief that Brown had behaved improperly, she still made an extra effort to please him, fearing that what had happened late on Tuesday night might further jeopardise her future employment.

So here he was; again by the parlour fire, again with wine, but now feeling miserable. His diary was not completed, there was no food in his belly, his Sunday service had been rushed and careless, he had given his maid a good drubbing and he had lain with her. He stood up determined to shake himself free of this self-pity, and he returned to his diary, but just as he was about to record that on Tuesday morning he had written a letter to the Bishop of Lichfield, he was interrupted by a knock at the front door.

'Reverend Thomas Brown?'

'Yes?'

'Reverend Joseph Holmes.' The man offered his hand, and Brown shook it.

'Please come in. This is no night to be outside,' Brown said.

Brown ushered him into the Parlour and took his wet and heavy cloak, overcoat and hat, draping them over chairs to dry. Brown was used to visits from other rectors, although usually they were preceded by a letter.

'Now then,' said Brown, 'you will join me in a glass of wine!' He remembered using the same words last Tuesday but tried to put that out of his mind.

'Come and warm yourself by the fire, and then you must tell me what you are doing in Tideswell and how, given this truly abominable weather, you travelled here.'

They sat down, either side of the fire, and Holmes began his tale.

'I took a coach from London which, and with just two changes, I reached Cromford on Tuesday. I conducted some business in Cromford on that day, and I have been attempting, well struggling, to get here since. I managed to get to Bakewell and stayed there last night, and I have walked from Bakewell to Tideswell today.'

'Goodness me,' Brown said, 'have you eaten?'

Brown knew that Bakewell was eight miles and in this weather would have been a very tiring journey.

'Not since breakfast.'

'We will go to the New George. It's very close, and we may get some food there. There's not much in my pantry here. Then you can tell me what brings you here, and you will sleep here tonight of course.'

Brown knew the New George quite well as he drank in there two or three times a week. The Inn was reached through a side gate from the churchyard, and they were soon there. Brown ordered two quarts of Ale, but Katy, the young barmaid, was on her own, and there was no food to be had. There were only two other customers, and Brown concluded that his evening's congregation of nine or ten, was probably quite a respectable number after all. They sat a little away from the other two customers but still close enough to feel the heat of the fire. The New George was a spacious place, but tonight much of this space was unlit. The only lamps were behind the bar and on the two tables with customers.

For those who didn't regard the church as the centre of Tideswell, then it was the New George. In the daytime, the coaches came and went, setting down at the front of the Inn, and although the Inn was not the Post Office, all of the post came and went via the New George, and on those same coaches. Brown put two more logs and a shovel full of coal on the fire and sat down. Holmes raised his glass, and Brown did the same, although at this point Brown still had no idea why the Reverend Joseph Holmes was here. Holmes was looking around the Inn.

'So, what happened to the old one?' he enquired.

‘Pardon?’ Brown was mystified.

‘The Old George – this is the New George.’

‘This was built when George the second came to the throne, that’s why it’s the New George. But there is an Old George Inn here in Tideswell.’

Brown was hungry and imagined Holmes was too.

‘We can drink this and go back to the schoolhouse. I have wine, and I’m sure I can find something.’

Brown knew that he had very little food at the house. He had glanced around the pantry earlier, and there was not even any bread. All he had seen was half an ox-cheek pie. That might have to do, but for now, they had ale to drink.

‘My parish is Saint Giles in London,’ began Holmes, ‘I have been given the opportunity of saving some young children, but not just saving their souls, saving their lives and their futures.’ He looked around and lowered his voice slightly. ‘Allow me to explain. The workhouses in London and in particular in Saint Giles, my parish, are overflowing with young children - children who have no future as they grow up, other than a likelihood to enter into prostitution for the girls and probably a life of crime for the boys. It also costs the parish a great deal of money in feeding, clothing and housing them. Word came to us that there was a fast growth in factories, especially cotton factories in parts of Derbyshire, Yorkshire and Nottinghamshire, areas where there is not a plentiful supply of labour,’ Holmes leaned a little closer to Brown. ‘The scheme is that the children are apprenticed to the mills so that the mill owners effectively take over from the workhouses, with the mill owners providing food, clothing and housing the children. Whether the mill owners pay the children any wages over and above this is up to them. Some mill owners pay nothing, some a ha’penny or penny a week. The children come with new clothes and a guinea, which is theirs but is usually kept safe by the employer. This scheme is already running in some of the silk mills in Hertfordshire and Essex.’

Brown was impressed by Holmes' confidence. Although he appeared very young, of small build, a boyish face and could easily be taken for under twenty; his delivery was composed, clear and came from an older more experienced man.

Homes continued, 'everyone is happy, and everyone gains something. All three groups that is: the losing parishes, the mill owners and the children. So what I am hoping is that you will help me find the local cotton factories as I have heard there are many in this area, although I have already visited Mr Arkwright's factory at Cromford.'

Holmes thought he had done a reasonable summary and raised his glass again. Brown mirrored him.

Back in the schoolhouse, Brown divided the ox-cheek pie, serving it with a good helping of rhubarb pickle. This, he hoped, would disguise the dryness of the pie, but both men were hungry enough not to care.

'So,' Holmes spoke first after putting down a clean plate, 'How come you are in the schoolhouse and not the vicarage? I tried the vicarage first, but it appears empty.'

'There is a legal dispute over the vicarage,' Brown went on to explain, 'The last rector, Richard Shuttleworth, left in a hurry and with many debts. I was offered the schoolhouse until the vicarage problem is resolved.'

Brown poured two more glasses of wine. 'How can you spare so much time away from your parish?' he asked.

'Well I'm not the official parish rector of Saint Giles. I don't actually have my own parish, but I've been assigned for three months to this venture. I represent the parishes of Saint Giles and Saint Pancras.'

They had sat in silence for a little while now. Finally Brown spoke.

'I will arrange introductions to some mill owners tomorrow, but there is a matter that perhaps you could help me with? It is a rather delicate matter and has been troubling me. I just need some advice really, perhaps a second opinion?'

'Of course, what is it?'

'Well, my churchwarden and organist and general help, oh, and he engraves headstones, you need to know that too.'

The parson took a swig and partly missed his mouth. He wiped his mouth on his sleeve.

'His name is Nathan Booker and two years ago his brother William passed on. This was before my time here, but naturally, Nathan engraved the inscription on the stone in accordance with William's wishes. The inscription reads as follows,'

Brown got up and rooted in a drawer returning to the safety of the floor and the warmth of the fire.

'I love I lived, in peace with all I died
When I was buried, few there were who cried
But tho' on earth not one has mourned my loss,
In heaven He cares who saved us on the cross'

Holmes put down his glass and clapped.

'Now, there were those who frowned when they saw the stone; they thought that the second and third lines were not what we would expect, but the last line is serious enough, so nothing happened, and it stayed as it was. Anyway, as I said, this was all before my time and was almost forgotten when I took over. Then in the middle of November, William's widow, Sarah, died. I buried her, in the family grave, and a week or so later Nathan added an inscription for Sarah on the same stone. It reads as follows,

Sarah Booker here she lies,
Nobody laughs and nobody cries,
Where she's gone to and how she fares,
nobody knows and nobody cares.'

Holmes smiled, and his smile turned to laughter. He took the paper from Brown and read it again. He fell to the floor, lying on his back looking at the ceiling, his laughter now out of control.

Brown had previously failed to see anything funny in this matter, but the drink gave him a different perspective, and with Holmes' laughter proving infectious, he soon joined in.

They fell asleep, drunk on either side of fire, and the rather delicate matter remained unresolved.

Four

MONDAY 19TH DECEMBER 1796
LITTON MILL

Ellis Needham's office was not big, but just big enough to seat all of the managers representing the various functions of the mill. Needham held a meeting at nine o'clock sharp each Monday morning, a time chosen as it gave two and a half hours to sort out any early morning problems with the workers, the mill machinery and other day-to-day matters. The weekly meeting was a new idea of Needham's that he hoped would give his managers a better understanding of all of the problems of the mill. In addition, it gave Needham the opportunity to humiliate those who appeared not to be pulling their weight. He paid his managers well, and in return, he expected their commitment, long hours of attendance and hard work. He had done his best to recruit people to these positions who were not only well trained in their particular skills, but also intelligent and capable of anticipating problems and not just ruffians who might motivate the workforce through fear and violence. But, attracting workers to Litton mill, which was hidden in a narrow valley in the Derbyshire peaks and isolated from any large communities, was just one of many problems that Needham faced, and despite his ideals, he had to make do with who he could get.

Four men filed into the room and sat, slightly too close together for comfort on a high-backed settle that Needham had come by in the back of a barn. Not only were they too close together for comfort, but to a man, they were uncomfortable with this whole weekly meeting idea. Even those who were more relaxed in meetings, such as Richard Middleton, the counting house clerk, still saw little value in it. The men sat facing Needham who, across his desk from them, remained silent, making notes in his journal. Filling this silence was the thunderous rush of the river Wye that could be heard through gaps in the small window.

Needham lived for the mill, and spent all of his waking hours, and some of his sleeping hours, worrying about the problems there. His worrying sometimes woke him, and on those occasions, he would sit in his bedroom, jotting ideas and possible solutions to his problems. He was thirty-two years old and had built Litton mill nine years earlier, after inheriting the family estate near Wormhill. Needham's mother was still alive, but she had moved to live with her sister in York, and so, apart from one servant, Needham now lived alone. He had little interest in farming, and he had sold off large parts of the estate to finance the building of the mill. He had heard stories and seen for himself, the success of Richard Arkwright who was the leading industrialist, profiteering from the change from hand spinning to mechanised spinning. Needham planned to copy Arkwright, and he anticipated that he would make relatively easy money from cotton.

From a rustic and harsh farming background, he saw no need for excessive comforts, not at work anyway. His office was basic, the walls whitewashed and the furniture well worn, all of it second-hand. Needham saw no business reason to decorate the room any differently as all of his business dealings, which were mainly buying cotton and selling yarn, were conducted well away from Litton mill. The room though was clean, tidy and orderly, something he insisted on throughout the mill.

'Good Morning,' Needham said and finally looked up. 'Robert won't be here today as he is, I believe, stranded in Manchester due to the weather. But as you can see, it is now thawing fast,' He glanced out of the window, but the view of the limestone cliff face gave no indication of the thaw, 'and so I expect him back tomorrow at the latest.'

Needham smiled and looked at each of the men before him. He had a round face with a thick and wild moustache, a good head of black curly hair and bushy eyebrows to match. When relaxed he could be quite jolly, but when angry the same face took on a subtly different expression. The managers of his mill were never in doubt as to his particular mood. Middleton studied Needham's face. He concluded Needham was in a good mood.

The absent Robert was Needham's brother. Robert was now aged twenty-eight, and he was in charge of buying the raw cotton and selling the finished yarn. He generally travelled to Manchester each week to conduct this business.

'So,' continued Needham, 'can we start with Mr Palfrey?'

Samuel Palfrey was the carpenter, although in addition to carpentry, Palfrey was responsible for the masonry structures including the main buildings and watercourses. He also looked after the oil lamps and monitored the water levels and opening, and closing, of sluice gates.

'Thank you Sir,' Palfrey presented his report in the format of which he knew Needham approved. This was: what he had done last week, what he planned to do this week and what problems he foresaw.

'Last week we fitted new locks to the main cotton loading doors. We checked the lamp oil, and we reckon we now have enough oil to see us through this winter. We have just six more lamps to repair this week, and that is all of the faulty ones done. Water levels are high at the moment, and with the snow melting we should have no problem with power for the next week.' Palfrey looked up from his notes.

'Mr Simpson.' Needham barked; the tone negating any effects of the respectful *Mister*.

William Simpson was the blacksmith with responsibilities for the machinery of the mill. This included the mill wheel, gears and shafts, belts, all of the mill machinery and anything else made of iron. Many of the machine parts were timber, and when necessary he worked with Palfrey on these. The stables were alongside the smithy, and Simpson looked after those too.

'The mill wheel has been thoroughly checked and some minor repairs made yesterday. That was Sunday.' He added the Sunday reference to make sure that Needham realised they had worked Sunday, but Needham was well aware. 'We are low on spare belting, and some is on the way, but with the weather I don't know when that might come.'

Needham thought his offering rather lacking so asked, 'And what do you have planned this week?'

'Helping Mr Palfrey with the lamps. When that is done I should finish making the railings for the cellar steps and then, anything else that needs attention.'

Needham then turned to Robert Woodward. He was the chief over-looker and looked after all of the mill workers, particularly those involved in production. He monitored their output for quality and quantity and made sure that all work places were covered. He also hired and fired them and, unknown to Needham, he used, and encouraged, physical punishments to keep them in check.

'The main problem is still the labour supply. We could immediately use twenty more people. At the moment, we are running eight hundred and forty spindles, but we have three hundred and thirty-six idle. All of the spindles are serviceable; we are moving work around each month so that nothing is idle for too long.'

Needham sighed and sat back, 'That sums up the situation very well, but you used much the same words this time last week. My question is what have *you* done to help this sorry situation?'

'I have again asked all the workers if they know of anyone, but the only person to come was a man with one arm. Since last week I have placed posters in all the local villages, and I have written asking how much an advertisement for hands will be in *The Manchester Mercury* and *The Derby Mercury*.'

It was the turn of the last man in the line up, Richard Middleton, the counting house clerk. Middleton had his counting house on the first floor directly below Needham's office, an almost identical room. He looked after all things financial including monitoring the stock of raw and finished goods. He worked closely with both Needhams.

'Our cash flow is good. We have raw cotton to last just over one week. I hope that young Mr Needham will bring word on that today—'

'Probably tomorrow,' Needham senior interrupted.

'Similarly,' Middleton went on, 'we didn't get any finished yarn out last week. However the snow is melting, and we have two carts planned to go tomorrow.'

Needham looked at them all and smiled.

'Thank you gentlemen, I have nothing to add to that. I am here every day this week if you need me. You know where I am. Would Mr Middleton remain here.'

They began to file out, and Needham shouted after them, 'If your man with half his arms could do half a job, he could have half a wage!'

Needham was very pleased with his little joke and laughed out loud. The others joined in.

At the schoolhouse, Brown and Holmes were in the kitchen. The previous night they had woke up around two o'clock. The fire had burned down to embers, and they woke when the cold had reached them. Brown had shown Holmes to the spare room, and they had both slept until gone eight. Brown was the first up, and he had dressed quickly and visited the nearest butcher and the local bakers for bacon, black pudding, eggs and bread.

He was cooking breakfast when Holmes came down. Holmes still needed to discuss his own plans and arrange his visits to the local mills; he had expected to do all this the previous evening, but the wine had flowed quickly, and after a certain point, sensible discussion had not been possible. Brown spoke first, anticipating his concerns.

'There are two quite large mills near here: Litton mill and Cressbrook mill. I know the owners quite well.'

Holmes sat down at the kitchen table, and Brown poured two cups of tea.

'I think it would be best,' Brown continued, 'if I visited them this morning with a view to arranging a meeting with yourself as soon as possible. I doubt we will just be able to walk in today, so I suggest you stay here and rest a while. I know of some other mills too, but they are smaller, and I have no connections, although I can tell you where they are.'

'Thank you,' Holmes said. 'I have already lost a week on the schedule I planned, and I need to move on as quickly as I can. There is a coach to Nottingham on Wednesday. I would like to be on that.'

Brown served the breakfast and sat down.

'After breakfast I will collect my mare,' Brown spoke with a mouthful of bread, 'and go to Litton mill and then on to Cressbrook mill.'

'One thing I didn't mention last night,' Holmes now spoke, his mouth also full of bread, 'is that there is some extra money, usually around three guineas per apprentice, which we can divide amongst ourselves and the mill owners. Do you think a third each? The division would be simple!'

Brown was clearly thinking about this, and Holmes thought that Brown might see taking money for himself, as somehow wrong. Finally, after taking a swill of tea Brown spoke, 'I'm not sure that the mill owners, well the mill owners that I know, will need any further inducement. I would suggest we divide it between ourselves.'

Both men smiled, and they shook hands.

Brown collected his mare and rode off towards Litton mill. As he rode up the hill out of Tideswell, the sun was shining and the snow melting very quickly. Most of the fields were still white, but water was running down the lanes, and the journey, though not fast, was not too difficult. He passed a number of parishioners on his way but kept his conversation to a simple, 'Good morning.'

Litton mill is two miles from Tideswell with the village of Litton halfway between the two. As he rode through Litton, he waved and shouted another 'Good morning' to Molly Baker. She was the landlady of the Red Lion and was swilling out as he passed. After Litton, he began the descent to Litton mill. He passed Littonslack, a small hamlet of mill workers cottages and carefully, and steadily, as the track was now steep, made his way into the steep sided valley, towards the river Wye and the darkness of Litton mill. The valley was so narrow and deep, that the mill spent the entire winter in shade; for the remainder of the year the sun could be caught warming the cold stone of the mill, but only for a short time each day, in the late afternoons.

Needham and Middleton were still discussing various figures and options and had been doing so for almost two hours. Middleton turned another page in his book, explaining his calculations to Needham.

'If we run eight hundred spindles for fourteen hours each week day and for six hours on a Saturday, then deducting fifteen percent for times where there is no water or power, machinery breakages, cotton supply problems and so on, then with the present profit margins on cotton, and the present wages and other overheads, the mill will turn in a profit of around four hundred pounds a year. The break-even point is when the percentage reductions reach twenty-eight percent. Of course if there are fewer stoppages, or if we could get more hands for the idle spindles then the yearly profit could be over a thousand, even up to two thousand pounds.'

Needham had taken all this in easily. His problem was that there were too many uncertain numbers in these calculations. There were too many guesses. Wages and some of the overheads to run the mill were well understood and stable, but buying prices and selling prices were volatile, and the mill was vulnerable during dry periods, it only having a small mill pond to stack up water for the wheel.

As Needham and Middleton gazed at the numbers on the page, there was a short knock at the door, and Parson Brown was in the room.

'Good morning,' Brown said and feeling invigorated by the fresh air and short ride, continued, 'Ellis, I have some good news. News that I think you will be pleased to hear.' Brown was smiling and looking quite flushed. 'Can you be at the Red Lion tonight at, say, seven? It will be to your advantage!'

Needham's head was still swirling with numbers and worries, and so he answered simply, 'Yes, seven is fine.'

Needham and Middleton, still leaning on the table, poised over the top of the books, looked up at Brown, waiting to see if he had more to say but he hadn't.

'Then, as I see you are busy, I will be on my way! Good Morning.'

'You will be paying for the ale I presume?' Needham quickly added.

'You need not worry about that!' Brown shouted back.

With Brown gone, Needham and Middleton moved on to look at transport costs and the possibility of using the same cart to deliver the finished yarn and then bring back the raw cotton.

Cressbrook mill was just half a mile downstream from Litton mill, but the path down the riverside was dangerous and underwater for much of the winter. The alternative, which Brown was forced to take, was a ride back up the hill to Littonslack and then down the other side of the hill into Cressbrook. Cressbrook mill was about the same size as Litton mill, but it had many differences. Whereas the valley was very narrow at Litton mill, with the river rushing noisily past, the same valley opened up at Cressbrook mill; here the river was much calmer, and there was a much more agreeable view of lush green fields. Cressbrook mill had a huge mill pond, and so even in the driest of weather, the mill pond would fill up overnight with enough water to keep the mill running all of the following day. The owner of Cressbrook mill had no need to sell off his estate to finance the mill, as he was from a wealthy family, his father owning both a cotton plantation and a sugar plantation in Jamaica. But like Litton mill, Cressbrook mill did struggle for labour, that they had in common.

William Newton was the owner, although he had never intended to become involved in the family businesses. As a young man had sought schooling in engineering, but he had found no immediate opportunities for his skills, and he had slipped back into the fold of the family. The family ventured into cotton spinning, and William seemed the obvious choice; managing a cotton mill seemed the best use of his skills.

On enquiring in the mill yard, Brown was told by a young man leaning on a broom that Newton had not been there all day.

'Probably at his house,' the man said.

Brown turned his mare around and made his way to Cressbrook hall, an imposing building reached down a drive of tall poplar trees.

No one answered the door so Brown let himself in. As he stood in the grand hallway, the wide staircase disappearing into darkness in front of him, he heard a voice. He moved towards the room the voice was coming from. It was Newton's voice. Brown listened at the doorway, cautious of interrupting something important.

'Thy praise resounding? Happy could I gain
Access, tho' hard, within the Muses' fane;
And thee behold, so high my thoughts aspire
Thy honoured temples by the sister's bound'

Newton was reading some flowery verse, at least that was what Brown thought, but was he reading it alone, or to someone else?

'With their bright chaplet of unfading hue
Graceful. Ah blest, might I, tho' far beneath
Thee peerless, with every bud and flowret crown'd
Of Poetry, gemm'd with Aonian dew,
Add one poor field-flower to thy blooming wreath!'

His question was answered when he heard polite applause and a woman's voice.

'Enchanting, enchanting,' said the voice. 'No one has written a sonnet for me before. A wonderful effort, especially for a self taught man.'

Brown calculated that he could either, leave, wait, or knock. If he left, he might be seen, which could be embarrassing. If he waited, what was he waiting for? So, he concluded, he might as well declare his presence. He knocked firmly on the door, but didn't enter.

Newton came do the door, 'Thomas! How are you?' He brought Brown into the room. 'Anna, this is Parson Brown from Tideswell.'

Brown thought that Anna looked a good few years older than Newton, whose age he didn't know, but he assumed him to be early thirties. Newton was a serious looking man with a distinguished long face and long nose to suit; he had silver and thinning hair and always dressed in a suit. The stranger was wearing some sort of evening frock; she was thin faced and thin featured with long wavy hair and an elegant deportment. As Brown was anxious to get back to his guest in Tideswell, and equally anxious not to become involved in poetry reading, he quickly made clear the reasons for his visit. Newton agreed to the arrangement to meet at the Red Lion at seven and didn't question further what the meeting was about. Brown presumed that Newton didn't want to risk lowly discussion of mill matters in front of his guest.

Newton showed Brown to the front door.

'She is Miss Anna Seward,' Newton whispered. 'She is a famous poet and known as The Swan of Lichfield. She is friendly with Doctor Johnson.'

Brown was unsure just how famous she was.

Brown rode home. He had done well. With the exception of understanding how Aonian dew might differ in taste or composition from Derbyshire dew, he was well satisfied. He laughed on his ride back at the *Dew* and the Sonnet that

Newton had written for Miss Seward! After calling to see his cow at Litton, he arrived back to the schoolhouse, dismounting from his mare just after one o'clock. On reaching the house, he found Holmes asleep in a chair in the sitting room, and he presumed Kezia was back, and in the kitchen, as he could smell soup.

'Your favourite soup,' Kezia said when she put it down, 'Green Pease.' There was no response from Brown and she added, 'Should I wake your guest?'

'I'll wake him, in a minute.'

Brown, who had been standing by the window, moved towards Kezia, 'Kizzie, please take this, it is for your grandmother,' Brown produced a bottle of currant wine from behind him and presented it to her.

'Thank you sir, she'll be grateful, I know. So am I.'

Five

MONDAY 19TH DECEMBER 1796
RED LION INN, LITTON

Brown and Holmes sat in the schoolhouse parlour, both enjoying an afternoon pipe and chatting about church, cotton and workhouse matters. They discussed their careers so far, and they planned and plotted their futures. Brown helped Holmes devise a more sensible route from Derbyshire to Nottinghamshire and finally on to Yorkshire, and Holmes helped Brown with a solution to the gravestone problem. The solution to the gravestone problem was straightforward: the gravestone, or at least the second epitaph on it, had to go. They were both agreed on that. How to achieve that end and how to broach the subject with Nathan Booker, was much more difficult; Brown could not afford to fall out with him.

Holmes had put forward a couple of ways of approaching him.

'Give him a gift, or perhaps, buy him a drink,' he suggested.

Brown puffed on his pipe and dwelt on the matter a little while longer.

'Thank you Joseph, I will do both! I will give him a gift that *is* drink: a bottle of last year's currant wine.'

Holmes was happy with that, although he was giving away his wine rather rapidly, this being the second bottle today. The earlier gift had been successful, and he hoped it would be again. The conversation with Booker was still going to be difficult; he would need to choose the right moment, and the right words, but at least he now had a plan.

Kezia served tea at six so that the men could be at the Red Lion by seven. She dished up pork chops, boiled potatoes and cabbage. To follow they had custard pudding.

'Your maid is very capable,' Holmes said.

Brown had noticed that Kezia seemed to be making more effort since last week's incident. It was nothing he could put his finger on; no single act stood out, but she just seemed to be putting a little more care into her work. He worried slightly that she might be expecting something more from their relationship. She needed to be clear that it was a working relationship, of master and maid.

It was a dark uneventful ten-minute walk to the Red Lion; they had considered a drink in the New George, but time was against them. They passed no one on the way to Litton, and the first face they saw since leaving the schoolhouse was Molly Baker, standing hands on hips at the top of the cellar stairs.

'I'll get a jug of ale, shall I?'

Brown was about to reply but she had scurried down to the cellar for the ale. She knew Brown's tipple, and his guests generally had the same. The Red Lion was a much simpler place than the New George. Where the New George had some importance in the town and was in every sense a coaching inn, the Red Lion was a simple village inn with no bar and four small rooms for drinking. All of the drink was kept in the cellar, and Molly carried it down and fetched it up. Molly was a short and stout no-nonsense woman. She was mid forties, but looked older. She was married to Francis Baker who was the actual licensed victualler, but Molly was the face of the Red Lion, and it was Molly who was in charge.

Brown explained the relationships to Holmes, 'Francis Baker is married to Molly. They have just one child, Ellen. Ellen is in the West Indies at the moment, in Jamaica, with Lydia Newton. Now Lydia is William Newton's sister and Francis is William Newton's uncle,' Brown explained all this to Holmes, although part way through he wondered why, as he was not sure that Holmes was keeping up. 'William Newton is one of the mill owners you will be meeting this evening.'

'So Lydia and William Newton are cousins to Ellen?' Holmes enquired. He *had* been keeping up.

'Yes, Lydia and Ellen are around the same age, seventeen or eighteen I think.'

Molly Baker reappeared slightly flushed from the climb up the cellar steps, and Brown made the introductions.

'Molly this is the Reverend Joseph Holmes from London.'

'Pleased to meet you,' she said and awkwardly shook hands with her left hand, as the jug of ale was in her right hand.

'I was just telling Joseph about Ellen,' Brown said. 'Have you heard anything yet?'

Molly put the ale on a table and plunged her hand into her front pinafore pocket. She produced a letter and waved it in front of Brown's face, 'Here it is,' she said. 'Her first letter. It arrived this last week. Would you read it to me?'

'Have you not heard it read it yet?' Brown knew that Molly could not read.

'My younger sister read it to me, but that's all. Would you read it again? It's not long.'

Molly produced some tankards from the side, and they all sat around the largest table in the room.

Brown began,

'November 8th.

'Dear Mother, I am now safely in Jamaica. Our house is in Falmouth in the county of Cornwall. It is strange to be so far away, yet surrounded by so many familiar names! The journey here was awful. We left Liverpool as planned on August 29th, and we next saw land after a fortnight at sea, when we got to Fonchial in the Madeiras. The weather was very bad on the way there, and we were very sick. We stayed there just one day, and it took another six weeks to get to Jamaica, but the weather slowly got better and hotter. Three people died on the way!

'The house here is beautiful and spacious. I have my own room. There is a large courtyard where we sit in the mornings and read. I am improving my reading, and I am enjoying reading the sonnets of Shakespeare. It is too hot to do anything outside in the afternoons so we often sit in and sew. In the early evenings, we have been learning to play tennis.

'I hope you and father are well.

'Love Ellen.'

Molly wiped her eyes on her grubby pinafore.

'Thank you Parson,' was all she said, and she shuffled off into the back to have a little weep on her own. She was missing her only child.

'Well,' said Brown, 'everyone is enjoying their adventures except me! You are roaming all over England, and Ellen is roaming all over the world.' As he was speaking Ellis Needham arrived and he continued, 'and Ellis has roamed all the way from Wormhill! Good evening Ellis. Allow me to introduce the Reverend Joseph Holmes.'

Molly brought more drink.

'Right then,' Needham said, 'can we get down to business?'

'We are waiting for Mr Newton I believe,' said Holmes.

Needham shot Brown a look, but Brown spoke before Needham could.

'Look I know that you and Newton are competitors and don't always see eye to eye, but I have seen you together before. So, as this proposition is of interest to both of you, open to both of you and as Joseph has a very limited time here, then it made sense on this occasion to have just one meeting. I'm sorry if it will be awkward for you.' Brown took a breath and a drink.

'I'll manage,' Needham grunted, wiping beer from his moustache. 'So, what do we do until Newton arrives,' Needham asked. 'Sing Carols?'

'I have an idea,' said Holmes, but William Newton arrived before he could reveal it.

There were brief introductions, and when all the tankards were again full, Brown looked to Holmes. Holmes took the hint and began talking to the mill owners about his proposal. What Brown noticed was that his speech was identical to the one he had delivered in the New George the previous evening. This young man knew about shortcuts too. These words were not from the heart, but from detailed preparation and careful rehearsal!

After the speech, the mill owners' expressions remained solemn and unchanged. There was silence and Holmes was worried. This was his second attempt, and the indications were not good. His first attempt had been to Richard Arkwright the previous week. He had been lucky enough to speak to the great man, but was out of the door within two minutes, with Arkwright having explained that he would only take local apprentices, and as a parting insult, he suggested that Holmes and his colluders were no better than slave merchants.

Holmes meekly asked, 'Any questions?'

The questions started to flow

'What age are the children?'

'All ages, but generally upwards of seven.'

Are there boys *and* girls?

'Yes, slightly more girls than boys.'

'What if they are no use, can we send them back?'

'Yes, so long as this is within six weeks of receiving them.'

Holmes dealt with these questions easily and sensing there was at least some interest, thought it wise to point out the financial advantages in taking the apprentices. He began by asking what the mill owners paid their local apprentices who lived at home. Both Newton and Needham paid them three shillings and sixpence a week.

'I have some typical weekly figures here on what it costs to keep an apprentice under this system,' Holmes read out the following figures, 'Food, two shillings and tuppence; Clothing, nine pence; lodging and other, nine pence,'

Needham wanted to know what was included in *other*. This time Holmes had no answer, but made a mental note to either find out or make something up before the next time. There was again silence. Needham was thinking. He knew he could do better than those costs, providing he had a good number of apprentices. Newton made a note to ask his counting house man what he thought. Molly Baker put another jug of ale down, but even that didn't break the new silence.

As a final and desperate attempt to make some progress with the mill owners, Holmes started talking about Richard Arkwright and other cotton mill owners that he claimed to have visited. This time they took the bait; anything Arkwright was doing, they would be foolish not to, and the conversation, although still without any commitment, moved to the practicalities of arranging the movement of apprentices, the legal transactions in shifting people from one parish to another and of course, the exchange of money.

Holmes had nothing left to say, so he gave the two mill owners a sheet with who to contact at Saint Giles. On the reverse, it contained a long list of girls and boys names, their ages and a few words describing their abilities. Newton looked at his copy reading quickly, finishing with the summary, which he read aloud.

'The younger branches of the poor of this parish might be useful to you as apprentices in your factory. If you want any of the above, we could readily furnish you with children from seven to twelve years of age of both sexes.' Newton looked up. 'Well that seems to sum it up. Thank you both,' he said.

The conversation then moved away from cotton, and aided by the drink, they fell into a more relaxed and comfortable subject area. Or so they thought.

'I hear,' Needham said, 'that the Reverend Brown has been showering his maid with gifts!'

All but Brown laughed. 'How do you know that?' Brown asked.

'So it is true!' replied Needham, and they laughed again.

Brown was angry. How could Needham know this; he had only given her the wine a few hours ago? In his temper, and having nothing on Needham to come back with, he attacked Newton instead.

'Of course, if I had the skills of Mr Newton, I might have read her poetry instead!' Brown said.

Now they all laughed but Newton.

Newton smiled a weak smile, 'The lady that the Reverend Brown refers to, and she *is* a Lady, not a maid.' This was followed with more laughter. 'She is Miss Anna Seward, otherwise known as The Swan of Lichfield. Now, the parson is correct in that I am actively looking for someone to be my wife, but I fear Miss Seward is somewhat beyond my reach; she is very well connected and unlikely to regard me as anything approaching her equal. However, she clearly recognises my talents and has in fact named me,' he paused for effect and took a drink, 'She has named me "The Minstrel of the Peak."' Newton thought that this would impress them, but this time the laughter lasted for a very long time!

Holmes found the walk back to the schoolhouse sobering, and his mind slipped back to his job, the workhouse children and the fear of failure. Brown didn't find the walk especially sobering and his mind slipped to thinking of Kezia and wondering whether he *did* have feelings for her?

'I'm really trying to do the best for those poor workhouse children,' Holmes said. 'They deserve a chance, and this could be it. This surely cannot be compared to slavery, can it?'

Brown was not listening.

Six

MONDAY 10TH APRIL 1797
SAINT GILES WORKHOUSE, LONDON

No one knew where the rumour began, but spread by the inmates, it was around the workhouse in no time. The rumour was that a deal was being made between the churchwardens of Saint Giles and the owners of some big cotton factories in the North. It was true: the parish of Saint Giles was about to dispose of a large number of workhouse children who would be apprenticed in factories until they were twenty-one. Most of the children were fearful of going anywhere else; they knew the workhouse routine and they were comfortable where they were, but Robert Blincoe, then aged twelve, had a different view. He was desperate to leave the confines of the workhouse and prayed that he would be chosen to go. Six months earlier Blincoe had missed an opportunity to escape when a number of chimney sweeps had come to the workhouse and picked boys to be their apprentices. Blincoe was told that he was not considered suitable, although he never knew why.

On the Monday morning, all of the children were gathered together in the committee room of the workhouse, and a list of names was read out. The names were those who had been chosen, although this time the selection methods had been much less rigorous, and almost everyone over the age of seven, boys and girls, were to be moved. Blincoe's name was amongst them, and after a cursory examination by a doctor, they were addressed by one of the parish officers.

'Oh lucky children!' he began. 'You have each been selected to be apprenticed to a skilled trade bringing the prospect of infinite riches. You will shortly begin this exciting journey, but this is not just a journey on the roads of England: this is the beginning of your journey in life. If you do as you are told, then you will become ladies and gentlemen, fed on roast beef and plum-pudding, be allowed to ride your masters' horses, have silver watches and always plenty of cash in your pockets.'

This rousing speech changed the attitudes of many of the children from one of doubt and fear, to hope and excitement.

As the children filed out of the committee room they were given completely new clothes for the journey and neatly wrapped in brown paper parcels, two other sets, one for working and another set that were called holiday clothes. Finally, each of them was given a sixpenny piece, a new pocket-handkerchief and a large piece of gingerbread. They were then carefully moved from the workhouse to the wagons that would transport them. The way from the workhouse to the wagons was secured by parish beadles wearing their official robes. They were positioned in two lines to look like a guard of honour, but their main task was to prevent any nervous children from fleeing. There were about forty children to each wagon with the girls and boys separated; once the grated doors were locked, the wagons moved slowly away, with the children cheering noisily. The floor of the wagons were covered in straw to make the journey more comfortable, but the unsupervised children chose to throw it at each other. But a few hours into the journey, the sun began to fade and so did the fun; the children began to realise that this would be a long and uncomfortable journey. They travelled through the afternoon and night, stopping only for the necessaries, but after just one night in the wagons, many were wishing they were back in the workhouse. The heavy jolts on the rough roads gave most of them bruises, although the drivers tried to console them.

'Don't worry about a few bumps as when you reach the mills, the owners will look after you and they'll pay attention to all your wishes.'

The next day they arrived in Leicester where Blincoe managed to spend his entire sixpence on apples. He had little experience of money, and an unscrupulous stall-holder took all of his money in exchange for a large bag of apples, a bag that should have cost no more than a halfpenny. The children then changed wagons and drivers, with each wagon now destined for a specific mill. There was about thirty boys and girls in Blincoe's wagon and they travelled through the whole of the next day, until they arrived at Cromford in Derbyshire, where they stopped for the night. The girls were lodged in dwelling houses, and the boys were put in a barn, sleeping on straw.

In the morning, the cart set off, stopping next in Bakewell market place. Under the supervision of Ayres and Jones, and in groups of four at a time, the children were let out of the cart, to use the necessaries. They were then allowed to drink from the pump before being put back in the cart; the process then being repeated for the next four. Despite the security, one boy, John Emery, did attempt his escape. It was poorly planned, carelessly executed, and with his strength weakened by the rigours of the journey, he proved no match against the experienced hands of two local farmers; he had made it no further than twenty yards. He was thrown back in the cart in a matter of fact way by Ayres and without any further punishment.

When the children had all had their turn, Ayres, who did most of the talking, shouted, 'Right you lot, we won't be stopping again. Another hour, and we'll be there: Litton mill. You'll look back on those days in the workhouse with such happy memories!' He then laughed an affected evil laugh. Ayres delivered a much more pessimistic view than had the driver who took them from London, and Blincoe wondered which of the drivers was telling the truth.

Jones who was more in charge of the horses, manoeuvred steadily out of the market place. By this time, the children were barely speaking; the journey that had begun with such optimism and joy, was drawing towards its end in doubt and despondency. The children were tired, grubby and sore from the journey; no cheeriness remained. Ayres hadn't helped their humour, periodically telling them some horror story of where they were going and what dreadful things might happen to them.

Over that last two days, the roads had been rough in many sections, but after Bakewell, they became so difficult that to prevent the cart overturning, considerable care and skill was needed. The road was now twisty and narrow, and Jones, who had the better driving skills, was watching carefully for the ruts and bumps. Those that he could avoid, he did, but those that were unavoidable, he had to slow for.

The route had followed the Derwent valley upstream from Derby to Matlock, stopping at Cromford and then on to Rowsley. From Rowsley the route changed to follow the river Wye, passing through Bakewell, and now they were headed to Litton mill. After Bakewell, the countryside was untamed, the track frequently lifted up from the bottom of the valley; in some places rising hundreds of feet above the river. The river was dotted with mills. Most of them were new cotton mills, but water power was nothing new, and alongside the Wye, the cart had passed a flour mill at Rowsley, a marble cutting mill at Ashford and as they neared their destination they turned on to an even narrower track and passed a small paper mill. The children were unaware of any of this as they were exhausted and were concentrating on bracing themselves for the jolts that further hurt their fully formed bruises. The terrain had forced the road further north than Litton mill, picking up the river Wye about half a mile upstream of where they wanted to be. It was now just past five o'clock, and for this last half mile the track, though still narrow, was almost level, running next to the fast flowing river Wye.

Slowly, the three-storey grey stone building of Litton mill came closer. The cart fell into its shadow as it entered the gates, and when it stopped, they were alongside the high limestone walls of the mill. Blincoe was one of the last out of the cart; he was as weary and battered as the rest of them, but additionally he was suffering with bellyache, having finished all of his Leicestershire apples on the journey. Ayres and Jones lined up the children in two rows; boys in one, and girls in the other. Blincoe counted twelve boys and seventeen girls. In front of each of them were placed their brown paper parcels containing the other two sets of clothes that had been carried since London. By this time, Woodward, Needham and the Governor, Richard Milner, were there to meet and inspect them. Needham spoke first.

'Welcome to Litton mill. Good evening. I am Mr Needham, this is Mr Woodward,' he turned to look at each of the men he was introducing, 'and this is Mr Milner. We are just some of the people in charge here, but exactly who is in charge of what will become clear during your first few days. I hope you have an enjoyable and interesting time whilst you are here. Now, I know you have had a long journey, and a decent dinner is being prepared for you, so I will leave you now and hand over to Mr Woodward.'

'I am Mr Woodward,' he boomed, 'You will address me and all the other managers as, Sir. While you are here you will work very hard, but in return, we are giving you an apprenticeship, and by the time you are twenty-one, you will be highly trained.'

As Woodward was speaking, he walked in front of the children, looking at each of them carefully and scaring them when his eyes met theirs.

'We are feeding you, clothing you and providing sleeping quarters for you. In addition you will attend a Sunday school, and if all that isn't enough we will give you a penny wages each week. Why, I wish I could change places with you!'

This was meant as a joke, but the travel-shocked children did not react; the other man smiled and Needham who had slipped away, rode home on his horse. Woodward waited while the clattering of the hooves crossed the end of the yard and faded as Needham rode up the track alongside the river.

Woodward then looked at his notes and announced, 'Those of you who disobey instruction; who are late for work; who neglect their work; who cavort, at any time; who are insolent; who spend too long in the necessaries; who are found smoking anywhere; or who disobey safety instructions in the mill,' he then looked up and moved his head looking in the eyes of all of the children, 'will be punished severely!' After a long pause he struck up again, 'Anyone caught disobeying the rules will not only be punished here, at Litton mill, but you will ultimately answer for your actions before the Mercy of God, and I know that some of you will burn in Hell!'

The shy and tired Blincoe stood trembling. All this talk of punishment and Hell added to the severe discomfort that he already felt from his bellyache. When Woodward had finished speaking, he handed over to the last man, Milner. He too was a frightening looking figure. He was tall and fat with a big nose and ugly face, but his speech and his manner seemed friendly, certainly when compared to Woodward.

'Girls and boys,' he began, 'I will show you next to the apprentice house and where you will sleep and where you can put your other clothes away. Each of you has been allocated to an established apprentice who will look after you for the rest of today and over the next few days while you settle in. They are called chums, and as I speak they are helping to prepare a meal to welcome you. They will serve you the meal tonight and are there to answer any of your questions. Right, follow me in line. Girls first.'

The children followed Milner, and he showed them to the apprentice house and to the girls and boys rooms. The building stood alone a little away from the mill. At the near end was an arrangement of wooden stairs looking as though they had been added as an afterthought. Blincoe followed Milner and the line of boys up the stairs; they filed into the boys room placing their clothes parcels on some open shelves near the door. The inside walls of the large room were unpainted bare stone; above were dusty and spidery roof timbers, and the floor was bare boards. There was a door at one end and a window at the other. In the roof were three opening lights and beds at two levels running down each side of the room. On one side of the long room, there was a break in the beds where there was a fireplace, but there was no fire lit tonight, and it was cold. The girls room, unseen by Blincoe until the next day, was much the same, but darker as there were no roof lights.

After ridding themselves of their clothes parcels, they shuffled down to the lower room: the refectory. Here they were seated on long benches that were placed in front of long tables. As soon as they were seated, a door swung open, and the chums began bringing plates of food. Blincoe and the rest of the travellers tucked into roast lamb, potatoes, green beans and gravy. Blincoe was sitting next to Durant a boy he knew from the workhouse and who he had become friendlier with on the journey.

'This is good,' said Blincoe.

'Very tasty,' said Durant.

That was the entire conversation.

Whilst he was waiting for his pudding, and having taken his eyes away from his plate for the first time, Blincoe looked around. The room was the same size as the two above; the only difference being that there must have been a kitchen at the side into which he couldn't see. The established apprentices were sat at another long table, but they were not eating: they were watching carefully over the new arrivals and in particular, their plates. On the command of the governor, the old plates were taken away, those with any scraps on being the first to go. They were then replaced with full plates of apple pie. Blincoe ate his pie with his fingers and went to pick up a piece off the floor that he had dropped, but on seeing that the floor was just bare earth, he left it there.

'Robert Blincoe will go with Isaac Moss.'

Milner was reading out the pairings, of who would chum with whom. On hearing his name, Blincoe followed the pattern of previous children; he got up from his seat at the table and met up with his chum by the refectory door.

After the substantial meal, and after his chum had shown him where the necessaries were, he felt a lot happier. Eating so many sour apples was something he was not looking to repeat, but the meal had been good, as good as any meal the workhouse had dished up, and although Woodward may have shouted and talked mainly of punishment, it was true that they were getting a recognised apprenticeship. Blincoe's whole life up to now, or at least that part he could remember, had been in the workhouse. This was his first experience of anything different, and it was *very* different, but on balance, Blincoe decided that he was happy.

'I'm Isaac Moss. I'm from Hammersmith, that's in London. You?

'Robert Blincoe from Saint Giles, that's in London too.'

'I knew you were from London by your accent. I'll show you 'round tomorrow, 'though it's a fairly small place really. You'll soon work it all out. I expect you're tired. Are you?'

'Very tired. We've been travelling for three days, and now there's all this to learn!'

'Don't worry.' Moss was undressing now, and so Blincoe did the same. 'We'll get some sleep now, and in the morning, I'm to show you to the mill. Then I think someone will show you what to do. That's what happened when I started here.'

'How long have you been here?' Blincoe asked.

'Just a month now. You're the third load of apprentices to come here. I was in the second load. The first apprentices came in March.'

The boys put on their nightshirts and got into bed. Although they shared the same bed, they topped and tailed with two pillows, one of them at each end of the bed.

'Goodnight,' Moss said.

'Goodnight,' Blincoe replied.

Blincoe turned his head to face the wall, and despite the chatter and commotion of all the other pairings coming into the room, and despite all the confusion, questions, and fears of burning in Hell, all of which were whirring around in his head, he was asleep almost immediately.

Seven

THURSDAY 13TH APRIL 1797
LITTON MILL

Blincoe woke up in Litton mill apprentice house with Moss shaking him. This was a huge relief to Blincoe as just prior to this he had been fighting for his life at the top of a church tower.

It began with Blincoe at the top of a Church tower. The fires of Hell were burning on the ground, and licking and climbing towards the top of the tower. Then the church bell was ringing and he was fighting with someone. But he was losing the fight, because he couldn't move his arms. He tried to shout for help, but no sound came from his mouth. His assailant was now shaking him, and he was unable to fight back.

But suddenly, his ordeal became a welcome reality; he was awake and very happy to see Moss who had saved him from the nightmare.

'Come on. It's time we were up and dressed. The first bell has gone, and if Milner comes back and any of us is still in bed we'll catch it.'

Blincoe did as he was told and dressed quickly. It was still dark outside.

'What time is it?' Blincoe asked.

'Half past five. The bell goes at half past five. We have to be at work by six.'

Blincoe had no idea what to expect, and fearful of Woodward's earthly punishments, as well as his non-earthly ones, he copied precisely what Moss did and followed him out of the apprentice house. In the cold and damp of the coming dawn, Blincoe, Moss and a gaggle of other apprentices had a cursory wash from a pump, beneath which was a long stone trough. It was a very busy scene with almost eighty children scurrying about, their only light coming from the moon and a solitary oil lamp. Next, they were back into the refectory, and the pair went up to collect their breakfasts. There was no table service this morning, no food brought by chums. Moss explained how it all worked.

'Mrs Milner, that's the Governor's wife, does all the cooking helped by one or two of the apprentice girls. You also have your dinner here at one o'clock, and your supper here after work has finished. On Sundays breakfast is later, and dinner is at six.'

It was Mrs Milner who dished out their porridge, which was accompanied with a generous piece of oatcake. Blincoe was still quite full from his dinner the previous evening, and although he cleared his porridge bowl, he left a large piece of oatcake on his plate.

'You can't leave that,' Moss said. 'You don't leave anything here. You'll be hungry later. You see. Put the bread in your pocket for then.'

Blincoe again did as he was told.

Just before six o'clock, the new apprentices were stood in the yard in exactly the same place they had been the previous evening; their chums had disappeared into the mill to start their work. Blincoe's heart sank as the figure of Woodward appeared from the mill and again stood before them. He was accompanied by a number of other men,

'Good morning,' Woodward shouted, 'for those of you with a poor memory my name is Mr Woodward.'

Woodward paused, and Blincoe wondered if that was a joke, either way Woodward's name was the one name Blincoe had not forgotten.

Woodward then read out lists of who should go where. 'Emery and Blincoe will go with Mr Smith.' Smith collected the boys and they followed him up the steps and into the mill. On entering the mill, the noise was deafening; speaking to anyone else was impossible. Smith led the boys through an area full of noisy machinery, through various doors, up stairs, and then down stairs, until Blincoe was quite lost. Eventually, they arrived in a quiet area.

'We've come here so we can talk,' Smith said.

Smith then introduced himself and familiarised himself with the boy's names.

'You will have seen, well heard, how noisy it is in most of the mill, and the noisy part is where you will be working. The work though is very easy. All you will be doing is picking up waste cotton from the floor, underneath the mules. They are the big spinning machines. You then put the waste cotton into sacks. Blincoe is to work the river side of the room and Emery the other side. Make sure you keep well clear of the moving parts of the mule and well clear of the belts and shafting. Also there are other people working the machine. There's spinners and piecers; you must not interrupt their work. I will be in the room at the end near the door so if you want anything else ask me. If I'm not there someone else will be. Your job is known as scavenging, and you are called scavengers. Now then, do you have any questions?'

Blincoe, eager to show his best on the first day of his apprenticeship, got to work in earnest. The mill had already been running for almost an hour, and no one today, had picked up any waste. Blincoe was small and agile, and picking up cotton from under the mules was easy enough. The conditions though were miserable: the noise, the cotton dust in the air, the stench of hot oil, the heat of the room and constantly stooping for the cotton waste. These all combined to make Blincoe feel quite sick. At ten o'clock, Smith came over to Blincoe and tapped him on the shoulder. Knowing that Blincoe was probably not yet skilled in lip reading, which was how most people communicated in the mill, he bellowed in his ear, 'You can go for a ten minute break now, follow that girl there.' Smith pointed at one of the piecers who was heading towards the door.

In the yard outside, Blincoe made an effort to talk to to the girl. He found out that she was Irish, her name was Mary Turner, she was nine years old, and she came here with the first load of apprentices. She showed Blincoe the routine at the morning break, which was just a drink of water from the pump. If the weather was bad, the apprentices took this in the refectory, otherwise they sat around outside in the fresh air.

'You must keep your eyes clean,' she said. 'It's the cotton dust. You need to bathe them as often as you can. Watch me.'

Blincoe was eager to do anything to reduce his suffering, and despite the water being near freezing, he did the same as Mary.

Mary took handfuls of water and brought them to her eyes.

'Try to keep your eyes open,' she said.

The break time was soon over, and Blincoe was again picking cotton off the floor. On his return, John Emery was allowed to go for his break, but after just another hour of back-breaking work, Blincoe was feeling weak and so sat down on one of the large window cills looking over the river. No sooner had he sat down than Smith was on him. Smith didn't ask him any questions; he just shouted in his ear, 'Back to work lad!' Blincoe did as he was told but he was worried about falling against the machinery and belts, and so he worked slightly slower and took more care. He realised that he must settle into a work pattern that would get the job done whilst at the same time keeping him safe from any accidents. Over the next hour he developed this new technique working more methodically and taking extra care. Doing this he found that he could still keep the floor clean but with much less effort. Just before noon, another man came into the room and headed straight over to Smith. Blincoe saw that both men were looking towards him, and then Smith was pointing. Gestures that cut through the noise indicated that Blincoe was to go to them.

'You're to go with Mr Simpson, he's the smith.'

Blincoe had no idea why Smith was telling him that this other man was 'The Smith', but he followed Simpson out of the mill and to a building across the yard. They went inside and straight into a hot dark room which had a sickly sulphurous smell, but there was no cotton dust, and no noise. The room was cluttered with tools, pieces of metal of every shape and size, wheels, shafts, belting, gears, oil, grease, jars and tins; there was no surface clear of some mill part or other, though the names and functions of these items were, at this time, unknown to Blincoe. In the far corner was what Blincoe soon found out was a furnace; this was the source of the heat and of the smell.

'Robert Blincoe isn't it? I'm Mr Simpson. Now you can call me Mr Simpson, I'm not a Sir. If I was, and if the King had laid his sword on my shoulder, I don't think I'd be here!' Simpson laughed.

Blincoe studied the man. He had a strong Scottish accent, which Blincoe recognised, as he had come across two people in the workhouse with similar accents. He couldn't tell his age but he was not old. His face was hidden behind the biggest moustache he had ever seen, and his body was protected by a shiny brown leather apron. Blincoe, though, was more interested in whether he was going to behave like Woodward, or whether he might be someone he could get on with.

'Now the last lad didn't last the morning,' Simpson said, 'so I'm hoping you might do better than that!'

Simpson went on to explain that he was the smith, or blacksmith, in charge of the smithy and the next-door stables. He asked Blincoe about his background and the journey to Litton mill, and Blincoe decided that Simpson was by far the nicest grown-up he had met since arriving at the mill.

That was all the time they had before Simpson sent Blincoe off for his dinner.

Blincoe rejoined the other children in the refectory for the dinner of beef stew and oat cake. Mary Turner sat next to him and they chatted away about their mornings and their work. Mary's morning had been quite uneventful,

'Just hard work as normal,' she said.

Mrs Milner cleared away the stew-pot and then shouted, 'You need to back at the mill in five minutes, five minutes.' Blincoe had already wiped his bowl clean and after a quick drink from the pump. He made his way back to the smithy.

'Nails,' Simpson said, and held one up to Blincoe's face 'That's what we're making today. Nails. Things are a bit quiet at the minute so we've got the chance to make some and top up these tins here.' Simpson rattled a rod down a row of tins that were high on a shelf. 'We'll probably get called to the mill and not get any done; in this job things can change in a second, you'll see. Anyway, we'll start you with some wee ones.'

Simpson worked patiently with Blincoe, showing him how to make nails. It was one of the easiest things that the smith did, and it was one of the lighter jobs, so quite suitable for a young boy. Blincoe took to this very well, and although his speed didn't match that of the experienced smith, the quality was as good, and Simpson was pleased with his progress.

'There,' said Simpson interrupting Blincoe's hammering, 'you won't get that service anywhere else.' It was four o'clock, and the smith presented Blincoe with a hot cup of tea in a bent tin mug.

'Now, we're not supposed to do this, so if you hear anyone coming, you put it here, and quick.' The smith showed Blincoe a space on a shelf just behind a large can of oil where they could quickly slide their mugs.

'But as there's no one about, we'll just have five minutes.' Blincoe listened hard for those five minutes, fearing Woodward might catch him, but they were safe. He took this opportunity of finishing off the piece of oatcake from earlier. He wondered if he should have offered some of it to the smith, but it was too late; he had eaten it.

The afternoon and early evening passed without any interruptions from the mill. Blincoe carried on making nails on the small anvil, and by mid evening, he had learned to make four different sizes. Simpson left Blincoe making nails alone whilst he moved to making different sizes of horseshoe on the larger of the two anvils.

'Right young Robert,' Simpson was looking at his pocket watch. 'It's about time we did the lamps.'

'Lamps Mr Simpson? What lamps?'

'Ah well, to keep us from getting bored, one of our jobs is to light all the outside lamps. Sam Palfrey, he's really the carpenter, looks after all of the inside ones, although he's got the easy job as most of the over-lookers light their own, and he doesn't have gales blowing his lamps out!' Simpson took a small box from a high shelf and a lantern from the same place. He opened the lantern cover and opened the box. 'Have you seen a tinderbox before?'

'Yes, but not close up, and I've never used one,' Blincoe said.

Simpson showed him how to light the cloth and then from that he lit the lantern. He then immediately snuffed it out. 'Right, you try,' he said. Blincoe lit the cloth first time and then lit the lantern only slightly burning his fingers.

'Beginner's luck I think,' said Simpson and laughed. 'Come on lets go.' He took the lantern, from which he would light the others and a pole from behind the door, with which he would lift down the outside lamps.

Blincoe counted nine lamps outside and then some more in the apprentices' rooms.

'Apart from our own, in the smithy and stables, these are the only inside ones we do,' Simpson explained.

Blincoe had somehow expected the girls' room to look different, to feel different, maybe to smell different, but it was as stark and miserable as the boys' room. It was when Blincoe was in the boys' room that he saw his bed and realised how tired he was. He hadn't asked what time work finished, and no one had told him. Tired though he was, he had still experienced enough of the mill to know that in the smithy, he was in the better place.

It was nine o'clock when work finished and Simpson snuffed out their lamps and they stepped outside.

'You've worked well young Robert. You'll be here tomorrow at six.'

Blincoe was unsure whether that was a question, or an instruction, and so replied, 'Thank you Mr Simpson.'

'Do you know what our first job tomorrow is?' Simpson asked. By this time, he had locked up the smithy, and they were walking across the yard.

'No Mr Simpson.'

'Think about it! Goodnight Robert.'

'Goodnight Mr Simpson.' Blincoe headed towards the refectory, and Simpson disappeared in a direction unknown to Blincoe.

The remainder of the evening passed quickly. Supper was the same pot of stew that they had at dinner that day. Blincoe was later than most and could only find a seat amongst some established boys who chattered amongst themselves, mostly about girls, and ignored him. After supper, he went to wash in the pump, but his hands, oily and black from the work in the smithy, remained black. In bed, and after the room's lamps had been put out and the door locked, his chum was telling him about one of the new girls.

'Her finger was chopped clean off,' he said. 'Only an hour ago, in one of the mules.'

As interested as Blincoe was in this story, he was still asleep before the end of it.

Blincoe was outside the smithy before six. He wondered how he would manage with another day working until nine o'clock, but his belly was full of porridge, and he had an emergency oatcake in his pocket, so he was as prepared as he could be. He stood there with his still grubby black hands waiting for Simpson and trying to guess their first job of the day. He had no idea.

'Well. I thought you might have worked it out it by now,' Simpson said, 'What on earth have you been doing all night?' Simpson laughed and went on, 'It's the lamps; the outside lamps. We leave those on all night and so now, it's just coming light, we need to snuff them out and top up the oil.'

The morning passed quickly. The lamps were done, and Simpson showed Blincoe around the smithy a little more and explained some of the tools and some of the stock. Around eight o'clock a young boy came over to give Simpson a message.

'Sir, the old carding engine's broke,' the boy blurted out.

'Is it jammed with cotton?' Simpson asked.

'I think so.'

'Tell them I'll be five minutes.'

Simpson calmly gathered up tools that he might need and put them in a sackcloth bag for Blincoe to carry, and they made their way over to the carding room.

'Have you been in the carding room?' Simpson asked on the way over.

'No,' said Blincoe. 'What is it?'

'There's two machines in there that mix and clean the raw cotton, so that it's in a decent state for spinning. Someone will have tried to feed in too much cotton in one go, and it's all got jammed up. It's happened before.'

The carding room had two carding engines, and whereas it was far dustier than the spinning rooms, it was a little less noisy. Simpson was correct in his guess about the problem; he and Blincoe had to remove the feed rollers and then clean out the cotton. They worked well together and needed to, as the reassembly was tricky, needing one of them on each side of the machine to reposition the rollers accurately.

When they were back in the smithy, each with a mug of tea, Simpson spoke.

'If we don't get mythered by anyone else, then after dinner we'll have a ride out to Baslow coal-pit as the coal's getting a bit low. There's two coal-sheds across the yard there, but only one with any coal in at the moment. We don't need much, not now it's April as we're not lighting many fires in the mill, but the furnace still eats it up.'

There were no interruptions, and just before two o'clock, Blincoe jumped up onto the cart, and the horse pulled them away from the mill. Initially, they followed the same road that Blincoe had travelled on when he came to the mill, just two days before. His previous journey had given him no view as he had been imprisoned, but now, he was alongside the driving seat, and he was taking in a view he had never before experienced. For Blincoe, this was the first time that he had seen the Derbyshire landscape.

'It's so green. Everything is green,' he said.

Blincoe had grown up in the dullness of the workhouse; had been transported to Litton mill in a cage and then for the last two days had only seen the outside, and inside, walls of the mill. He now saw acres of grass, thousands of trees, thousands of smaller bushes, purple flowers, pink flowers, yellow flowers: he had no knowledge of their names, but he did have an instinctive appreciation of the natural beauty around him. He grabbed at some of the plants as they passed close to them, examined them and then tossed them away. Blincoe was smiling for most of the journey.

It was an hour to Baslow, an hour at the coal-pit loading coal, a quarter of an hour having a drink and an hour back. Blincoe concluded that life couldn't get any better than this.

It was on the way back that Simpson and Blincoe got chatting a little more. Blincoe, aware of his own shyness, was now making more of an effort to make conversation. There was a reason for this: although Blincoe had only worked in the mill for half a day, he had experienced enough, seen enough and heard enough to know that working inside the factory was not for him, and whatever else happened, he must keep the smithy job. He wanted Simpson to like him, and he thought that striking up a conversation would lead to a friendship, and that would help keep him in the smithy. During their chatting, Simpson explained to him that the factory worked Monday to Saturday and that on Sundays it was closed, and all Blincoe would need to do was attend Sunday school for an hour. Blincoe had been told this from his chum, but what he didn't know was what Simpson told him next, which was this coming weekend, Easter weekend, the factory didn't work at all on the Monday.

'So, I take it you've no plans for Monday then?' Simpson asked. Unknown to Blincoe, Simpson's conversation had been deliberate and leading towards this.

'No, nothing.'

'I've got a wee job on at Tideswell,' Simpson said and then added quickly, 'It's a job of mine, nothing to do with the mill. If you want to come and help me, you could earn yourself a penny.'

'Yes please.'

Eight

MONDAY 17TH APRIL 1797
LITTONSLACK

Mr Milner rang the bell, but not until half past seven. Blincoe was already awake; in fact a good number of the apprentices were awake, being quite unused to such a long lie in.

For the apprentices this was going to be an unusual day, as apart from their normal meals, little was required of them; the mill was silent as this was Easter Monday and a holiday. The previous day had been quiet too. The apprentices had attended the regular Sunday school in the apprentice refectory, but at the end of Parson Brown's Sunday school, Mr Milner had addressed them.

'The remainder of today, and all of tomorrow is yours to do, within reason, as you please. As your employer and keeper, we would remind you that your appearance and your behaviour reflect upon the mill.' As Milner spoke, he strode back and forth in front of the apprentices, not looking at them, but at the floor ahead of him. 'You are reminded that you should go no further than Cressbrook, Litton or Tideswell, and those of you who venture to these places should wear their holiday best. Those staying around the mill may wear other clothing. There will be just Mrs Milner and myself here with breakfast at eight and other meals as normal.' He stopped and turned to face them, leaning on his stick. 'Please enjoy this holiday, and please do not get into trouble as there will be severe punishments for those who misbehave.'

Blincoe was unsure what clothes to wear. He had three sets of clothes: his holiday best, his work clothes and the clothes he had worn to travel to Litton mill. He was going to Tideswell and so according to Milner, he should wear his holiday best, but he was also going to be working with the smith and so really ought to wear his work clothes. The clothes he had travelled in would have been a good compromise between the two, but these had been taken away for washing. Blincoe settled on his work clothes, but wore his best shoes and his best shirt. He was pleased with his efforts as he was both smartly dressed and, for once, clean. The cleanliness was partly due to a day free of work, allowing the grime to slowly fade with each washing and partly due to a tip that the smith had shown him on the Friday, which was to wash the grease off his hands using paraffin oil. Blincoe finished his breakfast set off for the meeting with the smith.

There were a number of tracks away from Litton mill. To the east of the mill, and downstream alongside the river, was a difficult path towards Cressbrook mill. Blincoe and his chum had attempted this path the day before, but halfway to Cressbrook, their way was flooded, and they had to turn around. To the west and upstream from the mill, there was the track that was the main route in and out of the mill; this was the route Blincoe and the smith had taken to Baslow the previous week. South, and across the river from the mill, were steep limestone cliffs. There was no established route to the south, although Blincoe's chum had said that there was a tricky climb through to a village called Taddington.

It was to the north, up a very steep and winding track where Blincoe had been instructed to go, and he arrived at the top of the track, out of breath and flushed, but well in time for his nine o'clock meeting with the smith. Simpson lived at a cottage; one of a row of ten which were collectively known as Littonslack.

The cottages had been built by Richard Arkwright when he was contemplating extending his cotton empire further up the river Wye. Arkwright had eventually given up with the idea of building mills any further North than Bakewell, and his interests, which included the Littonslack cottages, were sold and eventually came in to the ownership of Ellis Needham. Needham needed these cottages as there was little accommodation in the area, and owning them enabled him to advertise for skilled men to manage the various aspects of the mill and offer them accommodation. This was how Simpson, originally from Perth, came to be at Litton mill. All this was unknown to Blincoe at this time, as was the name of one of Simpson's neighbours: Robert Woodward. Blincoe sat on top of the gate, where he had been told to wait, picking at the blossom on a tree and whistling a tune from one of yesterday's hymns. Had he known that Woodward was just a few yards away, he might have behaved very differently.

Simpson arrived on time, or as on time as Blincoe could tell, as sitting on a gate in the countryside, he had no way of knowing the time. Simpson was dressed in his ordinary work clothes and carried three sackcloth bags.

'Right young Robert, We better make sure you earn your money, so you can carry the two lightest bags.'

They set of up the track towards Tideswell. Simpson knew the area well, and rather than keep to the main roads and established paths, he took what he called ruts across fields and along clumsy paths. This meant that they skirted around Litton village. On the way, Simpson explained what the job was.

'Today, young Robert, I'm working for myself, nothing to do with the mill.' Blincoe noted that he had already told him that. In fact so far all he had been told, and told twice, was that Simpson was not working for the mill.

'I, well we, have two mares to shoe. One is Parson Brown's mare and the other, which shares the same paddock, is Whacker White's. Four shoes for the rector's mare and two for Whacker's. Any questions?'

Blincoe, weighed down with the heavy bags was thinking. He moved the bags from one shoulder to the other. 'No Mr Simpson. No questions. Not yet anyway.'

Blincoe was greatly relieved when they finally descended down a slippery bank and into Tideswell. They crossed a road and went around to the back door of the vicarage. Blincoe stood behind Simpson and let the bags drop from his sore shoulders.

Parson Brown had recently moved from the schoolhouse to the vicarage. The previous rector, Shuttleworth, had died, and this had in turn removed the obstacles that were preventing Brown from living in the vicarage.

Brown came to the door looking grubby and dishevelled. His shirt was hanging loose, and he had nothing on his feet. Blincoe stood back, and although Brown spoke quietly, Blincoe could hear Simpson's side of the conversation.

'Aye, that's fine. I'll be about an hour and a half and then I'll be back for my one and ten pence.' The men shook hands, and the door shut.

The mares were in the paddock behind the vicarage. In the paddock, Simpson lined up all his tools, nails and horse shoes, so that everything was in easy reach. Blincoe's job sounded straightforward enough. He stood at the top of some steps so that he was at the same height as the horse, and all he had to do was hold the horse and keep it calm whilst the smith did his work. This was not easy, as Blincoe was small and no match for the horse's strength, but by holding on to the horse and reassuring the animal that all was well, he somehow muddled through. Blincoe was alarmed how rough Simpson was with the horses, tearing the old shoes off, taking nails out with big pincers and then hacking and filing away at the hoof.

'They don't feel anything,' Simpson shouted as he cut away at a hoof between his knees. 'Not unless you just catch them wrong. It's like cutting your nails.'

Blincoe still winced, especially when he saw, and heard, the nails being hammered home.

‘Keep hold, keep hold.’ Brown’s mare seemed unhappy with the hammering. ‘It’s not the nails that bother them, just the banging on the hoof,’ Simpson assured him.

‘Those bags you carried here,’ Simpson went on, ‘would have been a whole lot heavier if I hadn’t measured the shoe size before we came. Four and three quarters for this one; five inches for the other one.’

It was at this point looking down at the piles of new and used shoes and nails that Blincoe realised that his first day at Litton mill had been making the very nails that Simpson was using. At the same time, Simpson himself had been making the very shoes that he was now busy nailing on. Blincoe was sharp enough to work out the rest very quickly: one shilling and ten pence income, less one-penny wages, for the apprentice, less nothing for materials left Simpson with one shilling and nine pence profit for just an hour and a half’s work!

Brown was now dressed, though still unshaven, and he invited them into the vicarage.

‘You look thirsty,’ he said and led them into the kitchen. He cleared two chairs of the piles of clothes, books and jumble, throwing it all into a corner, and the guests sat down. The remainder of the kitchen was no tidier with the pump surrounded by dirty pots. In fact, there was no surface clear of the general clutter. Brown pumped up some water for the guests, swilled out some passably clean glasses and sought to explain.

‘My maid has had to go away,’ he said, ‘to look after her Great Aunt in Whaley Bridge. So I’m afraid the place is a bit of a muddle at the moment.’

‘It looks just fine to me,’ said Simpson, trying to console the parson, but it was so obviously not fine, that he immediately wished he had said nothing. Brown offered the glasses, and Blincoe drank his straight away, save the last half inch, which he had learned to leave. This was the half inch that generally had little crawlies in it; something common to Derbyshire he deduced, as the water in London had always been clear. Simpson and Brown chatted briefly about horse matters with Blincoe listening. The conversation eventually came around to payment, and Brown handed over the one shilling and ten pence. Blincoe noted that Brown's mare cost one shilling and two pence and Whacker's bill was eight pence. It seemed that Brown was paying both bills.

'Bill Simpson! We don't see you in here very often?' Molly Baker said.

'Well no, but me and young Robert here,' Simpson patted Robert on the head, in case she should have missed who he was referring to, 'have done a fair morning's work, and we thought a wee drink was deserved.'

Simpson and Blincoe sat at a table near the front window of the Red Lion. This was Blincoe's first taste of beer, and he quickly decided that he liked both the taste *and* the effect. About halfway down his pint he noticed himself becoming more relaxed, talking more easily, and as he later described it to his chum, 'everything seemed right.'

Simpson handed over a penny to Blincoe.

'Best we keep today's job to ourselves,' he said, 'other folk don't need to know about our business.'

'Of course,' Blincoe replied and becoming braver with his conversation, enquired, 'Do you do many of these jobs?' Blincoe was thinking how he might earn more money than the one penny he would receive from the mill each week.

'No not many, maybe every other week I do an hour or two. Not always shoeing though, often just general repair jobs. It's kettles and pans more often than not.'

Simpson, aware that there was already a pan in his workbag for the next day and concerned that the cloudy division between his own work and his job at Litton mill might make the conversation more difficult than it need be, he changed the subject.

'Did you see the state of the parson?' he asked. 'Definitely not a man that should be living by his self.' Simpson paused and then spoke in a lower voice, 'They say his maid's great bellied, and she has gone away because of that.' Simpson paused again, but Blincoe was looking mystified. 'With a child,' he added, pointing to his own belly.

'Aye, and there's those who says it's his!' added Molly, who had a knack of hearing everything. In fact, not only did she hear everything, but she was also capable of listening to three or four conversations at the same time, chipping in when she thought she could add something worthwhile.

'Are you hungry young Robert?' Simpson asked.

'Yes. I'm sort of always hungry though, and I think I'll have missed dinner at the mill now.'

'Right, well it's just as well I planned ahead! My Janet should be cooking us some dinner right now.' He took out his watch and checked the time. 'It's just one o'clock so if we go now we should be just fine. You can have your dinner with us.'

The sacks Blincoe carried back to Littonslack were no lighter, the new shoes and nails having been replaced with the old ones, although the beer somehow made the carrying of them less trouble. They stopped twice on the way back, to relieve themselves against the dry stone walls, and as they came closer to Littonslack, Blincoe, slightly nervous at the idea of going to Simpson's home for his dinner, began to ask questions about Simpson's family and about Littonslack.

'There's ten cottages at Littonslack,' Simpson explained. 'We live up near the far end. All of them living at the Slack, that's what we call Littonslack, are mill folk. Most of them are the managers, like me, and Needham's other top men. There's only your governor, Milner, who lives down at the mill.'

Blincoe was now even more nervous to be visiting an area so heavily populated with Needham's top men. He followed Simpson closely for the last hundred yards, close behind his heels like a frightened dog, but he needn't have worried, as he made it into the Simpson's cottage without seeing anyone else.

The ten Slack cottages were all the same size and all built to the same design. On the ground floor was one living room and a small kitchen, and then reached by a steep winding staircase were two bedrooms. That was it.

Blincoe expected the houses to be more imposing and luxurious, especially given the importance of the people housed here, but these were simple and functional and had been built to a limited budget.

The living room, the only room Blincoe saw, was simply furnished with a few chairs, a dining table and a sideboard that was far too big for the room. On one wall was a large fireplace, another wall was taken up mostly with the front door and front window, another wall displayed the sideboard, and the last wall was busy with decoration in the form of mirrors, of which there were two, some small paintings and various embroidered samplers. As Blincoe stood alone in the living room with Simpson talking to Janet in the kitchen, he became transfixed by the samplers; the vivid colours, the patterns of animals, plants, buildings and people; then he examined the words; they were generally religious and in the case of the one directly in front of his face, rather sombre:

Death, like a flooding midnight stream,
sweeps us away, our life's a dream,
an empty tale, a morning flower,
cut down and withered in an hour.

As Blincoe was trying to work out why anyone would want to put anything so sad on display in their home, Mrs Simpson appeared, a tall thin woman.

'Hello Robert. She wiped her hands on a cloth, stuffed it into her pinafore pocket and with a still damp hand shook his.

'Dinner will be in just a wee while. I wasn't sure what time you'd both be in.'

She disappeared back into the kitchen leaving Robert again contemplating the embroidery, but before he had read any more, a young girl bounced in through the front door.

'Hello, I'm Martha. Are you Billy?'

'No, Robert,' he said, 'Robert Blincoe.'

'I'm Martha Simpson. Hello Robert Blincoe.' She emphasised the words *Robert Blincoe*, practising them in her

Scottish accent, as though they were new words from a language she had never heard before.

'When's dinner Mam?' Martha shouted.

'A quarter of an hour. Why don't you look after young Robert until then? It's the first day it's not rained for a week, so why don't you take him outside?'

Blincoe supposed that Martha was about his age; she was certainly of similar height. She had long wavy blonde hair and a permanent smile, But what surprised Blincoe the most, was how lively and how sure of herself she seemed. This opinion was further reinforced when she took him by the hand and dragged him out of the house

'Come on Robert Blincoe,' again, she emphasised his name. 'I'll show you round about.'

As soon as they were outside Blincoe spoke, 'Can we go somewhere a bit out of the way? I'm not too happy as all the mill bosses seem to live up here.'

'Aye, no bother. Come on!'

She led him to the far end of the cottages passing a couple of people who gave Blincoe a strange look, although he was relieved when he recognised neither of them; they jumped over a gate and into a grassy meadow. The sun was out from behind the clouds, but there was a steady breeze, and so Martha sat them down in the shelter of a stone wall.

'We can't go far before dinner,' Martha said. 'We'll just sit here, and you can tell me all about yourself, although I know nearly everything about you already!'

'Why, what do you know?' asked Blincoe, quite alarmed that he might have been the subject of discussion.

'Well now, let me see. You're from London, you arrived from there last week, you work at Litton mill in the smithy and you still suck your thumb when you're asleep!'

'What? I don't suck my thumb! Who told you that?'

'I was only teasing!'

Despite the teasing, Blincoe was enjoying the company of Martha. She was so alive compared to all the apprentices at Litton mill who were mostly too tired to even pretend to be cheerful. Blincoe, swept along with this change in energy, joined in the banter.

'Well I know things about you,' he replied. 'Your name is Martha; your mam and dad's names are Janet and Bill, you have come from Scotland and you still wet your bed!'

Martha pounced on him, tickling him under the arms and only stopping when she saw one of the neighbours looking down on them from over the wall. The neighbour, unseen by Blincoe, wandered away without comment.

'I don't really know anything about you at all,' Blincoe said. 'But you are from Scotland, aren't you?'

'Aye, I was brought up just outside Perth, and when I was seven we moved to Manchester, and then when I was ten we moved here.'

They were both sitting, backs to the wall, so that when the sun popped out from the occasional cloud, they could feel it on their faces. Blincoe was playing with grasses, winding them around his fingers.

'So tell me all about you,' he asked. 'Why did you move here? Do you have any brothers or sisters? Do you work?'

'You are a nosey wee boy, Robert Blincoe, but as it's you, I'll tell you!' Martha slid down so she was lying on her back. 'Well, we moved around mainly for work for dad. He's always worked, but the Manchester job was better than the Perth job, and then the Litton mill job was better than the Manchester job. I work at Cressbrook mill. I'm an apprentice spinner, but because I don't lodge there, I get proper wages of three shillings and six pence a week.'

'Three shillings and six pence!' Blincoe interrupted. 'You must be rich!'

Martha laughed, 'Well, I would be if it was mine, but I give it to mam, and I keep a penny for myself.'

'Does anyone else live with you, brothers or sisters or anyone?'

'No, there's just us now. I did have a brother and a sister, but they died when they were young. They were born small and weak.' Martha was unmoved, talking of her dead siblings, but she still moved the conversation back to Blincoe. 'What about your family,' she asked.

'I don't have any. I was put in the workhouse when I was very young. I don't know who my parents are.' Blincoe paused looking at the green grass stains all over his hands. 'Perhaps my parents are the King and Queen, and one day I'll be rich; even richer than Martha Simpson!'

'King Robert Blincoe you'll be. No that doesn't sound quite right. What about King Robbie the first? Aye, that'll be you!'

Blincoe knew he was some way off being King, but he did have a penny, which he felt in his pocket every now and then to check that it was still there, but he was going to be rich: he knew it.

'Come on,' Martha said, 'let's go and see if dinner's ready. If we're late I'll be in big trouble.'

They washed their hands in the trough outside and went in. They sat at the table with Blincoe under the wall of decoration that he had already seen and he was now next to another of the samplers.

The angels saw the opening flower
And swift with joy and love
They bore her to a fairer home
To bloom in fields above

Now Blincoe understood. This one had been written for Martha's sister; the other one presumably for her brother. He was now confused over whether it was better to have no family, like him, or a family like Martha's where you might have difficulties of a different sort, difficulties that life and death could throw at you. There was no easy answer.

'Do you like them?' Mrs Simpson asked as she sat down with the last plate of food. 'All of them were done by Martha. She's very skilled in needlework.'

Mrs Simpson went on singing the praises of her daughter, and Blincoe replied occasionally with simple and expected responses. He was shocked how Mrs Simpson could be so happy with Martha's sewing of the samplers, when they represented such sad events. Perhaps Mrs Simpson was blinkered to what words said, or what they were about. During dinner, Mr Simpson said little, and Martha said nothing, although she kept herself amused by kicking Blincoe under the table, out of sight of everyone else.

Back under the safety of their wall, they chattered away. They compared mill stories, although most of Blincoe's were second-hand, as in truth he had, so far, seen little for himself. The clouds thickened, and as the afternoon became cooler, they decided to leave the field.

'Come on King Robbie,' Martha said. 'I'll show you the planting, and as you're too scared to go down in front of the houses we can go around the field way.'

'It's not that I'm scared.'

'Ach, I'm only teasing, I understand. Mind it wouldn't make a very likely King, being that scared!'

She ran, and Blincoe chased after her until they arrived at a long thin wood that stretched across the end of the cottages. They clambered over a wall and into the safety of the planting.

'Are you alright?' Martha asked.

'I just landed in some stinging plants.'

'They're nettles. Now that's not the sort of thing a King would do, is it!'

'If I was the King you'd have to lie down on the nettles, and then I would step on *you* instead and not get stung!' They both laughed.

'I think there's some dock leaves in here somewhere,' Martha said. 'They'll make it better.'

They sat at the end of the planting, overlooking Litton mill, and Martha wrapped dock leaves around Blincoe's leg. Unusually for them, they sat quietly for a few minutes, and then Martha spoke.

'I'm going to have to go now,' she said, 'I promised mam I wouldn't be too long.'

'Thank your mam for the dinner,' Blincoe said. He climbed over the wall that separated the wood from Slack hill, the hill that would lead Blincoe down to the mill. They stood now, either side of the wall with Blincoe unsure what to say next in this unusual parting.

'Go on now, off you go King Robbie, or I'll be in trouble with mam and my dad, especially if you're tired at work tomorrow.'

'Bye then,' Blincoe said and set off down the hill and shouted back. 'I'll blame you if I'm tired!'

Blincoe ran down Slack hill. He couldn't explain why he was running, except that he could.

He lay in bed that night, the events from a very busy day whirring around in his mind. He was more tired than if he had worked all day at the mill. But today had been great fun, *and* he had earned a penny, which was for now, as he was unsure where to keep it, safe under his pillow. He had enjoyed Martha's company, but by the end of the day, he was left with a strange feeling inside that he had never experienced before and couldn't explain. Was it to do with Martha, the girl who had teased him, kicked him and possibly been involved in his falling into the nettles? He decided, as the old nurse from the workhouse used to say, *to sleep on it*. But even without sleeping on it, he knew that he wanted to see Martha again.

Nine

MONDAY 17TH APRIL 1797
THE NEW GEORGE, TIDESWELL

'Thank you for coming Thomas,' Needham said. Needham was one of a small number of people to address Parson Brown by his Christian name.

'It was but a short walk my dear Ellis,' Brown replied. He slurred his words as he spoke and then rocked forward, his chin nearly hitting the table.

Parson Brown and Ellis Needham sat together in the New George. It was early Monday evening and Needham had asked Brown to meet him. Needham hadn't anticipated that Brown would be drunk, although in the event he wasn't surprised as the parson had not been coping too well lately. The matter Needham wanted to discuss was important, and although he had found Brown was the worse for drink, Needham hoped he would still be able to help, and so he continued.

'First,' Needham began, 'allow me to thank you for your Sunday school at the mill. I am grateful, and I'm sure the apprentices are, and whether they are or are not, it is important that they receive such schooling.'

'Not a problem, not a problem,' Brown replied, 'and thank *you* for having me, and thank *you* for paying me.' As Brown leant on the table, his elbow slipped and unbalanced, he lost a good amount of his ale.

'What I want to do is to give the apprentices more,' Needham continued. 'I believe that we should be giving them some general schooling, perhaps an extra hour, maybe two? They have little else to do on a Sunday. Now I'm not asking you to do this, but I wondered if you could suggest anyone, perhaps someone from the school here in Tideswell?'

Had Brown been less drunk, he might have argued against the suggestion of using someone from the school and argued for himself and for the money, that he presumed would come with the job, but Sunday was his busy day, and in his present relaxed and happy state, any greed and any need for extra money was diminished.

'Grace Ball,' said Brown. 'Grace Ball. She works at the school; she can teach anything, has no immediate family and so like your apprentices she has little else to do on a Sunday. She is a good all round teacher.' Brown paused and tried to focus on Needham's eyes. 'I have to add though, that she is dull and extremely plain, but perhaps you don't care about that? I don't know, but if you do, there it is, the facts, dull and plain.'

Needham didn't respond to Brown's last comment. 'I think I know her from church. Perhaps you could introduce us after next week's service?'

This time Brown didn't respond. His eyes had moved to two young girls on the other side of the room. He knew them by sight from drinking in the New George. He had been told that they were whores, and they certainly wore colourful and cheap clothes, matched by equally colourful faces, although at this moment he cared little what their titles were. The glimmering of their frocks; their painted faces and their deep red lips drew him in. The girls were looking towards him, and one of them pushed down her frock to expose more of her cleavage. Brown looked back at them, wondering if he could procure the two of them. At this point, Needham was still talking, but it was just a distant noise in Brown's ear. Brown decided that now was a good time to approach the girls, and he slowly stood, and with his tankard spilling the remainder of his ale onto the floor, he began to move uneasily towards them.

Needham had by this time, observed what was going on; he had seen the exchange of looks, and he knew that he had no choice but to intervene. Normally the shorter Needham would be no match for Brown's strength, but Brown, physically weakened through intoxication presented no difficulty for Needham who held him by his collar and steered him, pushing in the middle of his back with his other arm, towards the outside door. Needham kept his grip until they were in the safety of the vicarage. Brown had protested verbally, but only in a weak and pathetic way, and he had raised no physical challenge.

Needham made Brown sit at the kitchen table and then he looked around. 'Good God man, look at this place!' Needham shouted. 'You really are going to have to pull yourself together,' he moved close to Brown and looked him straight in the eyes, 'and that starts now!'

Needham was a good friend of Brown's, and they had known each other for over five years. Needham had supported Brown's campaign to gain the rector's position in Tideswell, using his position to influence the people who mattered. Needham now had many reasons to help Brown: his friendship, some business arrangements they had, and he felt that he had a duty to those who had, reluctantly in some cases, appointed the parson. Needham made some strong tea in the cleanest cup he could find; he deliberately used no milk or sugar, although it seemed unlikely that there would be any fresh milk anyway, and on the recommendation of an apothecary he once shared a hotel room with, he added a large spoonful of salt.

Needham stood over Brown for over an hour and made him drink two cups of his concoction. It was no use trying to talk to Brown about anything initially, and it was almost two hours after arriving at the vicarage that Needham thought Brown sober enough to engage in sensible conversation. Those two hours had given Needham plenty of time to think about what he would say, to choose his words and to practise them in his head. Needham suggested they moved to the sitting room, which although untidy, did not have the same dank stench of the filthy kitchen.

'Thomas, we have known each other a long time now, and I'm sure we consider each other friends. It is as a friend I wish to talk to you now.'

Brown said nothing, just nodded. His head was beginning to throb, and he sipped at the glass of water that his friend had provided.

'There is no other way to put this, Thomas. You *have* to pull yourself together and pull yourself together quickly. If you don't, then I fear that you are close to losing everything – everything that you have worked so hard for.'

Brown sat awkwardly in his chair. He had sat down in an odd position and had been too weary to move since then. He put his glass down.

'You are correct,' Brown said. 'You have said nothing that I haven't thought myself, but I have been weak, and if I am honest, I don't really know what to do.'

Needham had expected an argument at this point and was slightly deflated when Brown sat there like a scolded child and simply agreed with him.

'You need to sort this place out, and between us, we need to get you some help, someone to replace Kezia, but more than anything else you must keep away from the drink. I understand this is going to be difficult.'

Needham thought the situation was probably hopeless; he had tried to help and would continue to do so, but nothing was going to change tonight. Needham was himself now weary and hungry, and as he had sobered up the parson, and said his piece, he began to think about leaving.

'Now neither of us is going to sort this tonight, so what I would prescribe is this: you go to bed now and enjoy a good night's sleep. I will call in on my way to the mill tomorrow morning, and we will enjoy a good breakfast, and we can talk more then.'

Needham stood and gave Brown a friendly hand on his shoulder. 'You must keep clear of the drink,' he repeated. 'That must be your priority. I'll see myself out, and I'll be back at seven in the morning.'

Needham left, unsure whether his speech had been effective. It hadn't quite come out as he had planned; it was so well rehearsed in his head that, in the event, it seemed to lack any passion, and perhaps he should have been harder, or perhaps he should have stayed with him longer, or even stayed the night. Whatever might have been best, at least he had done *something*, and if he had achieved nothing else, he had averted a disaster with the whores in the New George.

Brown followed his friend's instruction and although he went immediately to bed, he could not sleep. He tossed, turned, and whatever he did, he could not get to sleep. He eventually lay on his back with his arms behind his head and wide-awake. He was staring at the stringy cobwebs swaying from the ceiling in the moonlight, but he was awake because his mind was too busy dealing with his problems to allow sleep, problems spelt out very clearly through the words of his friend.

There was no single moment that Brown could put his finger on where his life had gone wrong, but clearly it had. Not having Kezia, who left five weeks previous, was certainly a part of it all. At least she had kept the vicarage running, and his decline had been rapid since she left. But even here, in his thoughts, he was denying the truth, or at least avoiding facing it. His rapid decline had begun before she left, as the reason she left was because she was with child. Still Brown knew that he was facing only half, maybe a quarter, of the truth. He realised that he needed to bare all; at least to himself – how else was he going to find a way through all this?

'She is with my child,' he said aloud, his hands had now moved to a praying gesture. 'She has left because she is with *my* child.' He closed his eyes and continued, 'Hear my prayer, O Lord, and with thine ears consider my calling. Hold not thy peace at my tears.' Brown lay silent for a few moments, wondering why he had allowed himself to lie with her. 'Why?' he shouted. He decided he must keep on searching until he found an explanation for his behaviour, only then could he put it right. He needed to understand why he was drinking too much, and why he had lain with Kezia. Maybe it was simply that he was weak and had succumbed to the evils presented to him. If so how could he be better equipped to handle those evils in the future? He concluded that if he could find himself a wife, then the temptations of the flesh and the temptations to go out drinking would be immediately reduced.

That was clearly a long-term plan, particularly as he knew of no suitable woman in the neighbourhood, and even if there was, he was not at this moment an attractive proposition - but at least it was a plan, and it made sense. However, the immediate problem remained, in that he needed some practical help in the vicarage, and he needed, somehow, to recover any damage to his reputation. It was at this point that he made another, even bigger leap, although he was so shocked by the brilliance of it that immediately presumed it was not intuition but the result of his prayers. Again he spoke out loud, this time so that he could hear how it sounded.

'I will have Kezia back to live with me, on the same terms as before, and she can raise her child in the vicarage.'

It sounded good, and Brown carried on talking out loud to himself.

'She will receive her full pay, have a decent home to bring up the child, and I will have the help I need in running the vicarage. It is the Christian thing to do, and it will, and rightly so, make me appear charitable and therefore help regain some of my lost reputation. If I do all this openly, then no one will ever suspect who the father is. Now, many parishioners will disprove of a bastard child being brought up in the vicarage, but this will be more than offset by those who will not now assume that I am the father of the child.'

Brown moved to a praying position, kneeling at the side of the bed.

'O Lord, I thank thee, for thou hast heard me and has become my salvation. Amen.'

Brown still could not sleep; he was now excited at the plans he had made. He hurried downstairs and began the task of cleaning and tidying and getting the house back in some sort of order. He worked right through the night beginning by lighting the kitchen range, so that he had hot water for washing. By dawn, he had cleaned and tidied, to the best of his abilities, the entire ground floor. Only the bedrooms remained which he would do later, and a considerable number of clothes needed washing, but he could pay in the town to have those done. At six o'clock, he boiled enough water for him to shave and take a bath. He set down the bath on the kitchen floor, and by seven o'clock, he was dressed and had laid the table ready for breakfast and Needham's arrival.

Needham arrived with breakfast provisions that he had purchased on the way. He had been nervous as to what he might find: would Brown be angry, or drunk, or something else? He was surprised to find Brown up, bathed, shaved and dressed; he was even more surprised to see the kitchen restored to normal levels of tidiness and hygiene.

Needham cooked breakfast, and Brown told Needham everything, sparing him no detail of the past few months. He explained how he had lain with Kezia and described the day Kezia had told him that she was with child. He went on to explain how he came up with the plan for her to leave for Whaley Bridge and how he had agreed to help her financially for one year. He repeated all of his thinking of the last few hours regarding his desire for marriage and raising Kezia's child in the vicarage. Needham, who had barely spoken, took it all in, although it wasn't all news to him.

Rumours travelled fast in this close community. One morning, Needham had overheard the milkman at the mill talking to his governess, 'Have you heard about the parson's maid?' the milkman had begun, But the governess took the wind out of his sails by telling him much more than he knew, including the name of the father! Needham knew that these were only rumours, but he also knew that rumours have no bounds, and whereas they may begin, based in fact, they can grow, and in this particular case, and only four days after the milkman's conversation, Needham had been told that Brown was responsible for three bastards in Tideswell. So, what Brown had to say was, more or less, what Needham had imagined to be the case, having picked through the rumours.

'Will she want to come back here?' Needham asked when Brown had finished.

'I don't know. I will need to make my position very clear. I have decided to ride over to Whaley Bridge later this week.'

Needham was impressed with the change. Brown seemed very positive and determined. Needham had just one other worry: if Brown did meet someone who might be his wife, how would that all fit in with Kezia and Brown's child all living in the same house. Surely, that was a very big lie - too big a lie to live with. Needham said nothing on this point keeping his concern to himself. The last thing he wanted was to deflate Brown at this moment when he was motivated sufficiently to change, and change for the better.

After breakfast, the men shook hands, and Needham departed for his weekly mill meeting; Brown went to bed, this time to sleep.

Ten

TUESDAY 18TH APRIL 1797
LITTON MILL

When Needham arrived at the mill, it was in full power. As he approached, he could see the wheel spinning, and even above the noise of the river Wye, he could hear the clatter of his spinning machines. He was normally at work much earlier than this, but this later arrival gave him a new perspective on his fully working mill, one which he rarely experienced. He steadied his horse and took a longer moment to enjoy the view. At that moment he was a very contented man; he felt confident about his future.

The mill was running reliably and efficiently; the arrival of the London pauper children had given Needham, for the first time in the mill's history, sufficient labour to run all of the spindles. The labour supply was not the only factor in his favour; of late, the water supply had been good, and although this fine spring morning was dry, Needham was enjoying pushing his horse through the puddles of the previous night's rain. Rain was good and the mill had not stopped once this year due to lack of power. Needham was proud of his achievements, although getting to this point had not been easy; to finance the building of the mill, he has sold a significant part of his estate, and although he still had loans, the profit the mill was now making was easily able to cover the repayments.

Needham was well aware that his fortunes could change, and beneath his proud exterior were concerns around the reliability of a constant water supply to the wheel, but on this fine Tuesday morning, he put this worry to the back of his mind; it was not going to interfere with this contented and optimistic moment.

By the time he got to his weekly meeting with the managers, which, due to this week's Monday holiday was now Tuesday, he had long forgotten his confident arrival, and true to form, he concentrated on those matters that were not going well. It was Needham who brought up the matter of the water supply, and he showed all of the managers his plans and calculations to improve the situation. He turned the drawing around so that the group could see it.

'The plan shows how we will raise the height of the existing dam,' Needham said, and he stood so he could point out the new height on the plan. 'The height of the new dam will be two feet higher than it is now. Any more than that, and we think we will flood the road. Even at two feet, we may have to raise the road in places. We will then modify the mill race to meet the new dam and build a new sluice, here.'

Needham sat down and continued, 'We have tried, but concluded that it is impossible to calculate the precise benefit of this. Obviously if there is ample water, like now, there is no benefit. If the river dried up completely, the dam will do little to help, and again there is no benefit. But for those times when the river is medium to low flow, we can back up a huge amount of extra water each night, which will give us the power we need for the following day.' Needham looked up, 'Any questions?'

No one spoke, so Needham carried on. 'I thought someone might ask how and when we are to construct this, but I will tell you anyway. I have already made arrangements for the stone to be delivered to the mill. The new sluice is to be made in Manchester, and if, or when, we get a very dry spell, and the mill has no power, we will use all of our people to build this. With the number of people that we have, labour will not be a problem. I need Mr Simpson and Mr Palfrey to manage this; we three will get together and discuss a detailed plan later this week. The sluice will not be ready for four weeks, but hopefully the spring rains will continue for a while yet.'

Palfrey and Simpson exchanged a glance, but in the company of Needham, it was just a glance; it failed to express what either of them was thinking. Palfrey and Simpson had suggested this very plan over a year ago, but Needham had done nothing then, and he failed to acknowledge their ideas now.

Needham then asked for the weekly reports from each of the managers; Woodward's report was the one that was of most interest.

'We have lost three apprentices over the weekend. It appears they have run away. We have checked everywhere around the mill, but it seems they weren't in their beds last night.'

Needham scowled, 'Milner, can you add anything?'

'No sir. They weren't in their beds last night as Mr Woodward said.'

'They'll not get far,' Needham suggested. 'Will it affect production?' Needham was looking at Woodward.

'No sir,' Woodward replied. 'We can move people around.'

'Then good day to you all,' Needham said, and the meeting was over.

It was a good day for Needham: he had helped Parson Brown with his difficulties, the mill was performing well and he had devised a plan to improve the mill's reliability. There remained just one thing missing from his life: a wife. He was thirty-two and aware that this was a matter that now needed his attention. He needed a son to carry on the line of the Needhams and to inherit and take over his businesses. He was also quite lonely at times and often yearned for some female companionship. It wasn't that he hadn't already thought about all this, but there was no obvious suitable woman in the neighbourhood, none that *he* knew anyway, and given that the majority of his time was spent in the mill, he was unlikely to meet anyone. For the last few years, he had put all of his energy into the mill, but this would have to change; he would need to put aside some time for this new project.

Blincoe woke to the usual ringing of the bell and a fear that there would be trouble today. The rumour had travelled around the boys' room the previous night that some boys had made their escape. As Blincoe dressed, he found that the rumour was true; their beds were empty. As Blincoe moved his penny from his sock to his pocket, he decided that should he be questioned, he would claim no knowledge of any escape. Blincoe sat at breakfast nervously making conversation to his chum, Isaac Moss. At this point, the absent boys had still not been missed.

'So where do you keep your money?' asked Blincoe.

'You won't be paid until Friday,' Moss replied, unaware that Blincoe had an extra penny. 'The Governor will give you your pay, but you have a choice, you can have your penny, or the Governor will keep it for you. If he keeps it, he writes it in a book, but you can always get any of your money on pay day.'

'What do *you* do?' Blincoe asked, but he had to wait while Moss finished licking his bowl before he replied.

'Mine is with the Governor. If you keep your own pennies, you'll have them thieved in no time. Plenty have.'

Moss's answer didn't help Blincoe in making safe his extra penny. He couldn't give the Governor his extra penny, as he would assume it to be stolen, but in any case Blincoe didn't like the idea of the Governor keeping his money.

Simpson was working in the smithy when Blincoe arrived, and the furnace was already hot enough for Simpson to put the kettle on to boil. Blincoe stood watching and waiting to be told what to do.

'So young Robbie, how was the rest of your day after you left us?'

Blincoe thought briefly of confiding in Simpson about the missing boys but thought that this might give Simpson a difficulty between his loyalty to the mill and to his new apprentice; this was a loyalty Blincoe did not want to test. Blincoe was now clear in his mind: he knew nothing of the escape.

'It was quiet Mr Simpson, nothing much happening down here at the mill.' Blincoe decided that he would ask Simpson his advice over his money problem, and it would steer the conversation away from the previous evening.

'Mr Simpson. I'm not sure where to keep my penny; the penny from yesterday. I can't just carry it in my pocket every day.' Blincoe produced the penny from his pocket at this point to illustrate his problem. 'Do you know what other boys do?'

'Aye, I can see your difficulty.' Simpson handed Blincoe a mug of tea and looked around the smithy. 'Well you could keep it in here somewhere; we're not short of places you could hide it in here. Let me think,' said Simpson, and he again looked around. After a few moments, he took a small tin from a shelf.

'This is my idea,' he said. 'This tin contains three-quarter inch washers. Now we never use three-quarter inch washers, especially not these with a really narrow band; in fact I don't know why we have them!' At this point, he emptied the washers on the bench. 'So what you could do is keep your penny, or pennies when you get more, at the bottom of the tin. Hide them underneath the washers. What do you think?'

Blincoe was delighted with the idea; his money would be both hidden and secure in the smithy. He thanked Simpson and carefully set his penny on the bottom of the tin, added the washers and put the tin back on the shelf.

'Looks like we have company,' Simpson said. 'Put your tea behind that oil can.' Simpson had been looking out of the window while Blincoe had been depositing his cash.

It was Woodward. 'I need your lad,' he said to Simpson. Woodward was no more polite to his colleagues than he was with the apprentices. There were no niceties; it was straight to the point and more importantly, straight to Woodward's point.

'Three apprentices have disappeared over the weekend, so I need your lad to fill in.' He turned to Blincoe and stooped down bringing his face close to Blincoe's. 'I don't suppose you know anything about this do you?' The frightened Blincoe just shook his head. 'Mmmm, that's what they all say.' He stood up again. 'I'll take him with me.'

'I just need him for the next hour,' Simpson said, 'Then I'll send him to you.'

'Send him to the carding room, as soon as you can.' With that, Woodward was gone.

Blincoe didn't ask what he was needed for in the smithy for an hour, and the time passed without any real work being done. They just tidied one of the benches and moved some boxes around. Blincoe thought that keeping him for this hour was just part of a game, where Simpson was not going to let Woodward have it all his own way.

The carding room was not the worst place to work in the mill. The noise was slightly more bearable than on the spinning floors, and there was no permanent supervisor in the room. Every half hour a man called Merrick would come in, generally criticise what they had done and give them advice as to how they might improve the quality and quantity of their work. What was worse than other parts of the mill was the cotton dust that left a permanent choking cloud in the air. Blincoe's job was easy enough, and deliberately so, as Woodward had needed to move apprentices around in a way that meant that there was little or no training needed. In turn this meant that his production targets were unaffected by the absconders. Another part of Woodward's changes had involved moving the girl who usually helped Mrs Milner in the kitchen. The girl and Blincoe were set working together in the carding room, spreading and cleaning the raw cotton by removing seeds and any other impurities. The noise was bad, but whereas in the spinning room normal conversation was impossible and only achieved through exaggerated mouthing of the words and lip reading, in the carding room, it was just possible to hear each other.

'Hello I'm Robert, Robert Blincoe.' The girl replied with just her name.

'Phoebe Rag.'

Conversation was slow, and after a while, Blincoe gave up and just concentrated on his work. Blincoe concluded that the girl's personality was like her appearance: plain, pasty, dull, thin. What a contrast she was to Martha who was alive, interested, interesting, happy, full of colour and noisy! As he worked, Blincoe's mind wandered to thinking of Martha, and he wondered if, or when, he might see her again. Neither of them had spoken about meeting again, and now that he had been removed from the smithy, arranging anything was even more difficult. Perhaps the missing boys would return soon, and that would enable him to get back to the smithy.

At dinner rumours of the escaped boys' incredible progress, and rumours of the lack of it, circulated. One boy claimed he knew that by now they were on a ship and leaving Liverpool; another claimed they were in the cells at Tideswell, having been found hiding in a crypt. Blincoe believed neither, but prayed, for his own sake, that they would soon return.

Phoebe was a little more talkative after dinner. She was an orphan from the workhouse of Saint Pancras. She had been at Litton mill just one month, but had proved too frail to work in the factory and had been put with Mrs Milner in the kitchen.

'I overheard them talking about sending me back to the workhouse,' she offered, 'but nothing's happened yet.' She smiled. 'I suppose that's obvious as I'm still here!' She then laughed, and Blincoe smiled at her. Blincoe was warming to her slightly, but she would never be Martha.

It was early evening, and the monotony of the carding room work was ended suddenly by Merrick, instructing everyone that they must go into the yard. The mill machinery stopped, and the entire workforce assembled on the mill side of the yard. It was immediately clear what this was about, and Blincoe held Phoebe's hand as he feared that her frailty would not cope well with what was coming.

In the yard was a cart on which Woodward stood. Tied up in the same cart were the missing boys.

Even before Woodward spoke, Blincoe had the impression that he was going to enjoy his opportunity for showmanship. Woodward raised a hand to silence the general chatter.

'These three individuals have broken the terms of their apprenticeship indentures in the most inappropriate way imaginable. For those unfamiliar with the indentures, the relevant line reads,' Woodward now took out a piece of paper, 'nor from his master's service at any time absent himself.' He put the paper away. 'The individuals have now been returned to us, and to make sure that everyone understands the severity of disobeying the rules, they will now be punished.'

With the help of another man, the first boy was pulled from the cart. His wrists were already tied from the journey, but now the second man stripped him naked and tied his hands again, this time to the top of the cartwheel. Woodward descended from the cart and with a horsewhip proceeded to whip the boy across his back and backside. The first boy made no noise during the whipping and after his twelve strokes was made to stand, still naked, whilst the other two received the same. Only the third boy showed any fear and fell to the floor crying when he was untied from the wheel. To avoid the terrible sight, many of the apprentices looked to the ground, but with the mill silent, the cracking of the whip echoed around the walls and even passed through the fingers that some apprentices had pushed hard into their ears; there was no escape. Phoebe watched, showing no emotion, but she gripped Blincoe's hand tightly during each of the whippings. Woodward climbed, once more, onto the cart.

'To give these individuals time to reflect on their errors, they will now be put in the coal-sheds. This will be for a week, or until we think fit to release them. Their diet will be bread and water. Let this be a lesson to you all.' Woodward finished his show by announcing, 'Take them away!'

Blincoe knew the coal-sheds; he had unloaded coal there the previous week with Simpson. One of the sheds was still empty, but it was filthy, dark and damp; it had no windows and just a door onto the main yard. The three boys were going to have a very grim time there. Blincoe then realised that with the three boys not back in the factory, it looked certain that he would remain in the carding room, at least for the rest of this week. At this thought Blincoe unconsciously squeezed Phoebe's hand.

Blincoe lay in bed that night; he and Isaac Moss chatted away about the day.

'I think they got off fairly light,' Moss proposed. 'I've seen just as bad punishments given to apprentices for doing nothing wrong at all.'

'What sort of punishments?' Blincoe asked.

Moss laughed, 'You'll find out soon enough! I don't think that many of us get away without some punishment. You even get used to it after a while!'

'Get used to what though?'

'Well today, the boy next to me, Tom, had a rough time, and he didn't really do anything wrong; he was just a bit slow. To start with, the overlooker made him eat dirty pieces of candle; then later on, I saw the overlooker pinching his ears. Now that doesn't sound too bad, but some of the overlookers grow their nails specially long, so that when they pinch your ear, the thumb and finger nails go through your ear and meet. I've had that done to me, and I just had to carry on working with blood dripping everywhere.'

Blincoe was not enjoying this conversation and so changed the subject.

'Do you fancy a walk to an Inn one Sunday?' Blincoe asked.

'It's against the indenture rules,' Moss replied. 'We'd be well flogged if we were caught.'

Blincoe didn't know that it was in the never ending list of rules in this indenture that he had never even seen. There was silence, but a few moments later Moss spoke.

'I'm up for it if you are.'

'This Sunday?' asked Blincoe. 'Or perhaps the next one?'

'The next one,' said Moss.

Eleven

WEDNESDAY 19TH APRIL 1797
TIDESWELL CHURCH

'Come blessed children of my father. Receive the kingdom prepared for you from the beginning of this world. Grant this, o heavenly father, of thine infinite mercy and goodness, Amen'

Brown was quite used to conducting funeral services. Funerals where people had reached their three score years and ten were easy enough; it was often expected, and if not, it was never that big a surprise, but this funeral was for a child, and children were a different matter. Brown remembered a caution he had received on entering the church, 'You'll become familiar with them, but they won't get any easier.' Brown thought it one of the most fitting warnings he had been given.

Being a country rector, Parson Brown knew most of his parishioners; he shared in their happiness, and he shared in their misery. On this occasion, the misery was for a child of just four months. The child was Thomas Walker, the son of Thomas and Sarah Walker. Young Thomas had never been strong, and it had been a surprise to most people that he had survived this long.

It was a small group around the graveside on this damp Wednesday morning. The parents, grandparents and other relations numbered eight; friends and neighbours another four. All of the relations were farmers, and they were bearing up well. Their stoic nature carried them through this difficult service, and it would carry them through the difficult weeks ahead. The only others in the churchyard were Nathan Booker, the organist, who had slipped out of the church to join them, hoping for a conversation with Brown regarding a headstone and Sam Slater the gravedigger, who loitered at a respectable distance, leaning on his spade, ready to fill in the grave.

'May Jehovah bless us and preserve us, may he be merciful unto us, and look favourably upon us, now and for evermore. Amen.'

The service was over; Parson Brown bowed his head to the grave and turned to the mother, Sarah. He took her hand.

'This must be a very difficult time for you,' he said. 'I will call and see you, but if you need me, my door is always open.'

Sarah Walker had braced herself for the rigours of the service; she had some idea of what to expect, but she hadn't thought beyond the end of the service. The kind words from Parson Brown, that were personal and far more meaningful than the words he had read out from the prayer book, took her by surprise, and it was at that point that her knees weakened, and she half collapsed leaning heavily against her husband for support.

'Thank you,' she whispered, and she meant it.

Sarah's father took up the conversation with Brown.

'You'll come back with us to the farm?' he asked.

Tradition was that after the service, the parson and friends were invited to the home of the relatives. Sarah and her husband, Thomas, lived with Thomas's parents, Abel and Elizabeth, and they worked the same farm.

'I'd be very happy to come to you,' replied Brown.

A week ago, Brown might not have accepted the invitation, he might have preferred to visit a local inn, although the possibility of free food might just have persuaded him otherwise. But this was the new Brown: a Brown who had risen dramatically out of the ashes of the old Brown. It was a very simple, but radical, change and when faced with any difficulty, he turned to his religion for guidance.

Today the decisions were easy, and he would do what was expected of him as rector by attending the Walker's farm, offering any support he could. He hoped he would not be there too long as he wanted to ride over to Whaley Bridge to see Kezia, although he had told himself, that if there wasn't time to go there today, then he would find another time; he would not allow himself to be rushed at the Walker's.

Brown planned to change quickly in the church vestry from his cassock into his normal clothes, but on his way into the church he bumped into Sam Slater, his spade over his shoulder.

'I was just going to fill in the little un's grave sir.'

'Well done Sam, the sooner the better.'

'Did you want any more graves digging? There's just one dug ready.'

'I think we'll just keep one ahead Sam. The weather's not so bad now.' Brown started walking away.

'Just one more thing sir, have you heard from Kizzie?'

'No Sam, I haven't,' he shouted back, 'but ask me tomorrow. I might have some news then!'

Talking to Sam, changing his clothes and bridling his mare introduced small delays, and Brown was the last to arrive at the Walker's. The regular rain of late had made the Walker's farm something of a mud bath, and although he passed over the greater part of it on his mare and tethered her as close to the farmhouse as he could, there remained a tricky traverse through sludge and slurry which he dealt with by walking on his toes.

The door opened directly into a good-sized room with a large table in the middle. Brown's eyes were immediately drawn to the spread on the table; a hot joint of lamb was the centrepiece, which was surrounded by bowls of bread. There was a variety of cakes at the far end of the table and the best china tea service at the near end. The beamed ceiling was low, and Brown's height meant that he had to move carefully around. The mourners mostly sat on chairs that had been placed around the edge of the room, and he had to bend down to talk to them. He made sure he spoke to everyone and offered his condolences, but it was Sarah was the one he truly felt for. She was just turned twenty and had only been married eighteen months. He spent some time with her, but she constantly interrupted their conversation by making sure everyone's teacups were full.

People began to drift away, and Parson Brown sat down for the first time. He made a note in his diary to visit Sarah in a fortnight. He knew from experience that Sarah would be surrounded by family, friends and sympathy, but that this attention would only be there for the first few days, maybe a week. People would then forget, but Sarah would be still mourning her loss. She was part of a big family though and that might help. Parson Brown put his diary away and looked up. He shook the hands of the remaining mourners, said some more words to the remaining family and Sarah, and he tiptoed back to his mare.

He left the farm just before two o clock, and with Whaley Bridge thirteen miles from Tideswell, Brown had plenty of time to complete the journey and get home in the light. The weather stayed dry, and he stopped just once on the way to water his mare and clean his boots.

He found the house easily having asked just once for directions.

The door opened.

'Kizzie!'

'Parson!'

Kezia stood in the doorway dressed as normal; the only change a now noticeable bulge in her belly.

'I wanted to talk to you. May I come in?'

Although Brown hadn't thought exactly what to say, he was confident that the words would come to him. He had spent more time worrying whether he was doing the right thing, but he had concluded that given the situation he found himself in, that he was doing the right thing. His biggest fear was meeting Kezia's Great Aunt; if Kezia had told her that he was the father, then this meeting could be even more difficult. He had prayed that for some reason, any reason would do, that the Great Aunt would be out somewhere. The story that Brown was telling people back in Tideswell was that Kezia was looking after this Great Aunt. That was a lie; as far as he knew it was the Aunt who was looking after Kezia, but it was another lie that would end if Kezia came back.

'This is Mary, my aunt. Mary, this is Parson Brown from Tideswell.'

Kezia's Great Aunt was quite young, mid forties Brown thought, definitely not the deaf and senile old woman he had imagined. The Great Aunt was pleasant enough and given an unannounced visit from a rector, she behaved the way most women would. She insisted on being called Mary, and Brown presumed from her behaviour that she knew nothing about his part in Kezia's predicament. Mary appeared to be enjoying the parson's company, asking him all about his parish and the church at Tideswell and showed no sign of leaving the two of them alone, so Brown intervened.

'Kizzie, shall we take a turn outside? The weather seems quite fine now.'

The two of them walked together away from the house. Brown thought it seemed a most strange situation. Escaping with a young woman from her Great Aunt was not something he had experienced, but he imagined that it would look to anyone else as though they were sweethearts. Brown was anxious to dispel any idea that this was his intention; it was important he cleared this up with Kezia straight away.

'Kizzie, I have ridden out here this afternoon with a proposal.'

Had Brown planned what he was to say a little better, the word *proposal* would have been replaced during his very first rehearsal. It was an unfortunate choice, and he needed to recover quickly.

'My suggestion is that you come back to Tideswell as my maid, just as before. You will be paid as before and work for me as before – apart from your confinement period that is.'

Brown was now happy with the way this was going, and he continued. 'You can bring up the child in the vicarage and that will surely be a good place to bring up a child, *and* there are plenty of rooms for you both.' Brown stopped walking, turned and looked at her.

'What do you think Kizzie?'

'I don't understand why you have changed your mind. Only a few weeks ago you thought it was best that I left?'

Kezia had understood entirely Brown's earlier reasoning. As the local rector, he needed to avoid any scandal, and he couldn't have a bastard child being brought up in the vicarage. He had originally proposed a year's wage if Kezia went away. It had been a very generous and attractive proposition, and she had made no complaints.

'Kizzie, I'm not the man I was a few weeks ago. I have changed. I really believe that this is the right thing to do, the action of a Christian man, and I assure you that my behaviour will in the future be entirely appropriate and respectful.'

They continued walking. They were silent for a few moments. Kezia was thinking all this through and Brown was checking in his mind that he had covered everything.

'Of course, the fact that I am the father must remain a secret,' Brown added.

Kezia blushed, and Brown wasn't sure why. Perhaps he had made her remember them lying together. Brown carried on talking.

'Everyone in Tideswell will know the child is a bastard of course, but that would be no different to what the people in Whaley Bridge would think.'

Finally, Kezia gave her answer.

'I would be happy to come back to Tideswell,' she said. 'I think it will be a good arrangement for everyone.'

'Good,' said Brown. 'I will leave you the coach fare. There is a coach tomorrow. Could you be on that?'

Twelve

MONDAY 1ST MAY 1797
LITTON MILL

Today, the first day for a fortnight, Blincoe was back working in the smithy, and he was relieved to be back. He had visited the smithy just once since he had been put to work in the mill, but he had only slipped in during his break to deposit his second week's wages, burying the penny safely at the very bottom of his washer tin. He had now earned two pennies at the mill and one penny with Simpson, although one penny was in his pocket, as it had been kept back for the ale he planned to buy in the Red Lion along with Isaac Moss.

Blincoe's first week in the carding room had been difficult; the work there was monotonous, and the cotton dust meant that he was bathing his eyes at every opportunity. Even then he was kept awake some nights with itchy eyes. He had got to know Phoebe a little better; as the week had gone on, her guard had come down, and she had opened up just a little more. Blincoe found that underneath the emotionless and hard exterior, was a vulnerable and sensitive girl, an orphan like himself, and he had grown to like her.

At the end of this first week, the three boys, black from their coal house dungeon were allowed out, and whereas they didn't suffer humiliation from the presence of the entire workforce, as they had at the beginning of the week, there were at least twenty onlookers for the next event. The boys needed to be cleaned, and one at a time they were stripped naked; a rope was then slung under their shoulders and they were then dropped in to the mill race between the dam and the water wheel. The water at this point was very fast, and whilst two of the over-lookers held the other end of the rope, the boys were helplessly dragged under the water. Blincoe was surprised that none of them drowned, or came free from the rope, in which case they would have been under the wheel, but all survived. The boys were now much cleaner, but the fun wasn't over as they were then sat under the pump whilst pails of water were flung at them.

The boys had been well punished. It emerged that their escape was not really planned; it was more of an impulse. They set out late and hadn't travelled far before they looked for somewhere to sleep overnight. They found a barn, but then in the morning, hungry and still tired, having had little sleep due to animal and creature noises, they asked for food at the farmhouse near where they had slept. Going to the farmhouse turned out to be a bad decision as it belonged to Needham, and the couple they interrupted at breakfast were tenants of his.

With the three boys back at work, Blincoe had expected that, in turn he would be sent back to the smithy. He had no reason to assume any different, after all Phoebe, her eyes still puffy from the cotton dust, was back in the kitchen, but that was not Woodward's plan. Woodward used Blincoe, during that second week, to fill in for absent apprentices in other parts of the mill. On the Monday, Blincoe was told there were two sick apprentices, and although they were back at work by mid-week, another boy had crushed his hand between a pulley and a belt, preventing Blincoe's return to the smithy. Rumours about the injured boy went around the boys' room that night, the most far-fetched being that his hand had been cut clean off and had been replaced with a hook!

Blincoe had neither the experience nor the inclination to work well at these temporary jobs. His work-rate was slow, and rather than make allowances for this, the overlookers punished him. Barely a day passed when he wasn't physically abused.

On Monday evening, he was kicked so hard by the overlooker that he left the floor and then slid helplessly into a machine, cutting and bruising his head. On the same day, he experienced the ear pinching that Moss had described to him; Blincoe thought little of it then, but with his ears sore and blood running down his neck, he gained a different view. Tuesday was the worst, and partly for working slowly, and partly as some kind of initiation, he was tied up by his wrists to a cross beam and suspended over the machinery. Woodward put a great amount of effort in designing new punishments for apprentices, and this was one of his. Each time the machinery passed him, he was forced to lift up his legs to avoid it hitting his shins, but after only a few minutes, with his legs and shins already cut and bruised, Woodward deemed it too dangerous and ordered it to be stopped. Blincoe was pulled down, and even though he found it difficult to stand, he was put straight back to work; Wednesday brought a relatively tolerable kicking.

Much changed in the mill during this fortnight, and the cause of most of that was the weather. The weather had changed from the expected April showers, to a period of unusual warmth and much less rain. Gone was the regular rainfall that was needed to keep the mill in full power. During Blincoe's week in the carding room, the mill had kept going at full power, but towards the end of the following week, the lack of rain had its effect. By the early evenings, there was insufficient power to do anything. The mill stuttered to a standstill and fell silent. This brought frustration to Needham who could see his profits draining away, whereas in the previous few months, they had been stacking up nicely. It brought frustrations to the workforce, as the warm weather added a few degrees to the already hot rooms of the factory, making working much more unpleasant; and it brought frustrations to the managers, whose job it was to find work for the apprentices after the mill had stopped, else bear the consequences of the mischief they would make. The net result of this was more beatings and more punishments for many of the apprentices.

It was the Wednesday when the drier weather first took its revenge on the mill. The time the rain took to roll down the hills, pass through the ground and into the river, meant a lag of around five days, but no rain for a week meant the mill was struggling. By Wednesday evening, there was not enough water to give any meaningful power, and so the wheel was stopped and the sluice gates wound down, to back up water for the next day.

Normally there was another four hours work to be done, and the apprentices first thought that they would be free, but Woodward had other ideas, and they were put to work cleaning machinery, cleaning windows and cleaning anything the over-lookers could think of. There was tidying, sweeping, painting and whitewashing; plenty to keep the apprentices out of mischief on that first evening. They did finish one hour early, but by then it was dark, and they were tired enough to settle for an earlier night. Thursday evening was much the same, except the over-lookers were better prepared, having had all day to dream up tasks. On Thursday the apprentices found themselves painting floors, weeding outside and picking up rubbish from the bottom of the gentler flowing river.

On Friday, the whole factory was sent home at six o'clock.

'I thought we'd be washing coal tonight!' a boy had remarked to Blincoe. Blincoe then passed the comment on to others, as if it were his own thought. There was still some daylight left, and the apprentices gathered around in small groups. As on Sundays, only the Governor and his wife remained to look after them, although the apprentices found it easy enough to keep out of their way. Some had sweethearts, and it was straightforward to disappear out of sight, along the river, up Slack hill, or even around the mill buildings. Similarly, if anyone wanted to fight, or breach the terms of their indenture in any other way, this could easily be done away from the Governor's view. Blincoe thought that maybe the Milners were deliberately allowing them some freedom, but whether this was true or not, the Milners had no choice; there were far too many apprentices to keep track of. Not all of the apprentices were intent in breaking the terms of their indentures; some were happy to play along the river banks, walk innocently, or play games such as marbles or hop-scotch. Others just talked and gossiped, often fantasising about much grander futures. Blincoe fell into this latter category, and wary of any further punishments, he walked down the river towards Cressbrook mill with Moss and Durant. The usually flooded path was now dry and presented no difficulty. When they got to Cressbrook mill, they did nothing. The mill at Cressbrook was still in full power, and the boys just turned around and wandered back to Litton mill. They agreed that exploring Cressbrook any further would probably get them into trouble, and in any case, it was getting dark.

Saturday passed fairly uneventfully with the mill providing power until the earlier Saturday finish, with Blincoe counting the minutes until the end of day. Just before the end of day Woodward found Blincoe.

'You're back in the smithy from Monday,' he said and then muttered, 'hopefully you'll be more use in there.' Woodward was walking away as he made this remark, which was just as well, as Blincoe was grinning at the thought of escaping back to the relative comfort of the smithy.

On the Sunday morning, Blincoe and Moss were at breakfast; Phoebe was in the kitchen and assisting Mrs Milner with the breakfast and washing the pots. Phoebe hoped to get some extra food to Blincoe for being nice to her, but it wasn't possible as she was always in clear sight of Mrs Milner. Blincoe and Moss were unaware of Phoebe; they were engrossed in planning their trip to Litton and the Red Lion, although there was little planning to be done. They had to attend Sunday school, then they had to attend the ordinary school, which to distinguish it from Parson Brown's Sunday school was being called Litton mill school, and then they could set off to the Red Lion.

Since the capture of the three apprentices, a notice had been placed in the mill listing what they couldn't do. The important part for today read: *Taverns or Alehouses he/she shall not haunt or frequent, unless it be about his/her masters' business there to be done*. Blincoe and Moss speculated on the walk to Litton, whether they could, in some way, be going there to help their masters' business, but neither could come up with anything remotely convincing. Another part of the notice that had amused the boys was that they couldn't marry, and they had laughed about who they were, and weren't, planning to marry. Another part forbade *fornication or adultery*, but no one had known what that meant.

They were nervous on arriving at the Red Lion and peered through the windows to check there was no one there they knew. They nervously stepped inside, again looking for danger and walked straight into Molly Baker who had been watching them since they arrived.

'Are you lads wanting to buy some ale, or are you just going to creep around all day?'

Molly made no reference to recognising Blincoe, which disappointed him, as he had earlier bragged to Moss that he was a regular drinker there. Molly put them in a little back room on their own where they spent their wages, the two pennies buying them two quarts of ale. Moss hated the sour taste of this drink, but claimed to Blincoe that he enjoyed it. Certainly, by his second pint he decided it wasn't so bad, and the relaxing effect Blincoe had told him about was fun. The way home involved peeing up stone walls and seeing who could mark the wall higher, and they continued the conversation regarding marriage, which they developed into a game, discussing each girl and then deciding whether they should drown them in the river, or marry them! Blincoe knew fewer girls than Moss, and so he was at a disadvantage when discussing particular girls, but he did brag about a girl he knew from Cressbrook mill.

On returning to the mill, they found a delivery: a large can. It had been left in the mill yard and there was no one about, even though the mill buildings were open. After some debate, they took the can up to the counting house, where a closer inspection revealed that it was a can of treacle. There was still no one to be found, and Moss was determined to have a taste. Blincoe was uneasy with this, and after a quick lick of his fingers, Blincoe left for his bed, but Moss, affected more by the drink, stayed and gorged himself. Moss was caught in the act by Milner, his guilt displayed by a sticky mouth and sticky fingers. The following day he was beaten and whipped by Woodward and he spent the following two days in the coal-shed.

Blincoe slotted back easily into his relationship with Simpson. Unlike the other managers and over-lookers, Blincoe could talk to him, or ask him a question without fear of being beaten. On Monday morning, the day after the treacle incident, Blincoe spoke to Simpson.

'Do you know if we will finish early tonight?' he asked.

'It's up to Woodward.' Simpson stood up from his anvil and straightened his back, 'Woodward's in charge today as Needham's away somewhere. Mind, he's pretty much in charge most days, but I reckon we'll be done by tea-time again.'

Simpson returned to his hammering and Blincoe to filling some lamps.

'Of course,' Simpson said, 'if there was any planning ahead at this place, we'd have that new sluice gate, and we could be getting on with that.' Simpson continued talking in between his hammer blows. 'Better still, they should have built the mill on a decent bit of river. Do you know there's not a cotton mill further up this river than here?'

'No Mr Simpson I didn't know that.'

'Arkwright worked out that that this place was no good years ago and then sold it as fast as he could.'

Blincoe had been hoping that their conversation would come around to Martha, or that perhaps there was some work he could help Simpson with this coming weekend. What he really wanted was a repeat of last time, where he could earn a penny *and* see Martha, but it was now mid morning and there had been no mention of her. Blincoe realised that he was going to have to move the conversation that way, and eventually he thought of some words and plucked up the courage to say them.

'How's everyone at the Slack?' he asked.

Simpson looked up from his work and then at Blincoe.

'Everyone's well, thank you. Janet, that's my wife, has just got over a cold, but she's well enough now.'

No one said anything for a few moments.

'And Mr Woodward and his family, they are all well too.' Simpson added.

The conversation again went silent, and then Simpson started grinning.

'You'd be really asking after our Martha I imagine? Well, am I right?'

Blincoe smiled, and his face blushed a little. He didn't reply.

'Martha is *very* well. Why don't you come up and see her this next Sunday after your lessons? I'm sure she'll be glad to see you. I think she's a wee bit sweet on you.'

Thirteen

SUNDAY 7TH MAY 1797
LITTONSLACK

Sunday came, a typical breezy spring day. The clouds flew across the sky; the ground underneath flashed between sunshine and shade, but totally unaware of the weather, Blincoe ran up Slack hill for his meeting with Martha. After his lessons, Blincoe had changed out of his Sunday best into the, now cleaned, clothes in which he had first travelled to Litton mill. Blincoe was much more nervous than last time he came to Littonslack; last time he had been there, he had been under the protection of Martha's father, and his meeting with Martha had been unexpected. Today his meeting was expected, although what he could expect when he arrived was unknown, and he was a little anxious.

A red-faced and out-of-breath Blincoe arrived at the top of Slack hill. During the steep climb his attention had been concentrated on watching his feet and being careful where he trod; the last thing he wanted was to tread in a wet cow pancake. When he arrived at the top, his shoes still had their polish, and just short of the gate, he put his hands on his hips, took in a deep breath and looked up.

'What kept you?' Martha asked. 'I've been waiting here nearly a half an hour.'

'Oh, sorry!' Blincoe replied.

'Ach, it's fine. Dinny be so serious!'

Martha was sitting on the top of the gate that separated Slack hill from the short track that led to Littonslack. Blincoe jumped up and sat on the gate next to her. They both sat facing towards the valley where, with the mill silent, there was just the faint noise of the river.

Martha held up a bag. 'Mam's given me some pudding for us, a meat pudding. We can go into the hills if you want. I can show you lots of things.'

The sun then came out for what was to be a longer spell, and Martha slipped down on the other side of the gate, took Blincoe's hand and pulled him to follow her.

'Come on!' she said.

'Your hand's really soft,' Blincoe said as they walked up the track. He thought that saying something kind was the right thing, and in any case, it was true.

'It's a wonder,' Martha replied, 'the way they work us at the mill. Mind, mam makes me put oil on them at night. So that must be working then.'

'What do you do at the mill?' Blincoe asked.

'I'm a piecer. That's just piecing the broken threads for the spinners. I started off as a scavenger.'

'I know what a piecer is, and I've done a fair amount of scavenging.'

'Anyway,' Martha replied, 'we don't need to think about work today. It's Sunday.'

Although they agreed not to talk about work, they did. They had little else in common, and the conversation inevitably wandered back towards mill stories. From what Blincoe could gather there was not very much difference between the mills. The work hours were the same, the hierarchy of jobs and where the apprentices fitted in was similar, the food sounded equally miserable, and the punishments sounded as harsh, as frequent and as arbitrary. The big difference was that Martha was one of just three local apprentices at Cressbrook mill, who lived at home and received a wage. As far as Blincoe knew, there were none at Litton mill.

'Where are we going?' Blincoe asked as they climbed over another dry-stone wall.

'You'll see,' Martha replied. 'Trust me.'

Blincoe followed her, with little option other than to trust her and trust her knowledge of the area. She led him across fields and through a dark and damp wood and finally up a high and steep sided grassy hill. On the way, the mill talk and gossip continued. Martha's mill experience was much greater than Blincoe's, and although he was well aware that many stories were exaggerated, or even made up, he knew that if anyone could be believed and trusted, it was Martha.

'There's been three apprentices killed this year at our mill,' she said. 'One drowned, one was mangled up in the machinery and the other one was found dead outside. It seems as if she had fallen out of a second floor window, or maybe she was pushed.'

As she said this, she pushed Blincoe, but as they were still holding hands she pulled him back up again before he fell. Blincoe smiled.

'My dad has told me that I mustn't stay working as a piecer much longer as they end up all deformed,' Martha said. 'It's the same for the scavengers: all the crouching and reaching and stretching and everything for six days a week, makes those who stick with it become deformed. He says he's seen it in the mills in Manchester, and he says if you're young and still growing, and then if you spend most of your time, say, bent over, your bones will grow so that you're a bent over person.' Martha did an impression of a bent over person, and they both laughed.

'I like your accent,' Blincoe said.

'Aye, one or two folk have said that to me, but some of them canny understand me, and they dinny always answer me, and that makes it a wee bit difficult for me. Do you ken?'

Blincoe didn't answer, and they both laughed.

'So if you don't want to carry on piecing, what else can you do?' Blincoe asked.

'I'm hoping next year I can be a spinner; more money and not so much running around. That's the idea for the next year or so anyway.' Martha stopped walking and turned to face him. 'What about you now? What does King Robbie dream of?'

'I'm not sure really.'

'Well that's no' very exciting. Anyway here we are. What do you think?'

'Think of what?' Blincoe asked.

'Look. Look behind you! Can you no' see a big dark cave? And see just at the front there, there's some stones shaped like two chairs, so we can sit here, and if it rains, we'll be dry. You can see for miles from here, and if you go into the cave, it goes for miles underground. That's what they say.'

Blincoe peered into the cave, but he could only see a few yards, and then there was just blackness.

'Have you been in the cave, for miles I mean?'

'No, I've been a little way, but it's too dark to see anything. I've been a little further than I can see. You can just get to a stream where you can get a drink.'

'Aren't you scared?' Blincoe asked, now with a serious expression.

'No, but if the wind's up and in the right direction, it can make a noise like a ghost.'

'Do you believe in ghosts?' Blincoe asked.

'Oh aye!'

'I'm thirsty,' Blincoe said. 'Shall we go and get a drink?'

'Aye, Come on, hold my hand.'

As the cave became darker, they walked more slowly and more carefully. Their eyes became used to the dark, but then beyond a certain point, their eyes were no use. They were in total darkness.

'Can you hear the stream now?' Martha asked

'Yes.'

'If you let go of me, and put your hand down to the right, you'll be able to get a drink.'

In total darkness they drank from the stream and then stumbled back into the daylight. Coming out of the cold dark cave, the outside world seemed brighter and warmer, and Martha suggested they lay on the grassy slope in front of the cave. On their backs and still holding hands, they lay staring at the sky.

'Aren't you going to kiss me then King Robbie?'

Martha again surprised Blincoe. He had never kissed anyone before, although he had spent plenty of time imagining the moment. A part of him wanted to run away, fearful of making a mess of it, but a much bigger, and in the event more powerful, part of him longed to kiss her. He rolled over with Martha still lying on her back. He hesitated very slightly to check that she was serious, and then with his eyes open, and looking into her sparkling and laughing eyes, he kissed her. He broke off and checked that all was well, and as she put her arms around him, they kissed again, this time for much longer. When he next pulled away, Martha spoke.

'That was nice. I hope you're no' thinking of stopping!'

For ten minutes, they kissed. There were a few times when it went wrong: noses getting in the way and teeth colliding, but he quickly got the hang of it. Later he would try to describe the feeling to Moss. 'Warm and sweet and wet' but he knew there were no words that could adequately describe the sensation he had experienced.

Blincoe later recognised that this day was a turning point in his life. It was not only his first close experience of a girl, but more importantly, it marked a change in his outlook and was the point when he began to think about his future. Up until now, he had spent most of his life trying to escape the workhouse, a task that had taken far too long. Since arriving at Litton mill, just over three weeks ago, he had been preoccupied with survival and understanding what was expected of him, but now, following the prompt from Martha, he could move to the next step.

Lying on the hillside, gazing at the sky and holding Martha's hand, he realised that she was right: he needed a dream. There was no future here. He was apprenticed by indentures, that he still hadn't seen, until he was twenty-one, and that was still over seven years away. From his experiences in the brief time he had been at Litton mill, he knew that something had to happen before he was twenty-one. The probability was that if he did nothing he would end up crippled, maimed or dead. Today was the day that he began thinking more carefully about his future. There were no easy answers, but at least he was thinking about it now.

'Are you alright?' Martha asked. 'You seem miles away.'

'I was just thinking.' He rolled over to look at her. 'It's nothing.'

The two of them moved to sit in the stone chairs looking out over the view of the Derbyshire hills. Martha shared out the meat pudding.

'Were you about to tell me your dreams?' Martha asked. 'Do you have a plan? Surely you don't want to be working like a slave all of your life?'

'I don't really have a plan, but you're right: I don't want to be doing this for ever. Thing is, I can't really see any way out at the moment. Maybe if I could learn your dad's trade? That might lead to something, but it's difficult. Look around here. Look around now. What do you see?

'I can see sky,' Martha began, 'and clouds and hills and a few trees and some sheep, oh and you! How did I do?' Martha understood his point but tried to keep the conversation cheerful and jolly.

'You did very well. We are sitting up here, and we can see for miles, but we can't see one other factory or anywhere else we could work. There's just nothing else here. If we were at a mill in a city, like Manchester, I bet there would be loads of other places you could go and things you could do.'

'Aye, I suppose your right.' Martha replied. 'I dinny want to be in a mill for ever either. Even when I get to be a spinner, I dinny want that forever.'

'Do you have a dream then, for when you leave the mill?' Blincoe asked.

'Aye, I'm expecting a knight in armour to ride into the mill yard and rescue me. We'll charge off up the hill into the sunset, and we will marry and have lots of babies, maybe ten.' She stopped and squeezed his hand. 'Anyway, you should be concentrating on kissing me, all this thinking can wait!'

Blincoe did as he was told; that was not difficult. He kissed her lips, face and neck, and she closed her eyes and smiled. He soon forgot about his uncertain future and fell back into the arms of the magical Martha.

The clouds turned darker and more frequently blocked out the sun; the warm and sunny afternoon began to turn to a chilly evening.

'I think I should be going now,' Martha said.

'Me too.'

'I'll walk down to the mill gate with you,' she said. 'If you want me to that is?'

Blincoe had found his last parting with Martha difficult, and this one was more so. There were other apprentices gathered about both inside and outside the mill gates, and so Blincoe and Martha stood a little way back, so they could not be seen.

'Are you going to kiss me goodbye then? Martha asked.

Blincoe looked around, checking that they could not be seen, and then he kissed her.

'So,' Blincoe began, and after hesitating he continued, 'can I be your sweetheart, I mean, will you be mine?'

'Dinny be silly, I'm no' anyone's sweetheart. Now, away with you.'

Blincoe gave her one last kiss, and with the words of her rejection still fresh in his ears, he ran into the mill yard. He was angry with her for not agreeing to be his girl, and he didn't look back.

Fourteen

SUNDAY 3RD SEPTEMBER 1797
RED LION INN, LITTON

A dull, damp and generally cool summer had passed, and for Blincoe it had all passed very quickly. At Litton mill he had spent his days working only occasionally for Simpson in the smithy, as he had been more often than not needed to back-fill for absentees in the mill.

In the mill, Blincoe had found that accidents, injuries and death were commonplace. He had now witnessed many deaths, and although they were difficult to accept, they were a harsh reality in a busy mill and usually came as a result of carelessness through fatigue; the fatigue being brought on through insufficient sleep combined with the excessive temperatures. The worst was when he heard the cries from a girl who was taken up by the belting and was then smashed around. She later died from her injuries. The girl was Mary Turner who Blincoe knew a little, as she had helped him find his way around on his first day. Not one of her friends was allowed time off work to go to her funeral, but curiosity led Blincoe, one drizzly Sunday afternoon, to the back of Tideswell church and to the grave. Finding the grave wasn't easy; there was no stone, no flowers, and all he could see at this unmarked pauper's grave was a pile of freshly moved earth. He stood a while watching the now heavier rain splashing in the muddy puddles where the spade had been. Her life had been brief and hard; her death a nuisance and inconvenience to her masters; and now, Blincoe concluded, no one cared. Even amongst her friends, she would be quickly forgotten. He kicked the soil in frustration, but all he achieved was a mud splattered face, and he walked away wiping his eyes on his wet sleeve.

Injuries were not the privilege of the young apprentices, although generally they were the only group to receive injuries from their regular punishments. One of the spinners had her hair torn from her head, again in a machine, but she recovered enough to be back at work within the fortnight, pale faced with her head bandaged and covered further with a scarf. Blincoe had no way of knowing how the number of punishments, accidents and injuries compared to other factories, but as far as he could make out from talking to Simpson, it was much the same in every mill.

Then there was Martha, or more correctly, there wasn't. Blincoe had thought hard about how he felt about her, how he should behave with her and what the future might hold for them. He wanted to be with her, but the times he had spent with her had been tainted with frustration and disappointment; their relationship was somehow unequal with Martha having all the knowledge of the area and being unusually sure of herself. Blincoe was still finding his way and still very unsure of himself, and he had resolved after his second meeting with Martha that he would not pursue her. This had been a difficult decision and one that he probably would have failed to keep, had it not been for his general fatigue and tiredness. The constant tiredness meant that he could just cope with the occasional walk to Litton for a quart of ale with Moss on a Sunday afternoon, but the thought of the additional effort in courting Martha, which included washing, changing his clothes, followed by the probability of some disappointment, all combined to help him keep his resolve. The whole Martha thing was just too difficult, although there was one other factor that kept him away from Martha, and that was Phoebe Rag. He had become friendly with her quite soon after he arrived at

Litton mill and had remained so since. Phoebe was generally in the kitchen assisting Mrs Milner, but like Blincoe she was sometimes sent to work in the mill, and their paths naturally crossed two or three times each week. Blincoe had taken to Phoebe, although her character, behaviour and physique could not have been more different to those of Martha. Phoebe was thin where Martha was bonny; she was pale where Martha had a good colour, she was shy where Martha was outgoing; and Phoebe rarely smiled, where Martha did little else. On the few occasions that Blincoe made Phoebe laugh, he thought her very pretty, but the remainder of the time she slid back to her natural dour expression. With Phoebe, the relationship was more equal, with Blincoe being slightly the more confident of the two, a situation in which he felt much more comfortable. He had walked out with her a number of Sundays during the summer, and once they ventured as far as the ghostly cave that Martha had shown him. He thought about kissing Phoebe when they were at the cave, but it felt wrong, almost like a betrayal of what he shared with Martha, and so he didn't kiss her, and he still hadn't.

Apart from a few hours on a Sunday afternoon, there was little to do other than work and sleep, and whereas the days were long, with hindsight, Blincoe thought the summer had passed very quickly.

Moss and Blincoe sat in the small back room at the Red Lion. Molly always put them there, as they would be safe should any mill managers come in. Molly was happy to take anyone's penny for a quart of ale, and the boys' pennies were as good as anyone else's. There were a number of reasons that Moss and Blincoe frequented the Red Lion: escaping from the mill, the fun of breaking the rules and the effect of the alcohol, were all reasons they were aware of, but without realising, part of the attraction was that Molly looked after them and whilst they were there, she was almost a mother to them.

The boys were beginning their second pint, and Blincoe was telling Moss about ghosts, caves that he knew that snaked underground *for miles* and how experienced he was in kissing girls. The beer helped the stories flow, and Moss told his own stories, including boasting about the vast sums of money he had in his account at Litton mill. Blincoe was about to better his latest tale when Molly put her head around the door.

'There's a chap here wants to see you two,' she said. 'I'll show him through.'

In the few seconds that Molly was gone, so was Moss. He sensed his opportunity and he was out of the back door of the Red Lion and away into the fields. Blincoe had judged the situation differently. Without thinking it through, he trusted that Molly would not hand them in, and so his reaction was not to run; at least this is what he later claimed when Moss accused him of slow thinking, but when the stranger appeared at the door, he wished he had run away.

'This gentleman is John Brown,' Molly explained. 'He wants to talk to you two.' It was then that she realised Moss had gone. 'Well he wants to talk to an apprentice; anyway I'll bring some more ale.' Molly left, shutting them in the room.

Brown offered his hand, and Blincoe shook it.

'John Brown, journalist from Manchester,' the man said. 'The Landlady tells me that you are an apprentice at Litton mill?'

Blincoe just nodded. He was very nervous about this whole situation: He was in the Red Lion, which he shouldn't be; drinking ale, which he shouldn't do; his friend had run off, and now he was trapped with this strange man. Blincoe studied the man, and he was indeed strange. After taking off his hat, his face remained hidden behind a great deal of long black greasy hair, a sharp moustache and pointed beard. He looked quite young, but most of his teeth were missing, just short black stumps remaining, and this made him look much older.

'Let me come straight to the point,' the journalist said, his voice whistling past the stumps of teeth. 'I am writing about cotton mills, and I just need the view of what it is like working in a cotton mill from the apprentice's position.' The journalist leant forward and with foul breath that made Blincoe move backwards, he whispered, 'I am able to pay you half a crown for your time.'

Blincoe was now relieved that he not only appeared to be safe from punishment and was not about to be handed in, but he was actually to be financially rewarded! Bolstered by the pint and a half of ale that he had already drunk, his confidence grew; certainly, it was at a much greater level than it had been an hour earlier. As a result he argued for, and achieved, a higher rate.

'Three shillings and sixpence then.' The journalist leaned over the table again and shook his hand again, and whilst still holding it added. 'That is providing that the information is adequate for my needs.'

Blincoe decided, there and then, that he would make sure that the information was adequate.

'Tell me,' Brown began, 'about your working hours at the mill.'

'We start work at six and finish at nine. That's Monday to Friday. On Saturday we usually finish at noon, and on Sunday the mill doesn't work.'

'Are these times fixed, or do you sometimes start earlier, or finish later?' Brown asked.

'The earliest I have started is five. The latest I have finished is twelve, at night.

Brown made notes of everything that Blincoe said his little book. His questions were quite searching, and he continued with the working-hours theme.

'Have you ever worked on a Sunday?'

'Twice. No, three times. That was when we were behind due to mill stoppages in the week and needed to catch up.'

'What meal breaks, or other breaks, do you get when you are working?'

'We get three meal breaks, but there is barely time to eat the food that we're given, and sometimes we have to eat it whilst still working. Forty minutes is allowed for dinner, but half of that can be taken in cleaning the frames. Sometimes we can be there the whole dinner-time, on which occasion, a ha'penny is given, or rather promised. Sometimes, we work the whole day through, often eighteen hours, without rest or food!'

Blincoe had planned to tell the journalist only the truth, but this was a tricky matter. Blincoe knew that this thing called the truth was not always known. For example when Brown asked about the food, Blincoe told him that they were fed with 'an inferior sort of Irish-fed bacon,' but Blincoe had no idea whether this was true or not. It was what everyone said; it was what everyone believed, and it may, or may not, have been true. Similarly, when Blincoe told him that they ate without knives and forks, using just their fingers, he failed to mention that knives and forks were available, but most apprentices didn't know how to use them and preferred the speed of using just their hands. One newly arrived boy, on being seen eating with a knife and fork, had been jeered so aggressively by his fellow apprentices that he soon fell in to line. Telling the truth was difficult, and the journalist was all the time pushing for anything about the mill that was appalling or evil. Now Blincoe was able to provide good, honest and sometimes truthful answers, but he worried slightly that even if they were the truth, were they representative of what regularly occurred? Added to this difficulty were Blincoe's intoxication and his desire to perform adequately for his three shillings and sixpence. It was a concoction of confusion that Blincoe couldn't figure out, but eventually, it was the intoxication and the three shillings and sixpence that dominated his thoughts and words. Complicated ideas of truth and fairness faded as the jug of ale emptied, and Blincoe gave the journalist what he had come for. He changed stories he had heard retelling many of them as though they had happened to him; he embellished other stories and made them more bloody and cruel; he increased the numbers of such events and the numbers of deaths. Blincoe knew Litton mill was a harsh place to work, but he provided what the journalist wanted. Blincoe was now two pints more confident than he had been when Moss left him, and the usual shy and cautious Blincoe was replaced with someone else, someone who was much more outgoing and beginning to enjoy telling his stories.

'What were your first impressions of the mill?' Brown asked.

'After we had been shouted at by the over-lookers and masters in the mill yard, we were led to the apprentice-house, where we were given a meal It was water-porridge and oatcakes. We had been led to believe that we would be fed well, but neither roast-beef nor plum-pudding appeared! The porridge was really thin and not well made, the oatcakes, were about an inch thick and very dry. I ate very little and some of the new apprentices ate nothing at all and went to bed supperless. The apprentices that were already at the mill were watching us; any leftovers were quickly eaten by them. They said that our stomachs would wake up in a few days, and that we would soon be glad to pick from a dunghill, the mouldiest pieces we had flung away!'

'And your sleeping arrangements?'

'Our lodging-rooms are in the apprentice-house, up two flights of stairs. On the floor below is the girls room, and on the floor below that, which was partly below ground, the refectory where we eat our meals. The beds are like cribs, built in a double tier all around the room. We sleep two to a bed.'

'Tell me about your arrival at the mill.'

I got friendly with a boy called Durant on the journey to the mill and wanted to sleep with him, but I was put with a boy already there, Isaac Moss; he was my chum. My first impressions were not good; everything was much worse to what we were used to, and the smell, from oil and filth was everywhere. Moss just jumped straight into bed, and without saying a prayer, or anything else, fell asleep; I hadn't even undressed. I'll admit now that I turned to face the wall and cried and passed a very restless night. I don't think I slept for more than an hour. It never occurred to me, at least, not till long afterwards, that those in charge at Saint Giles had deceived me.'

'Tell me,' Brown said, 'about punishments you have suffered at the mill.'

'I was not long at the mill,' Blincoe told him, 'in my first or second week, and for no reason I was tied up by my wrists to a cross beam and suspended over the machinery. Each time the machinery passed by me, I was forced to lift up my legs to avoid it hitting my shins. I was there for over an hour by which time I was so weak that I couldn't lift my legs. My shins and legs were battered, bruised and cut. Only then, as I was on the verge of passing out did they pull me down. By this time I couldn't stand, and I was carried back to the boys' room where I lay for the rest of the day.'

'How are the sick treated?' Brown asked.

'No one looks at the sick, not until someone collapses; then the over-lookers need to decide if the person has collapsed through sickness or just because they are tired. With the pressure on to keep the mill running, many sick people are beaten, as they are assumed just tired. Those who are eventually diagnosed as being sick are often so poorly that they are put into a wheelbarrow and taken back to the apprentice house, and there they are left to live or die. There isn't any real nursing or medicines; the sick are just given treacle-tea, that's hot water sweetened with treacle. If there is an outbreak of a disease amongst the apprentices, then they burn pitch or tobacco in the room, and they sprinkle vinegar on the floor and on our beds. If the doctor is ever called, then it is very serious and often too late.'

The interview continued for almost two hours. It covered everything, food, accommodation, working-hours, punishments, wages, safety and accidents, training, indentures, freedom, schooling, religious education and health, and on all of these subjects, Blincoe's embellishments knew no bounds.

Blincoe took his three shillings and sixpence.

When Blincoe arrived back at the mill, he had missed dinner. Phoebe waved at him from the kitchen, but he didn't see her. He was though, just in time for the Sunday evening head count, and so he was almost home safe. The only obstacle now was if the governor should smell beer on his breath. At the head count, as they filed into their rooms, Blincoe held his breath. This was something that he and Moss had practised so that the beer would not be noticed; it worked, and Blincoe was soon in his beery sleep with three shillings and sixpence under his pillow.

Fifteen

MONDAY 27TH AUGUST 1798
LITTON MILL

The Monday morning meeting at Litton mill had just ended; only Ellis and his brother Robert remained in the office. Ellis shook his head.

'I suppose they're doing everything they can,' he said, 'but I wished they would try and think a little more, come up with some new ideas at least.'

Robert sat across the desk from Ellis. Robert was the younger brother and had no stake in the business; he was just an employee, but given his relationship to Ellis, everyone treated him with due respect. He had a young face, which still wore the marks of his teenage spots. His hair was long, and as he sat down, he flicked it back with a well-practised movement of his head.

'It's no one's fault,' Robert offered. 'The mill is running efficiently and reliably, and you know that to be the case. We've had the new sluice gate and the stone for the dam sitting in the yard for nearly eighteen months, and that shows how well the wheel has been running. If we'd have had a dry spell we would have raised the dam by now. It's the market prices that are hurting us. We have no control over the market, so if we are going to make any profit, we must reduce our costs even further than we already have.'

'You sound like you have thought about this,' Ellis said. 'Do you have a proposal?'

'I have an idea, but the difficulty is that we can't actually reduce many costs at all. As I said, the mill is running efficiently. The only area we might make some savings would be the wage bill, but rather than reduce the rate of pay, what I think is a better solution is this: work the mill longer, something like twenty percent longer. If we do that without increasing the wages, then that would cost next to nothing, and our processing costs per bale would consequently reduce by around twenty percent. That should put us back into profit.'

'Do you think the workers would put up with an increase of that much?' his elder brother asked.

'We can explain to them that the alternative is a cut in pay, or in jobs,' Robert said. 'Anyway there's no other work for them around here, so they don't have a lot of choice. Twenty percent works out at an extra two and a half hours each day. So, I propose we start an hour earlier, at five and finish an hour and a half later, at half past ten. On Saturdays we would finish at one thirty.'

Ellis jotted the proposed times on his pad.

'Do you have any better ideas?' Robert asked.

Ellis did not have any better ideas, but before he had time to tell Robert that he liked his idea, there was a knock on the office door and Milner's head appeared.

'Mr Newton to see you sir.'

'Come in William,' Ellis said. 'Come in and sit down.' Ellis pulled up a chair, and now both Ellis and Robert sat in behind the desk. 'So tell me, what brings you to my mill? I hope you're not here to steal my ideas, or my workers?'

Ellis's words were friendly and in jest, but they were false; he had no time for Newton. They were competitors, and from Ellis's point of view, Newton appeared to have been handed his business by his wealthy family, whereas Litton mill had been built from the ground up by himself, and he was proud of that.

'I have come to congratulate you,' Newton said, 'on your new found fame.' Newton then placed three newspapers on the desk.

'Have you seen these?' Newton asked. The Needhams looked blank and made no response, and so Newton continued, assuming they hadn't seen them.

'What we have here is three articles in a newspaper called The Lion. All three articles tell the story of a young apprentice and in particular, what a terrible time he has endured at a place called Litton mill. It makes very interesting reading, very interesting indeed.'

Robert picked up the first newspaper and having found the article, began reading it. Ellis made no movement and said nothing.

Newton continued his gloating, and smiling he said, 'Now I can see you are busy, and as you both have an enormous amount to read I will bid you good day! Oh, and congratulations on your fame once more; we must have a drink, and you can give me some advice!' Newton left the room and could be heard laughing as he skipped down the stairs.

The articles were long and detailed; they were wholly about this one apprentice from Litton mill, and apart from a brief introduction and two paragraphs on his upbringing in the workhouse, they were entirely about his experiences at Litton mill. The two men spent half an hour reading and re-reading the articles. They occasionally let out gasps, they challenged what was written and made short suggestions as to how this apprentice might be punished for this act of betrayal. Ellis Needham's face grew red with rage, and Robert became more agitated.

'Well, how are we going to find out who it is?' Ellis asked. He was the last of the two to finish reading. 'Do you think Woodward might be able to help?'

'I think he might,' Robert said, 'especially as he is mentioned much more than the rest of us.'

'Fetch Woodward and send Middleton up too.'

From information contained in the articles, they quickly reduced the list of suspects to an arrival of apprentices on the thirteenth of April the previous year. Of those paupers, thirteen were boys, and the one they wanted was amongst them.

Woodward and Middleton were asked to read the articles for any clues that might further identify him. Middleton then spotted his age in the first article, and the list of suspects fell from thirteen to four.

Robert then saw a piece on punishments and thought that might help Woodward make the connection to a boy.

'What about this,' he asked. '"I was tied up by my wrists to a cross beam and suspended over the machinery. Each time the machinery passed by me, I was forced to lift up my legs to avoid it hitting my shins. I was there all afternoon, and when they eventually pulled me down my right leg was broken, and I was so badly cut that I nearly died through losing too much blood."'

Woodward immediately knew that the name they wanted was Robert Blincoe, but he did not want to admit to his involvement in this punishment. Half of the tale was lies, but he didn't want to have to explain what he really did. Woodward looked hard at the newspaper in front of him, trying to find something less condemning; he needed some other passage from which he could claim to identify Blincoe. Woodward could have lied and blamed that particular punishment on others, but as the minutes slipped by, it became more difficult for him to go back and react to what Robert had read out. Then, reading the second newspaper, Woodward found something.

'It says here that he doesn't trust his wages to the keeping of the mill and he takes them each week.'

Middleton scurried off downstairs, returning with the apprentice ledger. He checked off the four boys names.

'Robert Blincoe,' Middleton said. 'He's the only one of the four whose money we don't look after. That's him, Robert Blincoe.'

'Damn him,' Ellis said. 'It's difficult enough running this place without devils like him causing trouble. We must be careful though; this publicity is likely to attract the factory inspectors and goodness knows who else, and we can't have them arriving to find Blincoe missing, or harmed in any way. You all must understand that.'

Blincoe was alone in the smithy arranging his coins. Simpson had gone to see someone in one of the spinning rooms, and Blincoe had used this opportunity to take down his tin. He looked at the money in it, and even though he knew precisely the total, he counted it again. He had now been at Litton mill for eighteen months and very careful spending, whilst earning any extra pennies or even farthings where he could, now gave him the sum of nine shillings and five pence halfpenny. He replaced the coins, poured over the top layer of washers, put back the tin, high on a shelf and then began the job he had been given: Mucking out the adjacent stable block. But only five minutes into mucking out, Milner appeared.

'I'm to take you to Mister Needham's office,' Milner said. 'I think this time you are in a lot of trouble. Do you know why Blincoe?'

'No sir.'

Blincoe truly had no idea why he was being called there; it was, after all, almost a year since he had been interviewed by the journalist in the Red Lion.

The Needhams and Woodward had agreed that Ellis would quiz Blincoe on the content of what was written, after that, Robert would whip him and then Woodward would take him to the coal-shed. The plan was that he would remain in the coal-shed whilst they worked out precisely what to do.

'Perhaps best if we sleep on it tonight.' Ellis had proposed. 'We'll probably see clearer tomorrow.'

Milner left and Blincoe stood before them all; he was the only one in front of the desk, the other men were now sitting behind, with Ellis Needham in the middle.

'Three articles have appeared in this newspaper, The Lion,' Ellis began. 'The articles detail your time here at Litton mill. Are you aware of these?'

'No sir, I haven't seen them,' Blincoe said.

'But you have helped write them, and you know the author. Is that correct?' Ellis looked at one of the articles and then named the author. 'Mr John Brown; do you know him?'

'Yes sir, I have spoken with him.'

It was almost a year since Blincoe had met with John Brown, and he had long forgotten about the meeting and never thought of the consequences.

'There are two issues here, boy,' Ellis said, 'the first is that you have broken the terms of your indentures. Your indentures say that you must faithfully serve your master, keep his secrets and do him no damage. It seems to me that this is not being faithful to me at all.'

Woodward and Robert Needham were shocked at how calm and business like Ellis was being with all this. Each of them would have happily murdered Blincoe on the spot!

'The second point is that much of what is written here is complete lies. How do you explain that?'

Blincoe was now beginning to shake, sensing some dreadful punishment. 'I only told the truth sir,' he replied.

'Well let us have a look shall we? This is from the first article. "Breakfast is porridge made with water and oatcakes, badly made and often allowed to grow mouldy." Now tell me, how often have you had porridge made with water?'

'Just once sir.'

'That would be when the milk couldn't get through,' Woodward interrupted. 'The roads were all deep in snow.'

Ellis Needham was now becoming agitated, and he waved the newspaper in Blincoe's face, 'But this suggests *all* breakfasts are made this way. And what about the mouldy bread? When have you eaten mouldy bread at Litton mill?'

'Only when I have kept it too long sir,'

'So why in God's name have you said all this?' Ellis struck him over the head with the newspaper, once for each of the words he spoke, but it was a newspaper and did Blincoe no harm.

Seeing his brother becoming flustered by all this, Robert stepped in.

'What hours do you work here Blincoe?' Robert asked.

'Six 'till nine sir.'

'And on Saturday?'

'Six 'till twelve sir.'

'So why,' Robert asked, 'does this newspaper say this,' Robert cleared his throat. '"We start work at five in the morning, although sometimes it can be four-thirty, and the first bell goes half an hour before that. The finish time is generally half-past, ten, but can sometimes be eleven, on Saturdays we work until two o'clock." Well?' There was no reply, and Robert then shouted. 'How did Mr John Brown come to write that?'

'I don't know sir. I only told him the truth.'

Robert and Ellis looked at each other not knowing what to do next. Any further questioning was just going to make them angrier as they revisited the articles and then listened to Blincoe's fixed response that he *only told the truth.* The meeting was probably at an end, and whereas there remained the urge to ask more questions, the dilemma was resolved when Ellis noticed the growing dark patch on the front of Blincoe's trousers and the small puddle of urine next to his right boot. This brought the meeting to an end.

Ellis looked at Woodward, 'Put him in the coal-sheds until tomorrow. Woodward, you be here at eight in the morning, and we'll discuss this further.'

'Are we not to give him the lash first?' Woodward asked.

'Tomorrow,' Ellis said. 'we'll sort out his punishment tomorrow.'

Woodward left with Blincoe. He had one hand on Blincoe's collar and the other was twisting his arm up his back. Woodward struggled down the narrow stairs making sure Blincoe could not escape, but at the same time inflicting as much pain as possible. Part way down the last flight of stairs, and seeing that the outside door was shut, Woodward changed his grip so that he had both Blincoe's arms up his back. He then curled his right foot around in front of Blincoe's ankles and then gave him a swift push. Blincoe fell, and with no time to bring his arms forward, he was head first down the stone steps. He ended up slumped against the outside door with blood gushing from his head. Blincoe was still moving around, and Woodward had inflicted enough punishments in his time not to be worried by Blincoe's injuries. Woodward pulled him up and marched him to the coal-sheds. Woodward was disgusted with the timid way that the Needham's had thus far handled this situation, but as was usually the case, he presumed that the responsibility of Blincoe's welfare would eventually return to him, and then he could deal with the matter properly.

Woodward shouted across the yard to Simpson. 'Can you fetch the lock for the coal-shed? Your lad needs to be kept safe in there. Safe from himself too, he keeps falling down stairs!' Woodward threw Blincoe into the darkness, shut the door, and then he stood with his arms folded and his back to the door, until Simpson had secured it.

For Blincoe, the rest of the day passed slowly and the night even slower. At some point, Milner brought some bread, a small piece of cheese and water, but that was it. When Milner came, Blincoe stayed back in the darkness, fearful of a further beating. Had Milner seen the state he was in, he might have bandaged his head and possibly brought him fresh clothes, but it suited Blincoe to stay looking like this. He thought that Woodward might get into trouble with Needham if he saw what injuries had been inflicted. He made himself a bed in the coal heap and tried to sleep, and although he lay still for much of the day and night, his headache and worries about the next day meant he slept fitfully.

His plans to get one up on Woodward came to nothing. In the morning, Woodward asked Mrs Milner, to clean him up. 'He has to see the masters, and he must look his best,' Woodward said.

Mrs Milner made sure that Blincoe was clean, in clean clothes, and she tended to his head, which with the dried blood washed off, did not look so bad. Woodward stood guard outside during this time; his prisoner was not going to escape. He then took Blincoe to the counting house where he was again guarded whilst Woodward discussed the matter with the Needhams on the next floor up.

There was no agreement at the beginning of the meeting. Woodward was all for applying the most severe punishment possible. Ellis was particularly worried that factory inspectors would descend on them and seek out Blincoe. Whether Blincoe had told the truth, or not, was immaterial; if he was beaten or maimed, Ellis, as the owner feared he could well end up in court. Robert tried to steer a middle ground and come to some pragmatic solution, but there was nothing that satisfied everyone. In the end, it was Woodward who came to the rescue.

'I have an idea,' he began. 'You do not need to know all of the detail, but first, I believe that Blincoe should be punished in an appropriate way. He should receive the lash from Robert as we agreed. As he has broken the terms of his indentures, that is fair and would be seen to be fair, but then I have an idea to get Blincoe *on our side*, so that if he was interviewed in the future, he would not be a liability. Will you trust me?'

Both Ellis and Robert were tiring of the matter, and as there was other mill business to deal with, namely the future and profitability of the mill, they were happy for Woodward to take charge of the Blincoe business.

'Fetch him for his whipping.' Robert asked.

Blincoe entered the room clean, but showing a long cut and swollen and bruised forehead.

'What has happened here?' Ellis asked.

'The lad went a bit mad last night,' Woodward replied, 'I could hear him running, again and again, into the coal-shed door. I think he may be deranged.'

'Take his clothes off,' Robert said.

Sixteen

SUNDAY 2ND SEPTEMBER 1798
LITTON MILL

It was Sunday morning and Blincoe's sixth day living in the coal-shed. Although it had been tough living in a small, dark and damp space, he found it much less tiring than working in the mill. Working in the mill meant that you woke up tired and went to bed more so; working in the mill also brought with it a high risk of injury and an even higher risk of a beating. In comparison, Blincoe found the coal-shed experience was quite restful. It was uncomfortable, and the days passed at a crawl, but the opportunity to rest and sleep, was a reward, one that the masters had presumably overlooked. Blincoe spent the first days following his whipping, sleeping and dozing during the days, with the result that he lay awake through most the nights. The nights seemed even longer than the days with none of the daytime outside noises or movements for him to hear or see. The coal-shed door was of a simple wooden construction. It opened outwards and fitted up against the outside wall, but the outside wall was built of rough limestone which left gaps between the wall and the door, and if Blincoe pushed his face close to the door, and if the chain and lock had not been put on too tight, then he could see people moving about the mill yard. Most of those people were unaware that Blincoe was so close to them, and at no time was he in a mood for conversation or being ridiculed, so he stayed quiet. Watching them was not only frustrating, but also painful as he had to push his nose hard against the splintery wood, and after the first day, he only looked outside when there was some incident that sounded worth the effort.

The gaps let in enough light for Blincoe to find his piss pot and eat the scraps of food that were delivered twice each day. The food was not a lot worse than the apprentices were routinely given, porridge and oatcake for breakfast, bread and usually some kind of stew at night. He also had a bowl of water. Woodward always claimed that those locked up in the coal shed were given just bread and water, but Milner, who generally brought his food, provided better than that.

His daily routine began after the apprentices had started work, with Milner letting him out to use the bog house and have a wash. Milner always escorted him and Milner always attempted conversation, but Blincoe gave little back.

'How are your cuts healing?' Milner asked on Wednesday morning.

'Slowly,' Blincoe replied.

Milner's visits were Blincoe's total human contact.

The long days gave Blincoe plenty of time to think, time to think about Phoebe, about Martha, about how he might actually get away from this place, and what he would do when he left. His ideas though, were more dreams than actual plans. He imagined being a successful entrepreneur, running a workplace where everyone was happy; he imagined being married and spending time with his wife; he imagined playing with his children on long hot Sunday afternoons, but this was all imagination, and he had no idea how to go about achieving any of this.

During Thursday morning, he noticed a spider near to the top corner of the door. The spider was quickly and skilfully, repairing the web, which must have been broken when the door opened for Blincoe's breakfast to be delivered. When the web was repaired, the spider waited patiently. Blincoe, with nothing else to do, waiting patiently too. The first fly flew into the web, but somehow freed itself and flew back outside. The second was not so lucky, and the more it struggled, the more it became entangled. The spider then ate the second fly just leaving some, unappetising pieces of wing. Blincoe decided that the next fly into the web would represent his chances of getting free that day, but when the next fly was devoured, Blincoe decided that there was no connection between himself, spiders and flies. He dashed the web to pieces with a piece of coal and lay back in his coal heap to doze again.

On Sunday the routine changed. It all began the same, but partway through the day, the door was unlocked, and he was escorted, by Milner, to the Sunday school. He was the last to arrive and Milner, much to Blincoe's embarrassment, led him in into the already full room. As he was being shown where to sit, at the only remaining place on the front row, he caught sight of Phoebe, her face expressionless as it often was. Parson Brown smiled at him and then began the Sunday school, but all Blincoe could hear, or all he thought he could hear, was other apprentices sniggering behind him. When the hymn that signified the end of the Sunday school was done, Blincoe was led back to his cell.

'It was Parson Brown,' Milner said, 'who insisted that you attend the Sunday school. Knew you by name he did. He says that everyone who is fit and well, should attend.' There was no response from Blincoe and Milner continued, 'No one's said anything about the ordinary school, so it's back to the shed now.'

It was as Milner and Blincoe walked back across the yard that Blincoe noticed something. As he walked towards the coal-shed door, he noticed that the door hinges were just hung on upright pins that were in turn attached to the outside wall, and if the chain securing the door was not too tight, then the door could be lifted off the hinge pins. Blincoe examined the door carefully as he came closer to his cell. He hoped Milner would not see him as he studied the length of the pins and tried to work out how high the door would need to be lifted to come free of the hinge pins. Milner had given up trying to make conversation, but as he began to close the door on Blincoe, he still felt the need to say something.

'Dinner will be around the usual Sunday time: about six,' Milner said.

As Milner was speaking Blincoe jammed a lump of coal, about the size of his fist, in the opening of the door. He hoped it was big enough so that when removed, it would give him more slack on the chain, but not too big a lump so that Milner would notice the increased gap.

Milner had gone and so far, the plan had worked. Blincoe had removed the coal and there seemed a fair amount of slack on the chain. But should he escape and if so where would he go? He knew of no apprentices that had made a successful escape. Plenty had tried and all had been returned. He decided that he would escape, but then return before dinner. His decision was made, but he couldn't be seen around the mill or meet anyone from the mill. He had no money, so going to the Red Lion was not an option. If he was to escape, his only choice seemed to be to go up Slack hill and try and find Martha. He hadn't seen her for a year, but they didn't part on bad terms. He had told himself that he was finished with her, but the truth was that he had spent more time thinking about her during his time in the coal shed than he had thinking about Phoebe.

'She probably won't be there anyway,' he said out loud.

Using the leverage of a coal shovel, the door lifted neatly off its hinges and landed, still upright, the chain holding it so. As the door hit the floor, there was some noise, and Blincoe listened before making his next move, but there was no one about; they were all in the school class. Outside in the mill yard, he used the same shovel to lift the door back on to its hinges and then propped the shovel against the wall, carefully moving it twice until he was happy it was in a position that would cause least alarm.

He was free. He ran out of the mill yard keeping low, as there was a point where he might be seen from the apprentice house. He began to run up Slack hill, but the combination of his whipping, and a week in the coal-shed had left him frail, and he walked up the remainder of the way. On a number of occasions, he wondered about returning to the coal-shed, but something kept him going forwards. There was the usual fear of bumping into Woodward or anyone really, but he told himself that if he was caught, there were few further punishments they could inflict on him. However, he kept his senses and kept his head low. He also needed to avoid Simpson, as although they had a good relationship, this could be ruined if he was to put Simpson in a difficult position. He carefully moved through the wood and then into the fields at the back of the cottages. He worked his way along the row of cottages keeping low behind the dry-stone wall until he reached Martha's house. His plan didn't go much beyond this point, but he slowly raised his head to look over the wall. Coming to meet him, on the other side of the wall, was Martha's dad's pig, which sniffed and snorted at him and then wandered off uninterested. In front of Blincoe was a small area the width of a cottage and about twice as long. Some cottages had vegetable gardens in this space, and others kept a pig. Beyond that was a rough track running in front of the cottages and beyond that, the cottages and Martha's front door. Blincoe stood watching the front door for a few minutes willing it to open. He concentrated hard, closing his eyes to help the door open and to help Martha appear, but there was no open door and no Martha. He sat back down in the field on the safe side of the wall.

Blincoe waited and gazed into the valley of the mill, wondering when he would escape forever. Was this the moment that he should seize? Should he set off now and head for Manchester or Sheffield? He was ill prepared for such a journey, and he knew it. Apart from his physical frailty, he had no plan, nowhere to go to, little in the way of skills to sell and no money. His thoughts drifted to nothingness, and he dozed a little. He was woken by the pig squealing and making much more noise. When he peered over the wall, he saw Martha feeding it. She was wearing a huge pair of boots that Blincoe knew were her father's.

'Hello,' he said, but the pig snorted and drowned his voice. He tried a little louder, 'Hello.' Still nothing. He was concerned that should he shout louder the whole row of cottages would hear, and so he picked up the smallest stone he could find and threw it in front of Martha. It worked. She looked up.

'Hello,' he said again.

She looked surprised, and seemed not especially pleased. Blincoe began to think that this was not one of his best ideas.

Martha moved towards the wall. 'I heard you were locked up,' she said. 'Have they let you out at last?'

'No, I've escaped.' Blincoe looked around him, signalling to Martha that this was not the best place to talk.

'Escaped?' She asked, rather too loud for Blincoe's liking.

'Sshhhh,' Blincoe mouthed.

Martha had now grasped the situation. 'Listen, go to the wood. I'll come as soon as I can. I've just got to feed Ellis.'

'Ellis?' Blincoe looked puzzled.

Martha smiled, 'It's Ellis because … oh never mind now I'll explain later. Now, away with you!'

'I haven't brought you any food. Are you hungry?' Martha asked.

'No, not really.'

'So what are you going to do now you've escaped? You can't stay here.'

'I'm going to go break back into my little prison. Break back into it in exactly the same way as I escaped. If all goes well no one will ever know. Well, no one apart from you!'

'So why escape then?'

'I don't know, just because I could and maybe to see you.' Blincoe looked at her, and he thought she blushed, just a little.

'I could try and get a piece of bread for you,' Martha said.

'No, I'm fine. I'll get some dinner at six. Do you know what time it is?

'It's about four.' Martha took a good look at him and smiled.

'So young Robert, or is it Robert the Free? So, Robert the Free, what are you going to do to keep me amused for the next two hours?

'I don't know, but you were going to tell me about Ellis?' Blincoe said.

'Oh aye. It's just the name dad's given the pig. It's the name of your master at the mill; he's Ellis Needham. Did you know that? Anyway that's all. It's one of dad's wee jokes. In fact, our last three pigs have all been called Ellis.'

Blincoe laughed. For Blincoe the joke was still funny.

'Mam's going to have a baby, not until next year, but it's definitely on the way. I know.'

Blincoe's knowledge of how babies were born was more or less correct, but unsure whether all of what he had been told was true, and to avoid looking foolish, he restricted his comments.

'That's good.'

'Aye, except it's making everyone grumpy; they think the baby might die, just because the last two did. We'll see.'

The two of them chatted easily. Blincoe was surprised how easy it was to talk to Martha. It was as though the year that had passed without seeing her, had never happened. Martha was very physical too, and physical contact, save beatings, was something that was totally absent from his life. She held his hand and circled her nail around his open palm, making the hairs on the back of his neck stand up. They lay back, and he rubbed the side of her neck, which she had told him she liked, and they talked for an hour, until Blincoe started to worry about his return.

'I think I might need to be getting back soon,' Blincoe said, 'and I might need some help to get back in.'

'Oh aye, and how's that?' Martha asked.

'Well I can lift the door up, but I'm not sure I can guide it back on the hinges. I'll be on the wrong side. Do you see?'

'Aye, you're definitely on the wrong side, living in a coal-shed, that's for sure!'

Blincoe's re-imprisonment was almost as easy as his escape. There was no one in the yard, and the two of them managed to put the door back. Blincoe lifted from the inside, whilst Martha guided the door hinges back onto their pins from the outside. It was only when he was re-imprisoned that he realised that he had planned to kiss her. The chance was gone, but with them on opposite sides of the door, and with him somehow safe from giving away any expressions of hurt, he spoke to her.

'Martha, will you be my girl?'

There was a pause. Blincoe shut his eyes.

'Ask me next year young Robbie the Prisoner. I'm away before I get caught!'

Blincoe spent a troubled night. He had dwelt on Martha's parting words and couldn't fathom whether she was serious about him waiting a year, or was that just a joke because it had been a year since they last met, or was she just being kind to him? That night, he dreamt of her.

Very early the next morning, before it was light, and before the mill had begun work, Blincoe heard footsteps approaching his door. They stopped outside, and a small brown parcel was slid underneath. He then heard the footsteps walking quickly away. The parcel contained a small piece of meat pie. Blincoe was sure it was Martha who had brought it. She would have been on her way to work at Cressbrook mill and must have set off earlier than normal. It was good pie, and he ate it straight away. It crossed his mind that perhaps she did care for him. An hour later, and the mill yard was becoming busy with people. Blincoe thought he might be going mad when he saw another brown parcel appear under the door. This was the same brown paper and on inspection, the same pie. This one must have been from Martha's dad; the time was about right for him coming to work. Blincoe chuckled as he ate the second piece of pie and imagined both Martha and her dad stealing a piece of pie for him. He licked his fingers, screwed up the pieces of brown paper and threw them into the darkness at the back of the coal heap. He felt a lot happier with the Martha situation now.

He would have been happier still if had been able to see the note Martha had scribbled on the brown paper.

I am thinking of you. Come and see me soon, Martha.

Seventeen

MONDAY 3RD SEPTEMBER 1798
RED LION INN, LITTON

'Here's your ale Parson.' Molly dropped a quart of ale onto the table. 'You here on your own then?'

'I'm meeting Mr Needham here. We have one or two matters to talk over.' Brown wondered if here had been the best choice of venue as the matters were quite delicate, and he didn't need Molly Baker passing it on to the rest of the parish. Brown moved the conversation away from himself and Needham.

'How are you then Molly, 'Brown asked, 'and how's Ellen getting on?'

Molly was always happy talking about herself and happier still talking about her daughter, of whom she was immensely proud.

'I've had another letter from her,' Molly said, and she sat down beside him, clearly excited by her news. 'This is her fifth letter, and I think it will be her last as they are coming home at the end of the year. She'll be a proper lady when she comes back. She'll be twenty-one next February. We're hoping she'll be back here for then.'

'Mrs Baker, good evening.' Needham stood behind her.

'Oh excuse me,' she said, standing up hurriedly. 'Let me get you some ale.'

'He can share mine,' Brown said. 'Just bring another tankard please.'

Brown had not stopped drinking completely; that was not possible in the society he moved in, but he was now being sensible. When at home, he limited himself to a maximum of two glasses of wine each evening and when in an ale house, a maximum of a quart in any one day. He had now kept up this regime for eighteen months and had made no slips.

'So, how's the drinking?' Needham immediately asked.

'It's under control,' Brown replied. 'It's not a problem. That's not to say I don't want to drink more than I do! But I am in control now, not the drink.'

'Good to hear. At least something's going well for somebody.'

'Go on,' Brown said, as clearly Needham needed to talk.

'Oh it's nothing, and it's everything. The cotton business is a tough business to be in at the moment. It's proving difficult to make it pay. From Monday next,' he looked around and lowered his voice, 'we're going to have to work the mill longer hours, and there's no more money for wages. Don't say anything. No one knows yet.'

Brown was about to speak and offer some words of support, but Needham having taken a quick swill of ale continued.

'Then we've had some, what you might call, bad publicity. Some journalist has got hold of one of our stupid apprentices; a lad called Blincoe, and printed a series of articles making us look very bad indeed. It was mostly lies, but the damage is done. Worse still, bloody Newton took great delight in being the one to tell me about it, but I'll get my own back on him, somehow. And finally, and if I'm being honest,' he took another swill, 'I can't seem to find a good and eligible woman to marry. I'm thirty-four, and it really is time I married.'

Brown knew about the bad publicity, and he knew about Blincoe. He knew Blincoe a little, and had spoken to him only the day before; he thought that he seemed a polite and bright lad, but he didn't say anything to Needham, as he clearly had a different view. He also knew that Needham was thirty-four, single and lonely. This was something he sympathised with very much, and though Brown could still claim to be in his twenties, he was twenty-nine, and he understood how Needham felt. The difficulties of the mill, and the new hours there, were the only surprise for Brown, although not that much of a surprise, as he knew the cotton business was becoming saturated with over production and there was bound to be casualties. In fact the difficulties in the business had a connection with why Brown wanted to see Needham this evening.

'Anyway, how are you?' Needham asked, ending his moan. 'How's it all working out at the vicarage with the child?'

'It's all working fairly well,' Brown said. 'Samuel has just had his first birthday; Kezia cannot do as much as before, but we get by. I'm not really sure what the parishioners think of the situation, but they seem nice enough to my face and my congregation numbers are rising.'

Kezia had returned to the vicarage straight after Brown's visit to see her in Whaley Bridge. On her return, she resumed her full duties, but as the pregnancy advanced, she did less. For a few weeks around the birth, she did almost nothing and Brown managed on his own. The vicarage may not have been dusted as often and his clothes not cleaned as often, but he managed moderately well, and most importantly, without descending into the mess he was in before. Kezia and Brown never spoke again about their intimacy; in fact, they never spoke about anything difficult. At the time of the birth, Brown made sure he was away. He didn't want to appear as an interested father, or someone who was paying too much attention to Kezia and her circumstances, and so he temporarily left Tideswell, making a visit to his Bishop in Lichfield to discuss how he might become involved in the anti-slavery campaign, a diversion that was beginning to become an obsession. The visit was justified but the dates of the visit were carefully timed and arranged by Brown, and on the night that Brown thought his child was being born he had wept himself to sleep. Kezia stayed at her Grandmother's for the birth, and when she returned to the vicarage, Brown organised both an upstairs room and a downstairs room, so that she could always be close to the child. Slowly she had returned to something close to her full duties, but Brown had to accept that the child would come first. He generally had nothing to do with the child, although on occasion, when Kezia was busy elsewhere, he picked him up. It was a miserable situation for Brown, although he observed that Kezia seemed happy enough and wondered if that's how it was being a mother. She seemed to be quite friendly with the gravedigger, Sam Slater, and Brown dreamt one night that they ran away together, freeing him from his burden, but Slater had no other work than digging the occasional grave, and in any case, no one was very likely to take Kezia with another man's child.

Needham ordered more ale, as he needed a drink. He also wanted Molly safely out of the way so he could speak to Brown about the Kezia situation.

'I have to tell you.' Needham whispered, 'that as far as I can tell, there is no suspicion that the child is yours; I have heard nothing on that front, nothing at all. There are plenty of parishioners who disapprove of you bringing up a bastard child in the vicarage, but there are an equal number who think it is an enormous act of charity, an act of kindness and generosity, true Christianity if you like.'

'What I have done for Kezia may be seen as Christian by others,' Brown said, 'but you and I know that it comes about from my sinning; I can never look to marry now, not while Kezia and Samuel are in the vicarage, but I think that is my punishment, and as difficult as it is, I must accept it.'

'More ale for you gents,' Molly pushed the second quart of ale onto the edge of the table.

'If I were you,' Needham concluded, now raising his voice, 'I would weave some appropriate story into a sermon one Sunday. Tell them what Christianity really means!'

Brown laughed, 'That's very good news, thank you, but as for the sermon, I am trying to increase my congregation, not infuriate them, or frighten them away!'

'Were you away from the parish at the end of last week?' Needham asked. 'Someone told me you were.'

'Yes I was,' Said Brown, 'but only for one night. I went to Manchester to the cathedral to hear Thomas Clarkson speak.'

Needham shook his head. 'Never heard of him,' he said.

'No, I didn't expect you would have. He is leading a campaign to abolish slavery, and I'm becoming more and more interested. Somehow, being rector of Tideswell, as busy as it is, isn't enough for me. I need something else.'

Needham had no interest in anything outside the parish and certainly abolishing slavery had no relevance in his world. He moved the conversation on.

'So, you wanted to see me about some parish matter?' Needham asked.

'Yes, It is rather delicate, and difficult, and let me apologise in advance if any of what I am about to say upsets you.'

'I'm on my knees already,' Needham said. 'I can't fall any further, so come on, spit it out!'

'Some of the Litton parishioners, and I don't want to name any names, but some of the parishioners, and yes, they do understand that the cotton business is tough and that you are facing somewhat difficult times and an uncertain future; those parishioners are concerned that should the very worst happen, that the Litton parish would become responsible for all of your apprentices.' Brown could see Needham's blood rising but before Needham could speak, Brown continued.

'Please, hear me out. There is a solution to this. Now Litton mill sits on the river which itself divides the parishes of Taddington and Litton, and I believe that you lease lands on both sides of the river. Is that so?'

Needham nodded, trying to follow where this was going.

'If an additional apprentice house was built on the Taddington side of the river, and half of the apprentices lived there, then we have immediately halved any potential liability for Litton parish.'

'And what would Taddington say about it, and who would pay for it?' Needham asked.

'Well, Litton is my parish, not Taddington, but I would have thought that a problem, if there was one that is, is better shared. As to paying for it, there is some money available from the parish and some money from myself.'

'Why on earth would you contribute?' asked Needham.

'Well I have the money that I have been receiving from the parish of Saint Giles, my portion of the apprentice money that is; I have to say that I have become increasingly uncomfortable receiving this money. People have said that we are trading in people; there have been comparisons made with the black slave trade.'

'It's not the same at all,' Needham said. 'We are giving these children a chance.'

'Well, I don't think this is the best time for you to persuade me otherwise, not when there is cash on offer.' Brown sat back. 'There is a total of ninety guineas available if you agree.'

Needham worked out very quickly that he would not build a second apprentice house, but actually move the first one to the Taddington side. That way he could re-use the stone and most of the timbers; the material costs would be next to nothing. If he used his own labour, which would include apprentices, then the labour costs would be nothing. Overall, he would make almost ninety guineas.

'Very well then,' Needham said. 'I'll do it. I'm not going to argue.'

The men sat in silence for a while after that, Brown taking tiny sips of his ale, to limit his intake. With their important talk finished, Molly, who had heard most of it, thought it timely to get one of them to read Ellen's last letter. She had heard it read half a dozen times, but once more would be nice.

With the three of them sitting together, Parson Brown began reading.

'June 27th.

'Dear Mother, All is well here, I hope you are all well too. The big news is that Lydia and I will be coming home at the end of this year. We are booked on a ship that should sail from here on October 10th. The ship is called *The Surprise*. If all goes well we should arrive in Liverpool early in January, but hopefully sooner.

'The house we have lived in is to be sold. The reason is that the cotton crop has again been poor this season, and the next crop will be the last. It seems that worms have again destroyed much of it. Lydia's father says that they will now concentrate entirely on sugar cane. The house and land where we are will be sold, and they are to expand the sugar plantation. Some of the negroes working in the cotton will be taken to the sugar plantations, but many of them will be sold too.

'Lydia and I spend a lot of time thinking about home and how nice it must be walk around in the cool green valleys of Derbyshire.'

Needham grunted his disapproval, 'She'll not be back long in the damp and the rain, before she's wanting to be back there.'

'The corn on the other man's ground always seems more fertile,' Brown added.

'I would be more than happy to spend three years in Jamaica,' Needham said, 'thinking about *here*. Well, occasionally thinking about here.'

'Shall I continue?' Brown looked up for everyone's approval.

'Lydia's father says that we are now young women, and we should return to England and look for suitable partners for marriage. I hope you have found us some fitting suitors!

'I hope you and father are well. Love Ellen.'

'There you are,' Brown said looking at Needham, 'an eligible young woman for you to court!'

'I'm sure Mr Needham would be suitable,' Molly said standing up and taking back the letter. 'He can join the queue!' She then ruffled Needham's curly hair in the way only a mother, or Molly, would be allowed to do, and then she walked away.

As the men left the Red Lion, Needham whispered to Brown. 'The last time I saw the girl, she was a plump freckly thing. Not really what I had in mind!'

Eighteen

TUESDAY 4TH SEPTEMBER 1798
LITTON MILL

Blincoe had been living in the coal-shed for one week and one day. It was mid morning on the second Tuesday, and nothing had changed, although it was about to.

The first thing was that Simpson unlocked the door and took a couple of buckets of coal. Blincoe didn't say anything, he just watched him moving about silhouetted against the brightness of the day.

'I'm fetching a cart load of coal today,' Simpson said, 'so you might need to nudge up a wee bit tonight!' It was some sort of attempt at a joke, but to Blincoe, not particularly funny. Blincoe listened as the chain was locked again, and then he heard footsteps fade.

As Blincoe's eyes slowly became used to the dark again, he saw that Simpson had left on the floor a small pile of empty sacks. He presumed Simpson had left these so that he could make himself more comfortable.

'Thank you,' he said, but no one was meant to hear. He then worried that this might indicate he would be in the coal-shed even longer! It was at that moment, fearful of being locked up forever, that he made the decision that if he were not freed after two more nights, he would escape. He would find some way of getting hold of his money from the smithy, and then he would be gone. If this was to be his life, he had nothing to lose, and he would use his time in the next two days to plan his escape in detail and in particular, where he might go.

About half an hour later, he heard a horse and cart and that, he presumed, was Simpson, off to Baslow to fetch coal. After being imprisoned for this length of time, Blincoe would have done almost anything to be up on the cart with Simpson, in the fresh air and enjoying the freedom.

The second thing happened shortly after that. Again the door was unlocked, but this time the less friendly silhouette of Woodward stood in the doorway.

'Come with me,' he said, and he marched Blincoe into the smithy. 'Sit on this bench.' was his next instruction.

'Now I want you to listen very carefully to what I have to say.'

Blincoe saw Woodward reaching for some notes he had made; clearly, he was going to have a lot to say.

'Now I'm sure that you want to end your spell of imprisonment, and I have come up with a way that you can return to normal, return back to work as you were before. Is that something you would like?'

'Yes sir.'

'Right. Well first, you must agree that you will never do anything like this again. Agreed?

'Yes sir.'

'Next, if you are in the future interviewed by any officials, you must only praise the way Litton mill is run, especially praising its masters and the way you and your fellow apprentices have been treated. Agreed?

'Yes sir.'

'Next, if you are in the future asked about what you said to John Brown, the journalist, you must say that what was written was lies. Lies made up by him. Agreed?

'Yes sir.'

'Right, well nothing difficult there and no surprises I imagine. There is one final thing we need, and if you do this, you will be freed from your cell by this time tomorrow, and in the future will be treated much more favourably than you have been to date. Are you listening carefully?

'Yes sir.'

'The first thing you need to know and understand is that Litton mill is, at the moment, struggling to make any money and as a result finding the cash for the wages each week is getting more difficult. If nothing changes, than we will all find ourselves as beggars, or be sent to the poor house. You wouldn't want to be back in the poor house, would you?'

'No sir.'

'Of course if the other mill, Cressbrook mill that is, was unable to spin cotton, then Litton mill could take on their spinning, and we would make more profit. If, for example, there was a bad fire at Cressbrook mill, something not uncommon in cotton mills, then that would put it out of action for a considerable time. If that happened, then Litton mill could well benefit as a result, and our jobs would be safe. Do you see Blincoe?

'Yes sir.'

'I'm not sure you do, but let me make it clear what you are going to do. Before you go back to the coal shed, you need to gather up the things from here that you would need to break in to Cressbrook mill and start a fire there.' Woodward lowered his voice and moved his face closer to Blincoe's. 'Tonight, about an hour after work is finished, your lock and chain will be undone. You will then go to Cressbrook mill, break in to the bale store and start a fire in the cotton there. You will then return to the coal shed, and it will be locked again about an hour before anyone arrives for work. Do you understand now?'

'Yes sir.'

Woodward expected some shock on Blincoe's face at this point, maybe even some objection about what was being asked of him, but there was no visible reaction.

The punishment and pain of the last week had dulled Blincoe's senses and hardened his emotions, and nothing now was going to shock or surprise him.

'Now I imagine you will need a tinderbox, maybe two to be sure, and a bar. Do you think you need anything else?'

Blincoe thought about what he might need and then answered.

'No sir.'

'Do you know the layout of Cressbrook mill? Have you been there?'

'I know where the bales store is sir. I have never been inside though.'

'Good, so long as you know where the building is. Any other questions?'

'No sir.'

'In a minute you need to gather up the tinderboxes and the bar, but before that, you need to understand that we are the only two people who know of this plan. You also need to know that should you get caught, I will deny any knowledge of this meeting. I will say that I haven't seen you since last week. Now get your things, and just remember you are doing this not only to gain your freedom, but to help Litton mill stay in business. If you are successful, then tomorrow you will be freed.'

Blincoe was put back in the coal shed; Woodward was back at work with his morning having gone exactly to his plan. Blincoe was doing his dirty work, and if he stepped out of line again, he could be reminded, or rather told, as Woodward assumed he had little knowledge of capital punishment, that arson was a hanging offence. Occasionally young children were given lesser punishments, but only when they were considered too young to know the difference between right and wrong. Blincoe would not fall into this category; he was clearly sensible enough to know that premeditated arson was wrong. If he was caught tonight, he would hang, and if not Woodward would always have that threat over him.

Blincoe sat in the coal-shed and wondered if this was a trick. Perhaps he should have grabbed his money whilst he was back in the smithy, but taking his money would have been too risky with Woodward there. Surely Woodward would keep his word and set him free; he wouldn't want to risk a young apprentice squealing that he had been put up to setting fire to a mill?

Blincoe moved to planning his strategy for the evening ahead. He planned the route he would take, he imagined the interior of the bale store, he imagined how he would light the fire and he planned his return. He had practised with both of the tinderboxes, and they sparked well; both tinderbox cloths were well charred and dry. He was as prepared as he could be. He knew that Simpson would arrive back with a couple of tons of coal, and so he hid the tinderboxes and the bar behind some timbers in the ceiling. He was excited about his adventure tonight. He felt much the same as he did on Sunday before he escaped to Littonslack, but Blincoe had no idea of the magnitude of the offence he was about to commit and no idea of the punishment if caught.

Blincoe was released in the afternoon following the night of the fire, and he went back to work in the smithy. He had expected to be released sooner, and had begun to think that Woodward had lied to him, but Woodward kept his word.

In the days and weeks that followed, there was no conversation between Woodward and Blincoe. Blincoe thought this strange, but then having no contact with Woodward was good. Woodward was well satisfied with how events had unfolded. The fire could not have gone better. If it had been less severe, then probably no work would have come to Litton mill; had it been more severe, then the mill might never have been rebuilt. Woodward had done his duty to Litton mill, and he now had Blincoe where he wanted him.

Nineteen

WEDNESDAY 5TH SEPTEMBER 1798
CRESSBROOK MILL

William Newton looked down at his shoes that were now white: white with ash from burnt timbers and burnt cotton. He stood in the entrance of where the loading doors had been and took in what was missing from the view: there was no roof on the bale store, no roof on the carding room, no windows, no cotton, no doors. Then there were the items that weren't missing, but were damaged beyond repair and in some cases beyond recognition. There were lists to be made.

There were just two men with him, his clerk and his mill manager. Everyone else had been sent home for the day, although many, with little else to do, stood at a distance also observing the mess and speculating about how, and who, and why, and when.

Rumours were teeming through the distant crowd.

'They say it was William Newton himself who did it for the insurance money!'

'Apparently Jessie Bone's brother saw a shooting star and the next thing the place was up in flames!'

'I'm telling you, it was that little apprentice, Luke Swindle; he'd been handcuffed for a week, and they were only taken off yesterday.'

The fact was that no one in that crowd had any idea how the fire had started. The first anyone knew was at around one-thirty in the morning when the glow and noise from the fire woke some of the apprentices. The apprentice house faced the bale store, and a great commotion ensued. Many apprentices rushed out to try and help, but those apprentices, mostly girls, who didn't join in trying to put out the fire, had a grandstand view of the event.

The first adult on site was the mill manager. At this point, the fire was still contained within the bale store, and the roof was still in place. Through the slightly open loading doors, all he could see, from floor to ceiling, was orange fire, and he knew that that there was no way of getting into that building, not that way anyway. The bale store and the next-door carding room were in a large single story barn-like building, and this in turn connected to the three-story mill. The carding room was separated from the bale area by a stone wall, and there were initially thoughts of saving the room and its machines. Those thoughts came to nothing when the roof, common to both rooms, caught hold and quickly collapsed in. The efforts were then concentrated on preventing the fire spreading into the rest of the mill. This idea was much more realistic and proved relatively easy as there was just one simple door connecting the two buildings. After the attempts at saving the carding engines had failed, the door was shut, and it was kept doused with water from the mill side; that way the rest of the mill was saved. By dawn, the danger of the fire spreading was over. Timbers continued to burn and smoke, and although efforts were initially turned to putting out those smaller fires, there was nothing to be saved, and the mill manager decided to let them burn out. There had been a crowd of hundreds, but only half a dozen people were ever actively involved in preventing the fire spreading, and when Newton arrived, at around two o'clock, he ordered the apprentices back to bed and made sure that the villagers were standing at a safe distance.

Newton stepped up onto a step and kicked the ash from his shoes. 'Any thoughts on how it started?' he asked of the two men now with him. 'Are there any clues?'

'I was pretty well first on site,' the mill manager said, 'and the first thing that struck me was that the main loading doors were open. I don't mean wide open, but they were unbolted. Now the fire wasn't so fierce at this time, so it wouldn't have forced them open. The second thing is there was a ladder up to one of the windows on the far side; so you can draw your own conclusions.'

'Interesting,' said Newton, 'any thoughts on who?'

The mill manager shook his head.

'Can we keep that information to the three of us?' Newton said, 'It would be simpler for the insurance claim if we have no idea how it started. Agreed?'

The men nodded.

'Now, we must draw up some detailed lists,' Newton said. 'I will write to the insurers this afternoon, and I imagine ...' He paused, not finishing his sentence. 'What the hell is *he* doing here?'

Coming slowly towards them, on horseback, was the figure of Ellis Needham.

'You two go,' Newton said. 'I'll see to him.'

Needham stepped down from his horse, tethering it to some railings.

'What do *you* want?' Newton said, 'I am rather busy today.'

'I was just passing. I thought I would come and see how the downstream mill is, but I see you're not spinning today!'

'So what really made you come here today? I presume you heard about the fire. How though? How did you know about the fire?' Newton turned from surveying the scene of destruction and looked Needham straight in the eyes. His voice was now angry and much louder 'Did you have a hand in this Needham?' His arm swept out, needlessly displaying the scene.

'No, really,' Needham realised he had overstepped a mark. 'I swear on my mother's life, I had no knowledge of this until the milk arrived at Litton mill this morning.'

Newton believed him. Needham was a religious man and would not tell a lie, not against his mother's life.

'Very well,' Newton acknowledged. 'Well I may have some work for you if you are interested. It's going to be a few weeks before this place is up and running again, and I'm under contract to spin set amounts of cotton. Are you interested?'

'Yes,' Needham replied, 'if we can work something out.'

'Well I'll get my clerk to draw up what we need doing, and then we can get together and see if we can agree a price. We are busy with the insurance claim today, so shall we say tomorrow?'

'Tomorrow it is,' Needham said, and he walked back to his horse.

Needham came to an arrangement with Newton, and for three weeks Litton mill spun cotton for Newton's mill. Litton mill worked day and night, and Needham made good profits during those weeks. The burnt out buildings at Cressbrook mill were rebuilt by the dozens of idle workers and apprentices, and so the building grew quickly. Some second hand carding machines were bought from Huddersfield, and just over three weeks after the fire, the mill was ready for production.

On the Friday before Cressbrook mill recommenced production, Newton was given two, connected, pieces of information. The first was from his mill manager.

'The ladder I saw on the night of the fire,' he began, 'well, you wouldn't really need a ladder unless you were under five foot tall. I'm five foot six, and when we were fitting windows last week, I was able to get in and out of the windows without a ladder.'

'So do you think it was one of our apprentices?' Newton asked.

'I do. It certainly looks that way.'

In the afternoon, he received the second piece of information, although this was sent anonymously. The information came from someone who was by the river late at night. He was, presumably poaching in the river, and that is why he would not come forward. On the night of the fire, at about one-thirty in the morning, the anonymous poacher had seen a young boy running along the side of the river; he was running away from Cressbrook mill towards Litton mill.

Newton now had the evidence that he had sought. He now knew that Needham had lied to him and had been involved in the fire.

The following Monday, Newton left his home in the early hours of the morning. He walked down to his mill, surveyed the new building and walked around it, trying to imagine how the arsonist had seen it. He looked again at the height of the windows and then climbed over the wall where the arsonist must have done the same. On the river track, he walked towards Litton mill; he looked out for poachers as he followed the river upstream, but that night there were none. When he reached Litton mill, he didn't turn up to the mill yard, but instead carried on along the track, until he was between the mill and the mill race. The track ended here. It was where the mill connected with the mill race, via the wheel, but the termination of the track did not bother him as he was exactly where he wanted to be.

He looked around him. There was no one to be seen. It was just beginning to drizzle, and that meant there was even less chance of anyone being about. The mill wheel was motionless as the sluice gates were shut to allow the mill pond, such as it was at Litton mill, to fill up overnight. There was only a trickle of water under the wheel, and Newton dropped down into the wheel well, so that he was standing on the bottom of the wheel. The wheel was twelve feet in diameter, and so Newton's head was close to the central shaft. He took from his coat, two large wrenches and proceeded, carefully and methodically, to remove the nuts from the bolts where the arms of the wheel connected to the hub at the centre. At the other end of these arms was the outer ring of the wheel itself. The wheel had been in place for some years and there was considerable rusting of the nuts and bolts and the plates that held it all together. This was both a hindrance and a help: a hindrance as the nuts were difficult to shift, but a help as the bolts showed no sign of turning. Each arm had two bolts at the centre and there were eight wooden arms each side of the wheel. Just over an hour later, wet through from the drizzle and having removed all but three nuts that were seized too tight, he emerged. He calmly walked back along the river and fifteen minutes later, he was home at Cressbrook hall.

Litton mill continued throughout the next day with no problems; the mill wheel turned, and the spindles turned. On the day following that, again there were no problems. The third day began well, but just before five o'clock in the afternoon, the spindles stopped. Unseen by anyone the bolts on the wheel had slowly been working loose, and after a number of the bolts had fallen out, the wheel lurched and fell into the well. The outer wheel immediately stopped, but the centre, with the momentum of the mill behind it, continued for a fraction of a turn, and the arms where the bolts had not fallen out were then twisted and snapped.

Needham, Palfrey, Simpson and Blincoe all gazed into the wheel well looking at the mangled wreckage of the wheel. There was no indication at this stage that this was anything other than some kind of mechanical failure. As no one was rushing forward with ideas and solutions, Needham took control.

'I need all of this out of the well. Get anyone who can help and get the thing out. Lay it out on the mill yard so we can see what we need to do to repair it. Work all night if you have to. We'll see where we are first thing tomorrow.'

Before midnight, the wheel and all its components were laid out on the mill yard. The outer wheel had suffered some damage, but that would be repaired locally. The main damage was to the wooden arms and the connecting plates, but there were also signs that some of the nuts, those that Newton had been unable to remove, had recently seen a wrench; there was bright metal showing. Needham was anxious to know the truth and took Woodward to one side.

'Do you think it could have been the Blincoe boy?' Needham asked. 'After all he has access to tools and now has some engineering knowledge.'

'No, not Blincoe,' Woodward said firmly. 'Blincoe won't step out of line again.'

It was four weeks until the mill wheel turned again. Needham had explored sending his spinning to Cressbrook mill, but his margins were so slender. that had he done this, he would have made a loss. It had been four weeks with no income, and although he paid no wages, he still had to feed over eighty hungry apprentices.

Although it was not at the top of Needham's list, he did use this time to rebuild the apprentice house on the Taddington side of the river. He used apprentices to do much of the work, with them sleeping in the mill whilst it was out of action. Brown gave over the promised ninety guineas to Needham, and that kept the mill's finances fluid, just.

Twenty

SATURDAY 2ND FEBRUARY 1799
CRESSBROOK HALL

Since the New Year, the North of Derbyshire had been in the grip of a brutally hard winter. Long spells of freezing temperatures, snow, ice and sometimes wild winds had just made everything more difficult, and everyone was struggling. Litton mill struggled on too, although the weather was only one of many problems that faced the mill. To keep the business solvent, Needham had been forced to sell some more land from his estate at Wormhill, and as a way of keeping down his wage bill, he now had even more apprentices. There was now a much larger market for apprentices with many more mills and factories looking for cheap labour, and so Needham had been forced to take even younger children; some were just six years old.

Those responsible for the incidents at Cressbrook and Litton mills the previous summer, were never identified, although there was now a general belief that, somehow, each mill was responsible for the sabotage of the other. Parson Brown arranged to meet both Needham and Newton one evening and gave them some blunt advice.

'I don't know what's been going on,' he began, 'but I would very strongly suggest that you stop fighting each other and concentrate on your businesses. Goodness, from everything you tell me it's a difficult enough business to be in!'

The men sat there, nothing to say, their heads bowed slightly, like scalded schoolchildren.

'What you should be doing,' he went on, 'is where it is possible, to join forces, pool your resources, help each other.'

The men listened, and although as the weeks passed, they never brought themselves to help each other, there was an end to the sabotage, and the mills continued to work, Litton mill kept solvent by Needham slowly selling his estate and Cressbrook mill propped up by the wealth of the Newton family.

Lydia and Ellen had now returned from Jamaica. Their ship docked in Liverpool on Tuesday the twenty-second of January. They stayed two nights in Liverpool and were back at their homes in Derbyshire on the Friday.

Ellen's twenty-first birthday was the second of February, and following much deliberation, the decision was made to hold a combined party to celebrate both Ellen's coming of age and the girls' safe arrival from Jamaica. The first thought was to hold the event in the Red Lion, but when the guest list was finalised, they realised somewhere bigger was needed. Newton was resident in the Newton family home, Cressbrook hall, and this seemed an obvious venue with a much grander setting and a large drawing room that would accommodate all of the guests. Lydia's parents remained in the West Indies managing the plantations but Lydia still moved back into the family home at Cressbrook hall, with Molly taking on the role of her mother as much as she could. In the days leading up to the party there was much fussing and comings and goings. There were dresses to worry about, food and drink to organise and Cressbrook hall to decorate.

The guests began to arrive at seven. Mostly they were relations of the Newton's, but in addition, local dignitaries and some close friends were invited. Ellen and Lydia made themselves busy in Lydia's room, making sure they looked their best. Molly fussed around everywhere and especially hindered the girls, but eventually she left them alone so she could greet the guests.

Parson Brown and Ellis Needham were amongst those who had been invited, and they stood making small talk in the drawing room whilst waiting for the appearance of the girls.

'I was in Tideswell yesterday,' Needham began, 'and I thought I saw your maid walking with a man. I had ridden past before I had chance for a good look. Does she have someone?'

Brown seemed distracted and Needham wondered if he was listening at all. Brown then stood on his tiptoes, looking over Needham's shoulder and beckoned Newton over to the two of them.

'I was hoping I might get the chance to talk to you both tonight,' Brown said, 'and I'm afraid it's a money matter I need to talk to both about. It's another parish matter concerning Leisure house.'

Leisure house was a Litton parish scheme. The building had come into the ownership of the parish long before the mills were there. A man by the name of John Hooley had owned the house, but he died leaving no family, or at least none that anyone could find. The house stood empty for a year, after which time, the parish claimed it. Subsequently, they allowed a young homeless woman Nancy White, to live there rent-free. Nancy had some skills as a nurse, and the condition was that she provided care to the sick of the parish; Nancy was still there, now in her fifties. The scheme was that the church and the parish paid for the medicines, bandages and other items that were needed, but of late, the demands on the limited funds available had been tested in the extreme. The invasion of well over a hundred apprentices at the two mills meant that Nancy was run off her feet with sick and injured children. She couldn't cope, and the costs of medicines was a burden that neither the church nor the parish thought they should be liable for.

'I don't want to put a fixed price on it,' said Brown, 'or create any kind of tax, or charge per visit. What we are looking for is a contribution. It's up to you, but what if we said twelve pounds each, and then I'll come back to you when we need some more?'

Neither Needham nor Newton could think of any way out of this. There really was no argument against helping Leisure house, and so they agreed. Needham raised his glass and smiled across the room at Nancy. She had been watching and listening, but despite her best efforts, she had heard nothing.

It was at eight o'clock. Just as Parson Brown was making arrangements to visit Nancy, to discuss how they could best spend the new money, that the two girls finally made their entrance.

Both were in long flowing gowns, and both looked very well indeed. Brown, Needham and Newton, who by this time had separated from each other, each moved slightly to afford a better view of the girls. Lydia wore a peach coloured gown with her blond hair piled high on her head. She was tall, with a plain, slightly chubby face. She was a Newton, born into money and had that arrogance that came with it. William Newton made his way over to her.

'Sister,' he said, 'you look marvellous!' Newton had seen his sister many times since she got back; she had been living in Cressbrook hall for the last week, but none of the three bachelors had set eyes on Ellen for over four years. Newton's compliment to his sister was genuine, but also positioned so that he could easily pay a much more heart-felt compliment to his cousin, Ellen. He moved nearer to Ellen, taken aback by the transformation from the girl he remembered. Her childhood freckles were still just visible, but faded. The chubby child had gone and had been replaced by an elegant woman.

Ellen recognised her own beauty and the power that came with it. She had turned more than the drunken lecherous heads of Molly's Inn. Ellen had now turned heads of men with position, although all of them already had wives.

Newton fell in love at that moment, and he decided that he would pursue and court Ellen. *She* would be his wife. The match was perfect, and she knew the family well, a family that was respectable and wealthy. She had spent the last few years preparing herself to meet someone suitable; she need look no further. He wasn't sure exactly what he would do next, but later on he paid her some compliments on her dress, her complexion and her hair. Any further advance tonight though, would be too soon. Accidental meetings were likely to be easy as she would no doubt spend some time with Lydia at Cressbrook hall, and that would give her opportunities to get to know him.

In due course Parson Brown was introduced to the girls. He invited them to his Sunday service and enquired about their experiences in the West Indies and on their perilous sea journeys. Like Newton he found he had a considerable attraction to Ellen, finding Lydia a little too superior. Brown kept his feelings for Ellen suppressed, as he knew deep down that with a child at home, he could not look to marry, but the experience of meeting Ellen, coupled with his insistence in not acknowledging his feelings, led to a restless night. One of his dreams was of a wedding where he became married to two women at the same service, one standing either side of him before the priest.

The last, and most desperate, of the three bachelors was Ellis Needham. Under any other circumstances, he would have been happy to pursue Lydia, regardless of the family connection to his main competitor, but Ellen's beauty eclipsed that of Lydia. Needham only spoke to Ellen briefly during the party, and he didn't feel he made the best impression. On later analysis of their conversation, he realised he had talked mostly about himself and his mill business, asking Ellen little about herself, but he was still confident that he had finally found someone suitable to be his wife. She would be lucky to have him; he was a landowner, a mill owner and the biggest employer in the area. He concluded that there would be no difficulty winning her over, just a little courting and flattering, and she would be his.

The party went well enough. There was plenty of drink and plenty of food; plenty of people to catch up with and for some, beautiful girls to admire. The finale was a local singer Samuel Slack, who sang unaccompanied, a number of traditional songs. Samuel Slack was Tideswell's most famous parishioner, having sung before King George the Third. The idea for him to sing was Newton's, and as Newton was hosting the party, no one questioned it. Newton thought it fitting, although the girls were greatly disappointed, as they had expected to end the night dancing. Samuel Slack's deep lumbering voice brought a sobering end to the evening, especially his final, and rather melancholy, *Happy Birthday* song. After his recital, the guests began to leave, hastened by the worry of more bad weather and in particular snow, which was beginning to fall.

By the time Ellen got to her bedroom in the Red Lion, the snow was falling heavily and settling. Molly's husband, Francis, had gone to his bed leaving Molly and Ellen in the bedroom. Molly hung up her daughter's dress, brushing some imaginary marks from it. She wondered when it might be worn next.

'Well?' Molly asked. 'Did you enjoy it?'

'It was wonderful,' Ellen said. 'It is so good to be home. Everything seems so much simpler here, and now the snow is falling. I haven't seen any snow in the last three years!'

'And did you see any suitable men?'

Ellen made a weak attempt at being shocked to be having such thoughts, and such a conversation, but with this acting over, she was only too happy to talk about the men there.

'William paid me a lot of attention and gave me some compliments. He seems nicer than I remember.'

'Anyone else?'

'Ellis Needham seemed very eager to talk to me. I think he was quite attracted to me. He seemed very nervous, and he was perspiring a little, but he seemed nice too.'

'Well, that's maybe two people in the queue!' Molly laughed. 'Was there any others?'

'There was one other man, I think he was the only other single man there, well single man under sixty that is! That was Parson Brown. He didn't seem that interested in me, but I thought he was very attractive. He has a kind face, he seemed the caring sort.'

Molly knew the three suitors and wasn't surprised to hear their names come up. Molly's list was the same as Ellen's, but it seemed that the order of Molly's might be the reverse of Ellen's!

Molly was unsure about Parson Brown. She knew him when he was a heavy drinker and feared he could, at any time, slip back to that. She was also one of a small number of people who still thought that he could be the father of Kezia's child. He wasn't all bad though, but he was last on Molly's list.

Molly thought there wasn't much to choose between Newton and Needham, but on balance her choice was Needham for the top of her list. She thought Newton's attraction to poetry and the accompanying, and rather strange, circle of friends that came with it, not a good ingredient for a marriage. She also thought it would be better for her to marry outside of her family.

Molly pulled up the bed-clothes over Ellen and kissed her goodnight as if she was still a child.

That night the three men all slept badly; they were all smitten with Ellen, and whilst she remained free, their souls were tormented. They tossed and turned; frowned and clenched their teeth, and all of them woke up still tired. At the same time, Molly and Ellen slept very peacefully, both smiling as they slept.

TWENTY ONE

SUNDAY 3RD FEBRUARY 1799
LITTONSLACK

The heavy snowfalls of the previous night continued into the early hours of the morning, and all of it had settled. The dawn brought a bitter wintry day where everything that was frozen would stay frozen. Undeterred by this weather were Robert Blincoe, Isaac Moss and James Durant who set off in the snow to their goal: the Red Lion Inn. There were two reasons for this visit. The first was that every fortnight they went there anyway, although the weather made today more attractive, as Molly would have blazing fires. Even the small room at the back, where she put them, had a small fireplace, and if it wasn't lit when they got there, she would carry a shovel full of hot embers from one of the other fires, and it would soon be roaring. The second reason for the visit was that the boys had heard that there was a new barmaid at the Red Lion, Molly Baker's daughter. The barmaid, so the rumour went, was the most beautiful girl in the world; every part of her was perfect, and the boys naturally needed to see her. Blincoe, in particular, was keen, as he was now fourteen, and such matters were beginning to interest him.

When they arrived, there was no sign of Molly's daughter, and the boys were too shy to ask. They took in turns to tiptoe out of their back room and look around, but she never appeared. The fire was lit for them though, and they enjoyed the ale, the warmth the room gave them and a dish of roast pork rind that Molly brought in. The talk was mainly of girls, and the boys bragged about things they had never done.

The way home was cold and made much worse by a stiff breeze blowing snow about. The boys added to this and threw more snow at each other, the silliness encouraged by the alcohol. By the time they approached Littonslack, it was half past four; darkness was falling, and they were wet and regretting becoming so. Durant and Moss stopped just short of the cottages to relieve themselves; they tried to write their names in the snow as Blincoe had shown them half a mile back, but in the wind their efforts were feeble. Blincoe wandered on and stopped at Littonslack; as he gazed up the slope towards the cottages, the giggling of the other boys dulled into a faint noise by the snow, he wondered what Martha was doing. Blincoe was deep in his own thoughts, but was quickly brought out of them when a voice spoke.

'If you're thinking of mythering the Simpson girl, you've not picked a good time.'

The voice belonged to Palfrey, Litton mill's carpenter, he was just the other side of a wall.

'I've seen you here a few times before, but it would best if you made yourself scarce today.'

Blincoe finally located the voice and through the gloom, tried to focus on the figure of Palfrey.

'You see, her mam's having a baby.'

Before the conversation could progress any further, someone came running from the cottages. It was Simpson, and he nearly knocked Blincoe over. Simpson also failed to spot Palfrey, but on seeing Blincoe, he instantly recognised someone he could trust and give instructions to.

'Robert, I need you to run up to Leisure house and fetch help. Can you do that?' Simpson was out of breath, like a man who had ran a mile, although he had only travelled a few yards.

'Of course,' Blincoe replied.

'Fetch Nancy. Tell her that Mrs Simpson is having a baby and it's not going well. Have you got that?' Simpson leant forward supporting himself with one arm against the wall.

'Yes sir.'

'Off you go then. As fast as you can!'

Blincoe was already on his way. He never gave Durant and Moss another thought; they had hid fearing repercussions of some sort, and after Blincoe and the other men had gone, they slipped quietly back to the mill.

Blincoe did as he was told and ran all the way. Leisure house was just along the valley side about half a mile away.

He banged on the door loudly three times. It was a confident knock that Blincoe thought reflected the importance of his message. He banged again.

Inside Leisure house were two mill children recovering from sickness, Nancy Swindle and Parson Brown. Brown had been to Leisure house to tell Nancy about the extra money that he had procured and to discuss how they might divide it between medicines and additional help. He had just looked at his watch and decided that if he left before five, he would have half an hour to better prepare for his evening service. He was about to say his farewells to the children and to Nancy when Blincoe's frantic knocking came. Nancy had heard that knock many times before; she knew it was a knock for help. Brown was first to the door and looked down at the out of breath boy.

'Sir,' he began, 'I'm to ask for Mrs Nancy to come to Littonslack to Mrs Simpson. She's having a baby and it's not going well.' Blincoe quoted the words as they had been given to him. He didn't really know what *not going well* meant, but judging by Simpson's face, it probably meant it was going very badly, but he had no firm idea what the *it* referred to, and so he stayed with the script he had been given.

Nancy heard the conversation and was already gathering her bag and coat. She was experienced in most sickness and emergencies, and although she had no qualifications, she had seen enough over the years to deal with these events and deal with them at least as well as the local doctor. She kept a bag by the door with everything in it she might need; childbirth and its complications were routine matters to her.

'You can ride with me,' Brown said to Nancy. 'It will save time.'

After a few failed attempts, Nancy made it onto Brown's mare, and the two of them set off for Littonslack. The journey was not fast; it was now dark, and the horse needed to tread carefully in the snow. Blincoe followed on foot. He wasn't sure whether to turn down to the mill for his dinner, or carry on to Littonslack: He carried on to Littonslack. He felt a loyalty to Simpson and now felt involved, and maybe he could be of some more help. Alternating between running and walking, Blincoe was able to keep up with the mare, although he kept a respectable distance.

Blincoe loitered outside the cottages. He expected a scene of panic and people rushing about, but it was quiet and peaceful. He wondered if he should go, but then for the second time tonight, there was an unexpected voice, although it was the same voice as before: that of Palfrey.

'We can't stay out here all night,' Palfrey said. 'We'll catch our deaths. I think we better go in, and I'll make us a hot drink.'

Blincoe smiled and followed Palfrey into his cottage, the cottage next to Martha's. Palfrey concocted what Blincoe presumed to be a beef drink; whatever it was it was just what he needed. He looked around the parlour, surprised just how similar it was to Martha's.

'So who's next door?' Blincoe asked.

'Too many people if you ask me,' Palfrey replied. 'Well apart from the three of them, there's the parson, Nancy Swindle, my missus and Woodward's missus. There might be more, other people have been coming and going all afternoon.'

Blincoe was still too shy to ask, what was not going well. He thought that having a baby should probably be a private matter anyway. Conversation was difficult, Blincoe hardly knew Palfrey, and these were not the best circumstances to strike up a friendship. The room was cosy though, the fire blazing up the chimney, and Blincoe's body was already too comfortable to want to move.

But Blincoe's brief moment of comfort was ruined when Palfrey's wife burst in; Blincoe and Mr Palfrey stood up.

'They couldn't do anything,' she shouted, and she sat down where Blincoe had been sitting, sobbing into her apron.

'I don't think we could have done anything different,' she went on. 'Nancy said she had lost too much blood. The little baby's alive though, just.'

It was only now that both Palfrey and Blincoe realised it was Mrs Simpson who had died. They had both presumed it was the baby who was in danger. Blincoe desperately wanted to see Martha now, to put his arms around her and comfort her, but there was no opportunity, and Palfrey, now with his wife to console, showed him to the door.

'Tell the Governor you have been with me. Tell him I'll explain tomorrow if you like.'

The following day the weather was as bad: more snow and stronger winds. Simpson failed to turn up to work, and Milner let Blincoe into the smithy. Blincoe began work alone going through his normal routine of daily chores. At ten o'clock Woodward came.

'It looks as though Simpson won't be in for a day or two,' Woodward said. 'I need you to keep this place running until he's back. Do the routine stuff, lamps, horses and so on, and if there's any other jobs that come up that you can't manage, then see Mr Palfrey.' Woodward said no more. He didn't ask if Blincoe was capable of doing that, and he didn't ask if Blincoe had any questions, he just turned and went.

Blincoe had already snuffed out the lamps without being asked and lit the furnace. He was already enjoying this new responsibility and challenge, but at the same time, he was thinking of Martha and her dad. He couldn't imagine how they were both feeling. He decided that he would work hard, and he wouldn't let Mr Simpson down. He would do his best to keep on top of everything so that when Simpson did come back to work, there would be no work backed up.

Simpson didn't come back to work after the day or two that Woodward had suggested. Blincoe thought he might appear on the Wednesday, but nothing changed. He didn't appear on the Thursday either, and when Blincoe heard that Martha's mum's funeral was on the Friday, he realised that he would be on his own in the smithy all week. But that fact gave Blincoe a new dilemma: should he attend the funeral? If it was up to him, he would definitely attend; after all he worked closely with Mr Simpson, and he knew the family fairly well, but if he asked Woodward if he could go, the answer would be no, there was no doubt about that. Blincoe made up his mind; he would go. Woodward had put him in charge, and as such, he was authorised to make decisions. Blincoe knew that his argument was weak, and he could be in big trouble again, but he was going.

It was Friday, and it was still bitter cold. The funeral was at eleven, and so Blincoe set off just before half past ten, with the wind blowing and chapping his cheeks. It was a cruel day, but there were crueller things, and today Blincoe wasn't thinking of himself. He had never been to a funeral before, but he thought he knew the basics; church service followed by burial. This was also the first time he had stepped into Tideswell Church, and he had imagined something much smaller, not the huge space he found. He was the first to arrive and had planned to sit a few rows from the front in a discrete position, but there were pews all over the place, some at right angles to others, some in little rooms off to the side, and so, rather than sit in the wrong place, he stood at the back of the church looking at the windows, plaques and stone effigies of dead people. After some time two women arrived, and so he sat two rows behind them.

The organ was playing and the coffin was brought in, and trailing behind, just a handful of people. Blincoe was surprised that Martha's mum's death could summon so few people.

There was himself and the two women who had sat down earlier, Martha, her dad, Mr Palfrey and Ellis Needham. That was it! He knew that Martha's family were not local, but it seemed a sorry end to a life.

A little later, the same people gathered around the graveside, Martha and her dad holding on to each other for support. Martha had spotted Blincoe, and she was pleased he was there, but she couldn't speak, not to anyone. It was an upsetting scene for Blincoe, and he stood a little way back, ice cold tears trickling to his chin. When the parson had finished he too stood back, leaving Martha and her dad staring hopelessly into the grave, still clutching at each other. Needham was chatting to Palfrey, presumably about work, and the two women wandered off together, one waving at someone across the road. Parson Brown walked over to Blincoe.

'Thank you for coming,' the parson said quietly.

'I had to,' Blincoe replied. 'All of the family have been very good to me.' Brown and Blincoe stood together rocking in the wind.

'I might be in trouble though, 'Blincoe added, 'at the mill that is.'

'I'll see what I can do,' said Brown, and after a short silence added. 'I'll tell them I asked for you to be here.' Brown patted him on the shoulder and left Blincoe standing alone. Blincoe then ventured to the graveside and looked in the grave at the coffin.

Twenty Two

MONDAY 18TH FEBRUARY 1799
LITTON MILL

At least life was varied: that was what Blincoe decided about his lot on the Monday morning. He was a little early getting to the smithy that day and as he looked up from the furnace that had kept in from the day before, he could see, across the yard, the same people, apprentices and grownups, going into the mill. No one was running, no one was rushing, and few were even talking. They just shuffled in, not questioning anything; the life and any spirit they once had, beaten out of them through punishments and general fatigue. Everyone was now working ninety hours each week, and all they had to look forward to was ninety hours of the same; the same routine every day and a routine spent in the most awful of conditions. There was no opportunity to rest; temperatures were often in the nineties, and there was the terrific noise from the machines. Most of the workers were half-deaf from the noise anyway, but deaf or not, there was no conversation possible over the top of the clattering din in the mill. Blincoe's job, although not always easy, did not have that monotony, and he was grateful for that. It was now exactly two weeks since Simpson had last been to work and as a result, Blincoe's time had become more varied and more interesting. He was generally left alone, and he fitted in the routine work around the more urgent work; anything he couldn't do, he called on

Palfrey, but so far he had only needed him twice. The mill benefited from this temporary arrangement, as they were saving Simpson's wages, and so far, they had not suffered in any way from his absence.

Whilst Blincoe was sitting and watching the flames in the fire of the furnace, Simpson up at Littonslack was staring into the flames of his living room fire. Nothing was the same at Simpson's house, and Simpson knew that nothing would ever be the same again. A few years ago he had lost two children, and he had now lost his wife. It was an unbearable situation, and he was hundreds of miles from his two brothers and his mother who were back in Scotland. He just didn't know what to do, where to turn, how to make things better, or how to make things even bearable. He hadn't slept upstairs since Janet died; he couldn't bear the thought of sleeping in the bed she died in. The neighbours had cleaned, washed and scrubbed the room following that dreadful day, but he wasn't going in there. When he had slept, it was in his chair; when he ate, it was in his chair and he was now in his chair looking into the fire, but focussing somewhere beyond the flames; the previous night's barely touched dinner at the side of him.

Martha had left her job at Cressbrook mill. Her thinking was that she should look after the new baby, the house and her father, whilst he worked and brought in a wage - only there was no wage. Martha was missing her mam, and she was missing her father, who barely spoke. Mrs Palfrey had told her that he was mourning, and it wouldn't last too long, but Martha was anxious for him to be his old-self. In the mean time, Martha knew that the baby needed looking after, and she just naturally looked after her and took on all the other domestic work. The work kept her busy, and that made her feel useful. The previous Friday, a week exactly after Janet's funeral, Parson Brown had called to see the family, or what was left of it.

'Is it Martha? How are you?' Brown had said.

Martha was sitting on the front step of the cottage with the baby in her arms. It was quite cold, but Mrs Palfrey and Mrs

Woodward had said that the baby would benefit most from being out in the fresh air. Martha didn't mind the cold, and it had the benefit of getting her out of the room where her father sat.

Brown sensed that maybe Martha was not too well; she looked tired and probably not in the mood for conversation about herself, so before she could reply he spoke again.

'How is the baby?'

'She's very small,' Martha said, 'but I don't think she's lost any weight. What do you think?' She looked up at the parson.

'I'm afraid I don't have much experience of babies,' he replied, but this was only a half-truth as he had paid close attention to his own child growing up in the vicarage. On the rare occasions when Kezia slipped out on an errand, he had played with Samuel. One day he had held his face up to a mirror, and with both their faces together, Brown looked for any resemblance to himself, but there was nothing obvious, something Brown concluded was unquestionably a good thing. Had Brown been honest with Martha, he would have said that her baby sister looked very sickly.

'Have you thought of a name for her?' he then asked.

'Janet,' Martha said. 'My mam's name.' She faltered a little as she said that, and her eyes welled up with tears. Then she took a big breath, composed herself and gasped.

'That's what *I* thought anyway.'

The conversation moved on awkwardly, Brown choosing his words carefully so as not to upset her any further. He had no idea that Simpson had not gone back to work, and when Martha told him this, he went straight into the cottage to see him. Conversation with Simpson was even more difficult than it had been with Martha. Simpson said he was quite well, when he clearly wasn't; he said that they were managing, when they clearly weren't; he wouldn't admit anything was wrong, when everything looked so wrong. Brown said a prayer and left him.

Martha was still on the step.

'Has anyone been to visit you?' Brown asked. 'Apart from me, that is.'

'Only neighbours,' Martha replied.

'I'll ask Nancy to come down and have a look at the baby; she can take a look at your father too. How are you for money?'

'We have five shillings left.'

'Well don't you worry about money; the parish can help you. I'll come and see you this time next week, and if your father's still at home, we'll sort something out; I'm sure your father will be back to normal soon.'

Part of Brown's reason for visiting Littonslack had been to collect his one shilling and sixpence for the funeral, but he left empty handed; that would have to wait.

Monday came, and Simpson was in no condition to go to work. He had no thoughts about work or even any awareness of the time. He just sat, with his eyes still pointing towards the fire.

Blincoe swiftly moved the kettle from the hot coals and slid it under the bench.

'Blincoe.' Woodward announced his arrival, in his usual abrupt manner.

Blincoe had seen Woodward coming across the yard; a visit from Woodward was never good news.

'It looks as though Mr Simpson will not be back again this week, so I want you to carry on as you have been doing.'

'Yes sir. Is he poorly sir?' Blincoe asked.

'Bad with his nerves lad. Bad with his nerves. It's a very sorry business. I'll ask Palfrey to look in on you.'

Woodward disappeared as abruptly as he had arrived. Woodward totally neglected the pleasantries of normal conversation; he just launched straight into whatever he had to say, and when he'd finished, he left. Blincoe thought that if he just learned 'Hello' and 'Goodbye,' it would be an improvement.

At least Blincoe now knew the reason that Simpson was not at work. He knew the reason; he knew the words, but he had no idea what they meant.

'Bad with his nerves,' Blincoe said out loud and then shook his head. It meant nothing to him.

An hour or so later Palfrey came over. They chatted about the Simpsons, although Blincoe didn't learn any more about Simpson's actual illness or injury to his nerves, but everyone seemed very concerned. The conversation then moved to mill work, and Palfrey told him that Woodward and Needham had a huge argument over Blincoe attending the funeral.

'Woodward wanted your blood,' Palfrey said, 'but Needham was insistent that your absence from work should go unpunished. What surprised me was how lenient Needham was, and how aggressive Woodward was. Very strange!'

Palfrey sat down. 'I'll just take the weight of my feet for five minutes,' he said, 'and have a quick pipe. Keep your eyes open for anyone coming.' Palfrey made himself at home, and when his pipe was established, he spoke.

'Now, none of the other apprentices and spinners know this yet, so keep what I'm about to say under your hat.' Palfrey took a few more puffs on his pipe and then continued. 'On Easter holiday Monday, Needham is planning a big party for all the workers and their families. It will be here at the mill, and there will be food and drink and games and singing and dancing and it should be a real good time. Now if your gaffer isn't back by then, you and me are going to have a lot to do. Even if he is back, you'll still be busy. So next week we need to make a start. I think Needham is going to make the announcement a week today.'

Blincoe's face lit up. He had never been to a party like Palfrey described.

'What will we have to do?' Blincoe asked.

'Plenty, oh plenty. We'll be worn out come the Monday! We have to bring a lot of stuff from Tideswell: benches, urns and a great big organ. We need to build a platform to put the organ on. We have to build a shelter to keep the platform dry in case it rains. I've got a list of jobs as long as your arm!'

That afternoon the man from Manchester delivered some cotton to Litton mill, and then he appeared in the smithy.

'Hello,' he said. 'Your gaffer about?'

'No,' said Blincoe, 'he's off poorly. Looks like it might be a few weeks more too. He's bad with his nerves,' and then muttered, 'whatever that is.'

'Gone a bit mad in the head,' the haulier said, having heard Blincoe. 'At least I think that's what it is. Anyway, who's in charge of the smithy now?'

'I am.'

'Herbert Beard,' he said, and offered his hand.

'Robert Blincoe.'

Blincoe studied Herbert. Tall, thin, very confident, perhaps more cocky than confident, but he seemed likeable enough.

'Right,' said Herbert, clearly a little confused, and he rubbed his chin to show he was thinking. 'You see, I have a little arrangement with your gaffer; he repairs bits and bobs for me and sells me the odd thing, and I see him right.'

'What sort of bits?' Blincoe asked.

'Well metal bits – pans, shovels, fire guards, anything metal that can be fixed.'

'I can do most things,' said Blincoe. Blincoe knew he could only do some things, but he sensed an opportunity here to further fill his washer tin.

'I've got a list of everything,' Herbert said. 'Look here.'

They looked at the list together. Blincoe was fairly confident that he could do it all. Mostly it was riveting, soldering, brazing, replacing straightforward pieces of things, but the last item on the list was two and a half yards of chain that Herbert wanted to buy. Line by line, they went through the list and agreed a price on everything, but the chain was difficult, as Blincoe had no idea of the price, and he was nervous about selling what was the property of the mill. It seemed a step too far. Herbert produced an old list where the prices were shown, and Blincoe reluctantly agreed the same price on the chain.

'I'll bring it all over,' Herbert said. 'Everything is in a dolly tub; the dolly tub just needs soldering on the seam.'

Herbert was away to Nottingham next and so they agreed that he would pick it all up on his way back in two days' time and then he would pay Blincoe the ten shillings and nine pence that they had shook hands on. By the time he left, Blincoe had concluded that Herbert was agreeable enough, except he had an annoying habit of constantly addressing Blincoe as Blinkie.

The jobs had been straightforward enough, but Blincoe had struggled to find the time to do them and went in early one morning so that he could get on with them. At four o'clock in the morning, there was no one to catch him out, unlike the rest of the time, when he was constantly looking over his shoulder. Mrs Milner had seen him going to work early, and had thought he might be struggling to keep up with the workload, and so she had sent Phoebe over with an extra breakfast.

Phoebe appeared at the smithy door giving Blincoe quite a start. She just held out his breakfast. Blincoe turned to take the food off her and saw tears streaming down her face.

'Phoebe what is it?' he asked, but she just ran back to the kitchen. Blincoe then wondered if he had done something wrong. He wondered whether she knew about Martha. In the end, he couldn't make any sense of it. Perhaps she was bad with her nerves too. He carried on with his work.

On Thursday, Herbert returned, and Blincoe had everything ready for him all neatly packed in the dolly tub, including the chain, and all of it hidden under some sacks in a corner. Herbert was as good as his word and handed over the ten shillings and nine pence, which later on that day, Blincoe placed in his washer tin.

'So, you been at the mill long Blinkie?' Herbert asked

'Just over four years.'

'I'm thinking of setting up in business,' Herbert went on, 'and I'm looking for a partner. Someone that's sharp like yourself. You interested?'

'What sort of business?' Blincoe asked.

'Cotton waste,' said Herbert. 'There's loads of money to be made in cotton waste. Tell me, what do you do with the waste here?'

'We burn it, mostly.'

'There you are then. I bet you didn't know that there's two mills in Manchester that take in cotton waste, and they can re-use it for spinning. As soon as you get away from Manchester, nobody bothers; they all burn it, or give it away. But in Manchester, those mills will pay for it'

Blincoe was impressed. Herbert seemed to know what he was talking about.

'So what do you say about us setting up in business together?' Herbert asked.

'I would love to, anything to get away from this place, but I'm tied by my indentures up until I'm twenty-one. Running away wouldn't work either; everyone who's tried it has been brought back and flogged, and anyway, if I was still in the cotton business, I would have no chance; I'd be found easily.'

'Oh well, never mind,' Herbert said. 'If you change your mind, or something changes, let me know; I'll be around. It's not going to happen just yet, as I need the best part of ten pounds to get it all up and running.'

As Herbert rode out of the yard, Blincoe knew that he could find his half of the ten pounds easily. In fact, at the rate his tin was filling up, he could probably find all of the ten pounds by Christmas, but what he had said about his indentures was true. He was well and truly trapped.

Twenty Three

MONDAY 25TH MARCH 1799
LITTON MILL

It was Easter Monday morning, and the most important topic of conversation over the last few days continued to be the most important topic: the weather. A huge amount of thought and work had gone into making today a success, and although there were plans should it rain, they only provided a partial solution, as the covered areas could never accommodate the two hundred people who were expected. The conversation about what the weather might do, turned to what the weather was doing, and it was overcast and drizzling; not what anyone wanted.

The party was Ellis Needham's idea. He was aware that he asked a great deal of his workers, and this was a way of saying thank you. Easter Monday was a day when the mill didn't work, and so there was nothing lost in terms of production; also Needham would gain a subtle advantage over Newton and his mill, as Newton had done nothing like this. Needham and his team had organised the provision of entertainment, food and drink for everyone, although it was the provision of *drink* that had caused the most debate.

Ellis Needham was resolute that having alcohol available on a religious day was wrong, and furthermore it would certainly lead to trouble and fights, but his managers were of the opposite view, and they were unanimous.

‘It’s unthinkable to have a party and not be able to have a tankard of ale,’ his brother said.

‘Easter Monday will be like a village wake, and you can’t imagine a village wake without a drink,’ Palfrey said.

Eventually, Needham gave in on the point, but then argued that no drink should be served to any apprentices.

‘But some are aged twenty,’ his brother argued. ‘Surely you can’t refuse the older ones a drink.’

A further debate then raged. In between the extremes of serving all or none of the apprentices, there was an option proposed of only serving those fourteen and over, but this was deemed unworkable as the people serving the drink would not know their ages. Then a proposal of only serving those over four feet nine inches was considered, and rejected. In the end, they decided to leave the whole matter to the discretion of Molly Baker. Apart from the tea urns, Molly was looking after all of the drinks, and she could decide whom she would and would not serve.

The weather had no knowledge of Needham’s party or of the huge amount of work that Blincoe, Palfrey, Simpson and many others had put in. After spending four weeks at home following the death of his wife, Simpson had been back at work for two weeks. He was now back in the smithy with Blincoe, although he was not the same person, and everyone agreed on this when they spoke about him. Some days, Blincoe felt as though it was Simpson who was the apprentice and himself the smith. Simpson was slow to make decisions and never fully concentrating on his work; he was improving though, but desperately slowly. During the four weeks Simpson had spent at Littonslack, Martha had coped well, much better than her father who generally got in the way and didn’t help at all. She was also relieved to find that they didn’t need any handouts; a few days after Parson Brown’s visit, Simpson had produced some money from upstairs and given it to Martha for food. He would have given it to her earlier, but it was hidden in the bedroom, the last place he wanted to go.

Over the last week, the mill yard and the road towards the mill, where there was a wide stretch of grassland running between the track and the river, had been transformed. In the mill yard they had built a large raised platform, one big enough to take a pedal organ, which Blincoe and Palfrey had fetched from the Methodist chapel at Wormhill, and big enough to take a travelling band who would perform on the Monday evening. They had built a canopy over the top of it and laid out rows of benches in front of it. On the grassy area, they had built stalls where local people would sell food of various sorts, and they had built a larger stall where Molly could sell ale and wine. Two barrels had been delivered direct to the mill by the brewery, and they had already been moved to the ale stall so that the beer could settle. They had marked off areas for games, such as skittles and sack racing, and they provided a place where a pig would be roasted.

This was not a workday, but Blincoe and Palfrey still met at the normal hour of five o'clock. Everyone else was still asleep, and although the drizzle was heavy, there was still work to do. Simpson would not be helping them; Palfrey had told him he wasn't needed, and that was true, especially as he was generally more of a hindrance than a help.

The party was due to start at noon and there were notices informing what was happening, and when, and more general signs *Pig Roast, Skittles* and so on. Blincoe and Palfrey spent the first hour erecting these, as they had only been painted the night before. There were information notices giving the order of events, although as Blincoe and Palfrey discussed, there was some confusion around what was free and what had to be paid for. At noon was *Tea and Cakes*, they believed this was free. *One o'clock, Games; Two o'clock, Samuel Slack Sings; Three o'clock, Easter Service, Rev. Brown; Four o'clock, Games; Five o'clock, Roast Pig,* here again the rumour was that this was free, but no one was sure, and finally on the notice was, *Six o'clock, Irish Band.* It wasn't printed on the notices, but Blincoe had been told that in the evening everyone would be dancing to the band and in particular, girls dancing with boys; he was excited.

With the signs and notices erected, Palfrey and Blincoe set off in the cart to the Red Lion in Litton, where they collected wine, tankards and the pile of miscellany that Molly had put near the door for them. Blincoe still had not seen the beautiful Ellen and was hopeful of a sighting this morning. He remained disappointed, with no sign of her, although he did find out from Molly that she would be helping her later, at the party.

By noon the drizzle had stopped, although it was still overcast and gloomy. The trickle of villagers and locals collecting their free tea and cake was supplemented by dozens of mill apprentices, who immediately made the event busy and lively. The rumour, started by Blincoe, that the stunning Ellen would be there, had shot through the male apprentice population at an alarming rate. The result was that rather than queue for their free tea and cake, there was gaggle of young boys at Molly's bar. Not all of them were buying and Molly was at first confused. Blincoe was at the front of the queue though, and there she was, standing in front of the barrels, pouring ale. At first, he couldn't see anything that special about her. She was pretty enough, but so were plenty, but then as he watched her moving, very upright, very controlled, and he watched the way she looked directly at people with no shyness, and he watched the way she talked to them, perhaps standing a little closer than most would, he slowly began to see what the fuss was about. He tried to make sure that it was Ellen who served him, and he was disappointed when found himself in front of Molly.

The disappointment was brief though, as Molly closed his hand around his penny and said, 'Keep it. That's for doing a good job this morning.'

Later on, after a quart of ale and two pieces of cake, Blincoe joined in a sack race. He had never raced in a sack before and struggled to acquaint himself of the necessary technique. Out of eight starters he was running next to last, when the person in last place, having worked out what to do, caught him up, but then collided with him. They ended up on the ground still in sacks and struggling to get up. The spectators were laughing, and so were they. Blincoe looked at the person who had hit him. It was Sophie Grimes, a girl from the mill.

'Sorry,' she said, 'I've never done this before.

'Me neither,' Blincoe replied.

They untangled themselves and apologetically, returned their sacks.

'Do you fancy a walk?' she asked.

They walked along the river, upstream from the mill where it became quieter. Blincoe knew Sophie by name, but he knew nothing about her and had never spoken to her before. At thirteen, she was two years younger than he was, but much taller. The race incident and a quart of ale had removed Blincoe's shyness, and he asked her about herself and whether she had a sweetheart.

'Yes, I have a sweetheart,' she answered, 'but it's a secret, I can't tell anyone.'

Normally Blincoe would assume that to be a lie, but her blushing face told him that there was some truth there.

'Do you have someone?' she asked.

'Yes. Well I think so. It's not been going long.'

'I have a plan to get out of this place,' Sophie said. 'It's the cleverest plan you could ever imagine! But before you ask, I can't tell you what it is; that's a secret too.'

'I have a plan to get out too,' Blincoe said, 'but it just needs a little more work on it; a few details need sorting out.'

It was the strangest conversation Blincoe had ever had. They both just talked about vague ideas that were shrouded in secrecy, and Blincoe was aware that he was as vague and secretive as she was. A bell rang. This was the signal that the service would be starting, and the apprentices had been told that they must attend this.

'I'll just say a few words,' Needham said quietly to Parson Brown, 'and then introduce you, and then you can begin the service.'

Parson Brown and Ellis Needham were stood on the platform; there were just a few minutes to go before the three o'clock service. Nathan Booker was the only other person there, and although no one could hear it above their chatter. Booker was playing the chapel organ; trying to understand all the stops, whose labels had faded to nothing over time. When the apprentices were in the yard, and it seemed that no one else was looking to come in, Needham stood at the front and raised both hands to silence the congregation.

'Thank you. Thank you,' he shouted, and slowly the congregation became silent.

It was at this moment that the sun broke through for the first time today, and Needham briefly thought about making a joke about the *sun shining upon the righteous*, but he thought better of it.

'Before Parson Brown begins his service, I would just like to say a few words.'

He pulled out of his jacket pocket some notes he had made.

'First I must thank everyone for coming and thank all those who have worked so hard to make all this happen. I hope you all enjoy what we have provided, and there is still a free pig roast and a travelling band to enjoy later.'

Some people looked at each other, some nodded to each other; at least they knew now that the pig roast was free. Needham then began his prepared speech. His delivery was slow with long pauses between the sentences, and his voice echoed off the mill wall giving an eerie effect.

'My job is not a job where I receive a great deal of praise for my efforts. Indeed, mill owners seem generally to be a target for criticism. But I can tell you that I look to the Lord for guidance and follow his word.' Needham looked over to Brown at this point, Brown being nearest to the Lord.

'Just let me put a few facts to you. We now employ over eighty apprentices, whose lives before coming here were very uncertain. Most were from workhouses and their futures, had they not come here, were destined to a life of crime, or even worse. We have given these young people an opportunity to learn skills and earn an honest living. Not only that, but we now provide education in reading, writing and arithmetic and on religious matters.' He again turned to Brown, this time nodding towards him, acknowledging his work. 'We provide a roof over their heads, clothing and food, and we care for them. Look at them in their fine Sunday clothing; are they not a handsome group?' Needham paused and looked up before continuing. 'So, what about the adults you may ask. Well I can tell you that we pay better than any other employer in these parts; certainly better than lead mining, or labouring on farms, and there is little else to do. We provide housing for some of our workers, and in the last year, we have made arrangements so that if any of our workers are ill or injured, they will be looked after. Now, I said I would be brief, and I have been, but I ask you to think about what I have said. I will now hand over to Parson Brown for our Easter Sunday service.'

There was no applause, but then as Brown later explained to him, 'The end wasn't written in the right way to receive applause.' Brown looked at Needham's notes. 'It just fades out and slides into the introduction to me. Come to me next time, and we will go through it together.'

Brown's service was a simple one. He needed to appeal to a range of ages, from the youngest apprentice to the more mature members of the congregation, although it troubled him what the age of the youngest apprentice might be, in fact he had rather cowardly avoided finding out. The hymns were ones everyone knew, as there would not have been sufficient hymn books; there were short prayers, and a sermon that was straightforward and positive and on the subject of the crucifiction, as people would expect.

Unseen by Brown, just after the start of the service, the portly figure of a man slipped into the mill yard and stood to the side of the platform. He listened attentively to the service and to Brown in particular. Out of the hundreds of people, only

Brown would have known who he was: he was the Honourable James Cornwallis, Bishop of Coventry and Lichfield, and Brown's immediate superior.

'I need to speak to you, 'the bishop said after. 'It's sort of a parish matter.'

'Should we go back to the vicarage?' Brown asked.

The congregation, of mostly apprentices, drifted back to the games. It was still over an hour to the pig roast and the only organised entertainment on offer was games; there was nothing now in the mill yard until the Irish band at six. Blincoe was more tired than most, having been working all morning, and he sat on the end of one of the long benches and watched everyone go back towards the games, everyone except for Sophie Grimes that was. He watched her go into the mill. He couldn't understand why she would be going into the mill, and in any case, the mill should have been locked. After she had pushed the door to behind her, he ran across to the door and opened it slowly. He listened and could hear her feet going up the stone stairs towards the offices. The footsteps continued, and so she must have been going past the counting house towards Needham's office on the top floor. Then there was silence. At this point Blincoe could have left, or pursued whatever she was doing, but curiosity won the battle, and he tiptoed, making no sound, slowly up the stairs. When he finally reached Needham's office, he could hear noises from inside. There was a glass panel above the door, and so standing on a stool, he slowly and carefully raised himself up; slowly, his head moved towards the glass so that he could see into the room. Sophie was there naked on the desk, and climbing on top of her, naked apart from his shirt, was a man: Robert Needham. Blincoe had no need, nor any desire, to stay up there longer than he already had, and he was about to slip out in the same careful and quiet way of his arrival, when there were cries from outside. These were urgent cries, not playful ones, and they were loud too as they could be heard above the noise of the river. Blincoe thought Needham and Sophie might come out of the room to investigate the noise too, and so he jumped off the stool, and ran as fast as he could, down the stairs and into the mill yard. It was only later he realised that Sophie and Needham would have wanted to dress before they came out, and so he needn't have rushed so.

Blincoe followed the noise of the screaming and arrived to find a girl's body being brought out of the river by a villager. The body was limp and lifeless, and although some people did what they thought best, there was nothing to be done. The girl was Phoebe Rag, and she had been seen throwing herself into the river from a footbridge. No one knew why. No one really knew anything about her, except that she seemed unhappier than most.

'I have here,' the bishop began, 'an opportunity for you. It will mean you leaving the parish for around six months, maybe longer, but I think we can cover your duties by sharing them amongst the adjacent parishes. We've done that sort of thing before.'

Brown topped up their wine glasses and said nothing.

'I believe from our conversations in the past that you are quite passionate about the abolition of slavery. Is that still the case?'

'It is Bishop. Especially so since hearing the Reverend Thomas Clarkson speak.'

'Well, what I need is someone to represent our diocese in a group that they are calling *The Clapham Sect*. This is an organisation headed by John Venn. He's one of ours from Clapham, but the group also includes Wilberforce and some quite well known people.' The bishop paused and looked straight at Brown, 'Does this interest you? Shall I go on?'

'Yes it does Bishop, please go on.'

'I am coming under pressure from some of our wealthy, and important, and shall we say, generous, members to become involved with this abolition business, and so I thought you could join the group. This is something I've already discussed this with the Clapham group by the way, and then you can find out what more we can do. It will mean you moving to Clapham, although I will need to see you once each month.'

'I am very excited at this opportunity Bishop. When would it start?'

'I'm not sure. It may be a few weeks; it may be a month or two. There are still some details to finalise.'

'Whenever you say Bishop. I am ready'

'There is just one other matter you need to be aware of, and that is that we also have a good number of members, generous members again, who are involved, one way and another, in the plantations and with slaves and so on. It follows that they have a different view. Therefore, we cannot blunder into all this and lose their support, so we must tread carefully. I am sure you understand.'

Twenty Four

MONDAY 1ST APRIL 1799
LITTON MILL

It was just after half past eight on a rainy Monday morning, and from the smithy, Blincoe and Simpson watched as two men rode into the mill yard. The view from the smithy was muddled by the rain running down the window, but they could see enough. Before the men had tethered their horses, the blurred figure of Ellis Needham appeared. There was shaking of hands and then they were gone into the mill building. Blincoe and Simpson looked at each other, but neither spoke, as neither of them had any idea who the men were.

In Needham's office, there was now Ellis Needham; Richard Middleton, who was Needham's counting house clerk and the two men, who were busy removing their wet clothes. When they had removed them, they began.

'John Rumney,' said the taller man, and he held his hand out to Needham again.

'And Matthew Barber,' said the shorter man, also holding out his hand.

'We are commissioners of his majesty King George,' said Rumney, 'and we are here to conduct an inspection of your factory.'

'in particular,' continued Barber, 'we will need to interview most—'

'—possibly all,' interrupted Rumney, smiling.

'of your workers,' Barber concluded. He too smiled

'We aim to be here for two full days,' said Rumney.

'but it could be more, depending,' said Barber.

'We need lists of all of your workers,' said Rumney.

'broken down by their jobs,' added Barber.

'We will inspect the rooms in the mill this morning,' said Rumney, 'interview apprentices this afternoon and tomorrow morning,'

'and the other workers and managers tomorrow,' concluded Barber.

The men smiled.

Needham's eyes switched from one man to the other, never quite knowing who would speak next. They were a strange pair, he thought. Each thought he knew better than the other did and invariably there were additions to, and interjections within, sentences from the other one. Had they not been here on the business of inspecting his factory, he might have even found them amusing.

'I suppose you will need an office to work from?' asked Needham.

'Yes,' they both answered.

'Well you better have this one then. I'll work from downstairs,' Needham said.

The arrival of the commissioners, or factory inspectors as everyone called them, for their unannounced visit, had been the worst kept secret in the locality. The previous Wednesday the two men had taken rooms in the New George, and by late that same evening, they had been identified as factory inspectors. The news then travelled quickly to those who needed to know: Ellis Needham and William Newton. If there was any doubt as to whom they were, it was dispelled on the Thursday morning when the pair of them descended upon Cressbrook mill and spent the next two days there.

Neither Rumney nor Barber was entirely happy with the New George. Rumney, as a seasoned commissioner, was unhappy with the general cleanliness, and Barber appeared at Cressbrook mill on the Friday with bites on his face and neck.

After two nights at the New George, William Newton suggested they could stay at Cressbrook hall, and they accepted. This was the next rumour to circulate, and one that infuriated Needham.

'Surely,' Needham said to Parson Brown at the weekend, 'that cannot be just. Surely, you cannot inspect a factory and then take hospitality from the factory owner? He might as well give them money. He might as well write his own report!'

The inspectors' accommodation plans were just a very annoying detail that Needham had to live with, but he could not afford to dwell on it as there was work to do, and he was grateful that he had four days' notice that they were most likely coming to him next.

On the Saturday, the machinery at Litton mill stopped early at ten o'clock, and after that, the whole workforce was set to tidying, cleaning and painting. They cleaned the machinery, scrubbed the floors, cleaned the necessaries, painted walls and tidied anything away so that the place was spotless. After work had finished the apprentices were queued to sit with a barber that Needham had paid for. The barber gave all of the boys his standard short back and sides, and he did his best to tidy the girls' hair. At the end of the Sunday school, Ellis Needham lectured the apprentices.

'You should be grateful to be at a place like Litton mill,' he began, and after five minutes telling them just how grateful they should be, he ended with, 'If anyone should ask you what you think of your time here, before you answer them, think what else you might be doing now.'

Mr and Mrs Milner spent Sunday afternoon checking the apprentices work clothing, substituting better clothes for those that were frayed and torn and replacing any worn through boots where possible. They finished the afternoon by making sure that the apprentices were clean. On Sunday evening Robert Needham, took two of the apprentices, who were badly deformed through mill work and three apprentices with recent work injuries, to his cousin's farm near Bakewell. They would be shown on the books as having absconded during the previous weeks. Similarly two adult workers, one crippled and one having lost an arm, were visited on the Sunday evening. They were asked not to come to work the following week. They were shown in the books as *discharged*.

Needham was not solely in charge of overseeing all these preparations. On the Friday evening after Needham had gone home, Woodward asked to see Blincoe. Blincoe knocked on Needham's office door.

'Come in,' Woodward shouted.

Woodward sat comfortably in Needham's chair, but he left Blincoe standing.

'You may have heard, 'Woodward began, 'that we are expecting a visit from the factory inspectors next week.' Woodward leant back in the chair his hand in a praying position. 'I'm sure I don't need to remind you that if you are questioned by these people, that you will give a glowing account of your time here, and if necessary, make sure they know that the author of all those lies that were printed, Mr John Brown, is named as such.'

Blincoe nodded.

'If you choose to tell a different story, there will be consequences!' Woodward leant forward in his chair and put his hands on the desk. Blincoe realised the last time he had seen this desk, Sophie Grimes was lying on it, naked, and then he couldn't get the vision out of his head. He couldn't look away from the desk, but now the desk and Sophie were inextricably linked.

'Setting fire to buildings is a very serious crime,' Woodward said. 'It is called arson. Do you know the punishment for arson?'

Blincoe shook his head.

'Death by hanging!' Woodward shouted.

Blincoe took a step back, and his jaw dropped. The naked Sophie Grimes was out of his head now and instantly replaced with a vision of himself swinging from a rope.

'But I'm sure there will be no need for anyone else to know what I know,' Woodward said softly and then shouted. 'Now, back to your work!'

Blincoe again ran as fast as he could down the flights of stone stairs. Last time he descended these stairs, he had been running from the naked body of Sophie Grimes to the dead body of Phoebe Rag; this time he ran from the vision of himself swinging, hopefully towards something better.

He ran into the yard and almost into a cart that was stopped close to the door. Getting into the cart, with a blanket draped around her, was Sophie Grimes. He watched Mrs Milner help her onto the cart and give her a kiss, and then the cart moved off with Sophie staring back at him, her face grey. Blincoe was confused; he couldn't imagine why she would be leaving the mill. He tried to connect what he knew. She had said that she had the cleverest plan imaginable to escape from the mill. Was this it? If so what was the plan? He gave up trying to fathom what was going on and went back, still shaking, to Simpson in the smithy.

'Was she a friend of yours,' Simpson asked.

'Not really,' Blincoe said and then realised they might not be talking about the same person. 'Who?'

'The drowned girl?'

'Oh, sort of.'

'It's her funeral today,' Simpson said, 'but they're not burying her in Tideswell. She's to be buried in Taddington.'

'Why?'

'Well, they say that there's so many deaths here, that the Tideswell folk are not happy. Rumour is that Needham's spreading the dead ones between Tideswell and Taddington now!'

Accompanied by Needham, the inspectors had explored the factory. Needham had begun to explain the layout of the mill and how it all worked, but they paid little interest, and after a while, he let them lead the conversation. They had looked, poked, prodded and asked for locked doors to be opened. They had fiddled with windows, took measurements and counted various things, but they asked him few questions. Needham presumed that cotton mills were familiar territory to them. By eleven-thirty, they were done and back in Needham's office where Middleton had provided the books showing lists of all of the current workers. Middleton was downstairs leaving a nervous, and slightly sweaty, Needham alone with the inspectors.

'I understand that you have your job to do,' Needham began, 'but you need to understand that the business, Litton mill that is, is not in the best of health at the moment. If your findings were to result in us needing to spend money on the mill, then I fear that would mean the end of the mill, and all of the people that you are about to see, will be out of work.'

'Are you trying to blackmail us?' Rumney asked, 'into giving you a more favourable report?'

'We are here to make a fair and unbiased assessment,' Barber said.

'All factories must be judged by the same rules, otherwise what we do would be nonsense,' Rumney added.

'Aye, and your telling me that staying with William Newton won't affect your judgement of his factory are you?' Needham asked.

'It will not,' said Rumney.

'And it is all above-board,' added Barber.

'We have paid Mr Newton for accommodation, at the same rate as the New George,' said Rumney.

'So there is no personal gain,' said Barber, 'which is what I assume you are implying?'

Needham remained unconvinced about the Newton situation, but he had been honest with them. He was not just attempting to gain a better report; the mill really was in a mess. To keep the mill going, he had sold everything that he could easily sell and there was now nothing left in reserve. He had cut the wages to the minimum, leaning heavily on cheap apprentice labour, and he was working his mill long hours: over ninety each week. The profit on spinning had reduced, and he was just holding his own. If there were now any unforeseen additional expenses, or any further reduction in the profit margins, he had no more cards to play. He would be finished.

'Name?'

'James Durant.'

'Age?'

'Thirteen.'

'How many hours do you work each weekday?'

'Five till half past ten.'

'And on a Saturday?'

'Five till half past one.'

'How much time is allowed for your dinner break?'

'One hour.'

'And how much of that time is spent cleaning the machinery?'

'All of it.'

Rumney did some calculations on a pad and announced, 'Ninety-six'. Barber recorded the figure.

'What is the temperature where you work?'

'I don't know sir.'

'Is it hot?'

'Very hot sir.'

'Do you normally work without your shirt on?'

'Always'

'Are the windows ever opened?'

'No.'

'Are you excessively tired?'

'All the time.'

'Have you ever been ill?'

'Yes. Once with my chest and once with back pain.'

'What do you think of working here?'

'I think Mr Needham and his managers are very good employers.'

Twenty Five

SUNDAY 2ND JUNE 1799
LITTONSLACK

On Sunday, Blincoe was off to Littonslack again. He had to find a way out of this; a way of escaping from the death, misery and confinement of Litton mill. Littonslack and Martha felt like a lifeline. It was nothing he could put his finger on, but they seemed to have some sort of connection with the rest of the world, a world beyond Litton mill, and any connection might lead to the possibility of escape. The connection was that Blincoe was very fond of Martha, he worked with her dad, and the two of them came from Scotland. That was all, but it was something. He had only two other connections outside of the mill. The first was Herbert from Manchester; he was a connection with the outside world and a kind of ray of hope, although the ray was blocked out by the cloudy difficulties of indentures. The only other connection he could think of, was Parson Brown; Blincoe felt he knew him a little, as he had met him now on many occasions, and the parson had been kind. Now the parson had connections all over the county and maybe beyond, but Blincoe concluded that perhaps it was his job to be friendly and kind, and that maybe the parson didn't count as a connection that might lead to an escape route.

Blincoe's latest bout of frustration had begun a week ago when one of the mill boys he knew from the workhouse was killed late one night. The story was that he fell asleep and was caught in between a large pulley and its belt. He was freed and didn't look too badly injured, but he was gone. Then the very next night, a young girl, Eliza Dibble, did more or less the same thing. Her arm was mangled in the same pulley, and she was taken away. The story was that she lost her arm from just below the elbow and would not be returning to the mill. She was seven years old.

The long hours were difficult, and the only way many of the children kept awake, was from the beatings they received from the overlookers. Most of the accidents were now late at night, including those of William Mace and Eliza Dibble.

The accidents were one reason that accounted for Blincoe's despair; the other reason was partly his own fault: whilst Simpson was off, recovering from the shock of his wife's death, Blincoe was solely in charge of the smithy. Being a stubborn young man, Blincoe rarely asked for help, and partly to support Simpson, and partly to make sure he stayed in the smithy, he worked as hard as he ever had. As a direct result, questions were asked.

'If a young inexperienced lad can manage on his own,' Middleton asked of Woodward, 'then why can't an experienced smith, like Simpson, manage on *his* own? Why does he need a lad to help him?' Woodward agreed and spoke to Simpson about Blincoe leaving the smithy. Simpson fought as best as he could, and at the end of it all, a compromise was reached: Blincoe would work in the smithy on Wednesdays and Saturdays, and the remainder of the time, he would be in the mill.

In the most miserable of conditions, working in the filth, the heat, the noise and surrounded by death, Blincoe was now working in the mill. Four days a week he was there, and he was not happy.

Simpson saved up all the heavy work for Wednesdays, and as a result Saturdays, days where the work in the smithy had always been kept to a minimum, were the only work days that Blincoe looked forward to.

'What's the matter with you?' Simpson said one Saturday. 'You look like you've found a sixpence and lost a shilling!'

'Just thinking about the future,' Blincoe said. 'My future, that is.'

'And what about it?'

'Just that I'm trapped here for another six years, with no way out.'

'Aye that's true, but I suppose you have to make the best of it; that's all you can do.'

It was not the answer Blincoe wanted, and he gave Simpson a scowl, which made that clear.

'They say the apprentices here were sold to Needham by the workhouse,' Blincoe said, 'and now that we are owned by him, we are trapped and no better off than slaves.'

'It sounds like someone's been filling your head with ideas!' Simpson said. 'Look, I'm out most of this Sunday on a wee job. There's no money for you mind, but you're welcome to come along if you want a change. It would get you away from the mill.'

'No. It's alright.'

On the Sunday morning, Blincoe made his mind up to visit Martha, as he knew that her dad would be out of the way. He remembered the year before when she had helped him back into the coal-shed, and he had asked if she would be his girl. He could still hear her saying the words.

'Ask me next year,' she had said.

On the way up Slack hill, he picked some orchids that were growing on the bank. He hoped she would like them. When he reached the cottages, he avoided any neighbours by approaching from over the wall. The door was open, and so he stood just inside; out of sight of anyone. He knocked on the open door, and as expected, Martha came.

'These are for you,' he said and smiled as he pulled his flowers from behind him.

Martha looked at the flowers and then at Blincoe. Blincoe thought there was the faintest of smiles on her face.

'You better come in,' she said. 'I wasnee expecting anyone, so it's all a bit of a mess.'

'It looks tidy to me.'

'And I'm a mess too!' She held her arms out in submission, exposing her mess to Blincoe.

'You're not a mess,' he said. But she was; she looked tired and pale, probably working too hard he thought. He had seen enough tired girls and boys to recognise that. As well as the tiredness, she looked grubby, with her long hair tangled and matted.

The noise of their conversation, or possibly the waving about of arms, caused Janet to wake up, and she started crying. Martha picked her up, and she stopped immediately.

'Could you no' have told me you were coming?'

'It was a surprise.'

'Well, baby Janet,' Martha said to Janet. 'We better make King Robbie a drink, hadn't we?'

Martha spent most of her days on her own with Janet, and with no one else to talk to, she drifted into these one-way conversations. She looked up from the baby and looked at Blincoe. 'Do you want a drink?'

'Yes please.'

'Can you just hold baby Janet then, just while I put the kettle on.'

This was a first for Blincoe; he had never held a baby before. It was a strange experience, holding something so important, so precious, but so frail. But there was something else, the smell of the baby, a nice smell. It took him back to somewhere in his past, but he didn't know where or when. He let the tiny hands grasp his finger, and he rocked her gently, and they smiled at each other.

'You and baby Janet look like you've known each other a long time!' Martha shouted from the kitchen.

Although it had seemed like a good idea, and the right thing to do, in naming the baby after her mother, it had proved difficult using the word *Janet*. As a result, the baby became known as *baby Janet*, and that was a little easier for everyone.

Blincoe and baby Janet carried on smiling at each other, but he didn't reply to Martha; he didn't want to shout, not with the baby this close.

'So how is everything?' Blincoe asked when she had sat down.

'It's different, very different from before. Do you want me to have Janet back?' she asked, but Blincoe shook his head.

'Janet is doing well now. She's just coming up to four months and just starting to put some proper weight on.'

It *was* different. Martha was different, and it wasn't just her appearance that had changed. She was more grown-up and generally more serious. Where was the giggling Martha that he used to know? It wasn't the same, and although she was trying to make things the same, such as calling him *King Robbie*, it was forced and not something natural and playful like it used to be. Blincoe had not expected this. He had arrived wanting to ask her to be his girl, but now, all that seemed to belong to a different world.

'You'll make a good father, I think,' Martha said, watching them playing.

It was then that Blincoe decided he would say whatever it was he was going to say. What he had planned to say wasn't right anymore, and without much thought he opened his mouth.

'Martha, I want you to be my girl, and I want to marry you, I'm serious.'

At first, Martha looked surprised, but then her expression changed to an angrier one.

'Well that's a brilliant idea,' she said. 'but just tell me this: what is going to happen to baby Janet, and as you earn a penny a week, what are we going to live on? Or do you have a way of getting free from your indentures? Just answer those questions to start with.'

'I've got an idea for a job,' Blincoe said

'An idea?' Martha shouted. 'How on earth does an idea pay the bills? All you have is a stupid dream, but if you want to marry me, you need a lot more than dreams. You need to go away and think it all through a lot more than you have.'

Baby Janet was now crying and Martha took her from him.

'I better go,' he said.

They both stood up, and a single tear rolled down Martha's face. She already regretted getting so angry, even if she was right.

They stood near the doorway. Blincoe didn't want to leave without saying something, and with the baby in Martha's arms, they both leant forward at the same time to kiss. As awkward as it was with a baby between them, the kiss was a passionate, almost desperate kiss and all mixed up with the saltiness of Martha's tears and their confused emotions.

'I'll be back,' Blincoe said after they had separated; he was close to tears himself. 'You'll see,' he shouted back, with a lump in his throat, and he ran towards, and then jumped clean over, the garden wall.

Blincoe left there, more confused than ever. The lifeline that he thought Littonslack offered, seemed a dead end, and rather than bring opportunities, it brought even more difficulties and problems. He wasn't even sure who was the more trapped out of the two of them. Perhaps he should look for another girl, someone without complications. He kicked, as hard as he could, at some orchids on his way down Slack hill. He had to get away from the mill and earn some money. Perhaps then, everything else might just slot into place. The key to the whole thing was his indentures. How could he be freed from those? The idea came to him of simply asking to be released from them. He had never heard of anyone asking to be released from them; but why not. If it helped, he could offer to buy himself out; after all, he had over five pounds.

At Littonslack, Martha, in floods of tears, was arranging her orchids in a glass bottle.

Twenty Six

FRIDAY 7TH JUNE 1799
TIDESWELL VICARAGE

'Let me read it,' Parson Brown said, and he snatched the document from Needham.

Brown was as frustrated as Needham was angry.

'Where shall I start?' Brown asked, 'with Cressbrook mill or Litton mill?'

'Does it matter?' Needham shouted. Needham paced up and down in the parlour of the vicarage. Brown stood with his back to the mantelshelf of the unlit fire, turning the pages of the document.

'I'll start with Litton mill, but for God's sake calm down!' His reply was terse.

Needham had been in the vicarage a good ten minutes, having entered with none of the normal politeness. He saw no need for knocking on the door and waiting, not today. So far, Brown had got little sense out of him, except that he had brought with him *The Interim Report from the Commissioners of Factories*, and he had been waving that about furiously since his arrival. That, it seemed, was the root of his anger. Needham had then tried to read from it, but before he could complete any single sentence from it, he strayed from the document into a rant, complaining about the unfairness of it all.

Brown began reading, 'Litton mill – interim report from the commissioners of factories.'

Needham made a noise, and Brown gave him a look; a sort of schoolmaster look that suggested, he would not carry on, unless there was quiet.

'Perhaps you should sit down?' Brown suggested, and Needham did sit down, but he sat uneasily, leaning forward on the edge of a chair, and in a position where he could, if necessary, jump up to defend himself against any unjust accusation.

Brown continued, 'Note that no remedial action is necessary to comply with current laws. However, mill owners are advised to read appendix III showing the bill currently before parliament and the areas it is expected to address.' Brown looked up, 'Well that's good news, surely? You were concerned about the costs of any rulings.'

For once Needham made no comment, but gesticulated for Brown to read on.

'Overall, the mill raised a number of concerns. Although the work rooms in this mill were clean and white-washed, there was little ventilation, and temperatures, at the time of the inspection were in the mid nineties. The privies, lodging rooms and kitchen, are not well conducted. There are about eighty apprentices who are kept in a lodging house no great distance from the mill. These apprentices work late into the night, and due to the long hours were generally found to be exhausted. Many also appeared ill nourished. There was not always separation of males and females in the lodging house, where there is also some evidence of overcrowding'.

Needham grew redder in the face.

'Let me get you a drink,' Brown said, and he shouted to Kezia to fetch some water for them. Brown pointed to the document, 'There are some good points in here.' He examined it again. 'They like the white-washed walls and that your apprentice house is close to the mill.'

'And the bad points are?' Needham asked.

'Ventilation; cleanliness of privies, lodging rooms and kitchen; long hours; nourishment of apprentices; and overcrowding. Well that's not so bad. Open some windows and scrub around some of the rooms.'

'We can't open the windows; we need the temperature high for spinning.' Needham grunted.

'Well if we look at the list of criticisms,' Brown said, 'you aren't going to fix any of them immediately, but remember, you haven't got to do *anything*. It says that no remedial action is necessary. So I would suggest that you take note of the criticisms and try to work on those points; try and improve the overcrowding, the cleanliness and so on. What do you say?'

'Read Newton's report then,' Needham snapped.

'Cressbrook mill – interim report from the commissioners of factories. Note that no remedial action is necessary to comply with current laws. However, mill owners are advised to read appendix III showing the bill currently before parliament, and what it is likely to include.' Brown again looked at Needham. 'It seems to me as though these commissioners have no powers. This is the standard opening for every mill in the report.'

'They have no powers yet, but they will have. Keep reading,'

'Overall, the mill is well run. The workforce were generally healthy and their hours of work acceptable. The work rooms were well ventilated. The only concerns were the cleanliness of the floors. There are about forty-five apprentices housed in separate apartments a short distance from the mill. These apartments are clean, spacious and well conducted.'

'Now that's the sort of report you get when you give lodgings to the inspectors,' Needham said. 'There's just one little criticism in there, probably just to make it look believable.'

Brown thought that may well be true, but he was anxious to remain neutral in the fights between the two mills and ignored the comment.

'I'll just read this Appendix, then, I think, we will have read everything that matters.

'Likely areas that the new Factory Act will address: Adequate ventilation of factory rooms; Regular painting and cleaning of inside walls and floors; Children to be supplied with two complete outfits of clothing; Restrictions on the ages of children that can be employed; Restrictions in the number of hours children can work; Compulsory reading, writing and arithmetic for the first four years of a child's work; Male and Female children to be housed in different sleeping quarters; Children to sleep no more than two per bed; On Sundays, children to have an hour's instruction in the Christian Religion. There is likely to be a fine of up to five pounds for each offence.'

Brown sat down and took a drink of water.

'Well, that's not so bad; you're already doing around half of the points there.'

'And the other half will finish us,' Needham said. 'All those restrictions on the ages of the apprentices and the hours they work; that will finish us.'

'I will speak frankly,' Brown said and stood up again. 'I think you've got all this way out of proportion, and I think it is merely that you have been given a worse report than Cressbrook that is making you most angry. There is nothing in the report that you have to address, and the new Factory Act is probably years away, and when it is law; it will apply to everyone, and so you won't suffer unfairly, or on your own. If I were you, I would ignore the mill comparisons, but over the coming months and years, as you build your business, do so mindful of the coming changes in the law.

Brown sat down, his speech done. The men sat in silence; Needham was absorbing what Brown had said.

'You might be right,' Needham said

'You must concentrate on your own business; Cressbrook's success or failure does not impact at all on you or your mill. Looking at Cressbrook is just a distraction.'

Needham was now much calmer. Some common sense from Brown had dampened his anger, and the conversation eventually moved to other matters.

'I'm planning to propose to the Baker girl,' Needham said.

'Ellen?'

'Yes. Do you have any advice?'

'No. I'm sure you've as much idea as me on such matters.'

This was a difficult conversation for both men. Needham knew that all the single men in the world were attracted to Ellen and were therefore his competitors, and he counted Brown as single and one of them. Needham presumed that Brown was not looking to marry; not given his complicated arrangements at the vicarage, but just in case, he thought it wise to stake his claim to Ellen first, and he had now done this.

It was true that Brown was attracted to Ellen, but as Needham had surmised, he planned no approach to her. He knew why Needham was having this conversation, and he played his part in the game. Brown had enjoyed a similar conversation earlier that week with William Newton. He too was planning to propose to Ellen!

Just after noon, they shook hands and Needham left.

Needham's visit had been an unplanned interruption to Brown's morning; he had planned to enjoy some quiet time, thinking about his opportunity to travel to Clapham and his contribution to the abolition movement. He was nervous about all of this, as he had no direct experience of anything to do with slavery, merely a strong belief that all men should be treated equally, and the sooner the law changed to recognise this, the better he believed the world would be. Living in Tideswell, he was a long way from any direct contact with slavery, although he was aware of the connections through the cotton trade. The nearest place where he might encounter some elements of the slave trade was the port of Liverpool, but even that was seventy miles away. Before he left for Clapham, he had plans to spend a few days in Liverpool, to acquaint himself of whatever he could. He hoped to see on board some ships and perhaps see some Negroes, as there were no Negroes in, or anywhere near, Tideswell. In the meantime, he had arranged to meet Ellen, to hear her experiences of living on a plantation, and she was due to visit him this very afternoon.

Ellen stood at the front door of the vicarage. She was excited, but at the same time quite nervous. She found herself breathing quickly and took a moment to calm herself. She was certain that Parson Brown would propose to her this afternoon. 'Why else would he want to see me?' she had said to the mirror in her bedroom, and in case there might be any doubt in his mind, she had spent a considerable time in choosing her clothes, arranging her hair and on her appearance generally.

As she sat down in the parlour, Brown was again taken back by just how beautiful she was. He had thought long and hard about any possible relationship with Ellen, but given his position at the vicarage with Kezia and his child, he knew he had no choice but to continue as he was.

'Thank you for coming,' he began. 'I have to admit that I have invited you here for rather selfish reasons.'

Ellen did not look up. She could feel her heart racing and hoped that nothing unusual about her appearance was apparent.

'You see, I have been offered an opportunity to represent the church on the matter of the abolition of slavery, and I hoped that I might ask you about your experiences in travelling to and from the West Indies and on the plantations there. In particular I would like to know what you saw of the slaves and how they were treated.'

As his opening began, Ellen was still hopeful of him proposing, but by the end, she was less so. She retained her composure, and her expression remained fixed, as it had been since she sat down, with just the hint of a smile.

'To begin with, our experiences and contact with the blacks were quite limited. Our two sea journeys were long and difficult, but there were no black slaves on those journeys. My understanding is that the ships transporting the slaves usually travelled direct from Africa to the West Indies. When we were out there, apart from the servants in the house, we didn't come into contact with them very much. In fact, we were discouraged from talking to them.'

'Surely you saw some slaves in the time you were there?' Brown asked.

'As time went on we came into contact with them, and riding around we saw them at work, but as regards the treatment of the slaves, there are few laws to guide the plantation owners, least not any I know of, and you can imagine, the plantation owners differ wildly from each other in the way they treat the slaves. As far as the Newtons go, I don't think they were extreme in the way they treated them, although there were plenty of floggings and punishment for the sick, lame, lazy and anyone caught trying to escape. There were a good number died too, but mostly from illness, not from punishment. I seem to remember they talked of losing, mostly through death, about a third every two years. The first two years was called the seasoning period; if the slaves survived that, then they were usually reliable. We lived a little way from where the slaves lived, and we were discouraged from talking to them, but worse still, we were discouraged from having opinions on anything to do with the blacks. We were told that these were business matters. So, both our bodies and our souls were kept away from difficult matters. I think we naturally went along with this, as deep down we knew that if we confronted it, we would have had a truly miserable time in Jamaica. It was on my return journey when I was in Port Royal that I did confront it and it was then that I realised what slavery really meant.

'Port Royal?' Brown asked.

'Port Royal is the main trading port for the island.

Whilst Ellen had been speaking, Kezia brought in a tray of tea and some cake and left it on the table. Brown felt slightly guilty that he was treating Ellen so much better than he had Needham, but he decided that Needham had been in no frame of mind to appreciate tea and cake, and feeble as it was, that was his justification.

'Tea?' Brown asked.

'Thank you.'

Brown passed Ellen her tea and sat back down himself. She put the cup and saucer on the table, fearing her hand may be unsteady, following her earlier anticipation and excitement.

'Why did your opinion change through being in Port Royal?'

'My opinions became clearly formed on the journey home, from Port Royal to Liverpool. On that long journey, I had plenty of time to think, and it was all triggered by what I saw in Port Royal as we waited to board our ship. We arrived there a little time before we could board, and the area was very busy with people. There were three ships in the harbour. One of those ships was ours, and the other two ships were slavers. That is what they call the ships which are used to transport the negroes.'

'Some cake?' Brown asked.

'Thank you.'

'It was just a terrible sight; there was hundreds of negroes, chained and shackled together in groups of twelve. Most looked half-starved and ill from their journey; they lacked any spirit and had no hope. They came from one of the ships and were then put into wooden pens. This was the point when I realised the true horror of these people's lives. They were being treated worse than cattle. I'm not sure whether they were sold from these pens, or whether this was just a place to keep them secure, but it was very distressing. I had seen the slaves in the plantations and, yes, they were punished and worked hard, but this added another dimension to what I understood of their lives. Our journey to Liverpool took over three months, so I had time to think about the rights and wrongs of the situation, although these were clear almost immediately.'

'More tea?'

'I still have this, thank you.' Ellen's racing heart had returned to normal, and her hand was steady. She wondered if her nervous state had led her to talk too much and decided to answer any further questions with much shorter replies.

'I am very pleased for you Mr Brown, that you have such an opportunity,' Ellen said.

'Thomas,' Brown tried to correct her. 'Please, call me Thomas.'

'What are your plans now?' he asked. 'You say you spent three months thinking about the rights and wrongs. Is that it? Are you to forget it all now?'

'I cannot forget it. I will never forget it, but I do not think I will have the same openings to influence the situation as you have.'

This would be a good time, Ellen thought, for Thomas to propose to her; they could join hands and share Thomas's new challenge. Brown had become transfixed by a cake crumb just above Ellen's top lip, and had now lost the inclination to talk about slavery. How he wanted to reach forward and remove it, but he didn't, and as much as he longed to fall to his knees and propose to her, he maintained his resolution, which had been carefully thought through, and he said nothing.

Brown shook her hand. The crumb fell from her face and she left. Afterwards, Brown felt as though there was something incomplete about the meeting, and he sat alone, anxious and very confused.

Ellen was bitterly disappointed.

Twenty Seven

FRIDAY 21ST JUNE 1799
LEISURE HOUSE

'Is it Charlotte?'

'Yes.'

Charlotte McNally stood in the back doorway of Leisure house. She was wearing a grey coat that was way too big for her, and a brown scarf covered her head and most of her face so that only two big brown eyes were visible. Nancy stood inside the doorway, hands on hips looking down at her.

'I'm to give you this,' Charlotte said, her voice muffled by the scarf. She handed over an envelope. Nancy took it.

'Come in. Come and sit down here, and let's have a look at you.' Nancy helped her off with her coat and scarf, and pointed to a chair in the kitchen. After Nancy had slipped the envelope in a book on a shelf near the window and picked up another book from the same shelf, she sat down opposite the girl.

'Now then Charlotte, I just want to make some notes and then we can have a talk about everything.'

Nancy opened the book at a clean page.

'What's your full name?'

'Charlotte McNally.'

'How old are you?'

'Fourteen.'

'And how far gone are you?'

'Just three months.'

'Apart from that, are you healthy? Do you have any illness at the moment?'

'No.'

Nancy took a better look at her. She looked reasonably well. Her face was grey but that was probably the worry rather than any illness.

'Will everything be alright?' Charlotte asked whilst Nancy was writing. Nancy finished her writing and put the book down. She leant forward and held both of Charlotte's hands.

'Let me tell you what's going to happen, but I'm going to be honest with you Charlotte. At times, it is going to be very painful, and at other times, it will just be uncomfortable, but when you leave here, you'll be as fit as a fiddle.'

Nancy smiled, but Charlotte did not reflect the smile.

'Although you might want to think twice about getting yourself into this state again! It's not a good idea, not at your age.'

Charlotte first nodded, but then she shook her head, unsure what she was acknowledging.

'I know,' Charlotte said to clear up any confusion.

'And I don't want to know who the boy, or man is, that got you in this state, but if it's a man and he promised you this, that and the other, you need to forget him and not be taken in again by him, or by anyone else, 'cause they're all liars!'

Charlotte blushed, she had been promised things, and those promises, as Nancy knew, had come to nothing. Charlotte felt foolish, but she heard what Nancy said, and she wouldn't be taken advantage of again.

Nancy had heard that it was Richard Needham who was responsible for this one, but he was clever with words and could get what he wanted without the need for force. Charlotte was relatively lucky, as most of the girls came to Nancy following much more violent incidents, usually as a supposed punishment by an overlooker. Few girls wanted to talk about the details, and when a girl did name the man, it was quickly denied, and some boy was then named and punished instead.

Nancy didn't want to embarrass Charlotte anymore and so moved back to the practical matters.

'Now, this afternoon I'm going to give you something here.' Nancy patted between Charlotte's legs as she said *here*. 'That will relax you, and that'll stay there all night, and yes, it will be a little uncomfortable. Then about this time tomorrow, when you're all relaxed down there, we'll be able to see better what's going on, and then we're going to sort out the little problem. Then after a day or two, your body will flush it away, and that will be almost everything over; we'll keep you here around another week, just to make sure nothing goes bad. You'll have lots of baths and lots of rest. You should be back at work, let me see, maybe a week on Monday, if it all goes well.'

Nancy looked at Charlotte, who now looked quite frightened. Nancy had dressed up the detail of what was going to happen, presenting it as gently as she could, but without lying; she wasn't going to lie.

'Don't worry,' Nancy said, 'I've done this lots of times before. Lots and lots of times. Let's get started then.'

There were three empty beds in what was once the main parlour of the house, and Nancy had Charlotte undress and get into the bed furthest from the window. Meanwhile in the kitchen, Nancy took down a large stone jar. It sat on a high shelf next to other jars of potions and other paraphernalia of her work. The jar contained asparagus in an alcohol solution. Nancy removed pieces of asparagus and made up tiny parcels by wrapping a fine bandage around the asparagus pieces. When she was finished, she made sure that they were well soaked in the alcohol.

'It might sting just a little bit at first,' Nancy said, 'but not for long. I need you to keep your legs up now and later on, try and sleep with them up.'

She then tied a towel around, to help contain the potion.

'That's it for now, nothing more to do until this time tomorrow.'

Nancy was experienced in helping young girls who were in trouble. There was the occasional adult too, but mostly it was mill girls. A travelling salesman, or *drug merchant*, as he called himself, sold her both the asparagus potion and the pine sticks. Once the potion had done its job, a stick would be used to bring on the abortion. She helped one or two girls each month, and she hadn't lost anyone for eight months. The dangers were bleeding that couldn't be stopped, or infections, and more often than not, when she did lose a girl, it was to infections. Nancy had a special book set aside for this work, and she had a page for each girl. Over the last three years, she calculated that she had lost only one in every seven girls that had come to her, a figure that much impressed the sales representative.

'That's very impressive,' he said. 'Why the main hospitals lose more than that, and none of my other customers are anywhere near your figure.'

Charlotte let out a long and piercing scream.

After the scream had faded, Nancy whispered to her, 'That's it my love. The worst is over now.'

Charlotte's face turned white, and then she started shaking, shivering and perspiring; the more she shook, the worse the pain was, but she couldn't help herself. Nancy changed her towels and put more blankets on the bed.

'You'll be fine soon,' she said. 'You'll be helping me look after some of the others in a day or two. There's three upstairs you know.'

There were always a number of children in Nancy's care. She treated, broken limbs, illnesses, those apprentices made ill through punishments and of course, girls like Charlotte. By her fourth day, the miscarriage came, an event that she found particular frightening. The day after that, she was able to move around a little, and on venturing upstairs, she found two boys each with a broken leg, and a girl recovering from tuberculosis. The recovering girl moved downstairs where they shared the big room and made friends.

Nancy's work was part financed by the parish, partly by the mill owners, who would give money when Parson Brown reminded them, and abortion money. Illnesses and injuries were usually covered by the general fund, but it was the practice, a practice Nancy had implemented, to charge five shillings for each abortion. There was usually someone guilty enough, or embarrassed enough, to find the money, and in the case of the mill girls, she insisted that Needham's or Newton's businesses must pay. She was generally strict regarding the abortion money; otherwise she refused help to no one and rubbed along very nicely with the local doctor. He was pleased to be relieved of the difficult decisions that he might otherwise have to make, in whether or not to treat people who had no money. There were grey areas where he perhaps thought the patient could have afforded him, and Nancy sometimes had the same thoughts; there were matters, such as surgery that were beyond Nancy, and here the doctor had his place. On the whole, the partnership worked well.

By breakfast on Charlotte's sixth day, there had been just one new patient to arrive at Leisure house. A young girl had cut her hand badly at Cressbrook mill, and they couldn't stop the bleeding. Nancy stitched it and thought it best to keep her one night. Charlotte was now taking a bath twice a day and felt happier than any day since her arrival. She felt much stronger, although she still had occasional sweats and times when she needed to lie down.

It was around ten o'clock on the Thursday morning when Martha arrived. Charlotte was washing pots in the kitchen, but Nancy was quick to the scene and quickly steered Charlotte back to her room.

'Can you help me?' Martha asked, looking up from the baby in her arms. 'It's baby Janet.'

'Come in, come in,' Nancy said. Nancy took the baby from Martha and laid her on the kitchen table.

'Hello Janet,' Nancy said softly. 'Are you poorly?' Nancy put her hand on Janet's forehead and then turned to Martha. 'I can see she has a temperature; anything else?'

'She's been burning up for two days, but last night she just coughed all through the night, and this morning there was some blood around her mouth.'

Nancy had a good look in her mouth, but as she expected, the mouth itself was not the source of the blood.

'Have you given her anything?' Nancy asked.

'Nothing.'

'It looks like tuberculosis,' Nancy said. 'Best if she stays here.'

Nancy spoke as though this was a routine matter, but Nancy and Martha both knew that tuberculosis was a killer for a baby as tiny and frail as Janet.

'Oh well, you never know,' Nancy said and then realised she had said that out loud.

'Never know what?' Martha asked.

'Oh nothing,' Nancy said, but it wasn't nothing; Nancy feared for the child's life.

'Can I stay with her?' Martha asked.

'Of course you can. You can treat her too. I'll show you what to do.'

Nancy explained the treatment to Martha. 'We want lots of fresh air, so long as it's not too cold, warm baths twice a day, castor oil, which we'll rub on, and I've got some rhubarb and soda mixture, which is very good, so long as she can keep it down.'

Nancy moved Charlotte and her new friend into one of the upstairs rooms and made Martha and Janet comfortable in the parlour. When they were all settled, and as Martha was likely to be here at the end, she decided to be a little more honest.

'Martha, baby Janet is very weak, and although we will do everything we can, you need to know that in the end we may be beaten.'

'I know,' was all Martha said.

At Litton mill on Friday morning, Blincoe heard the news from Simpson, that baby Janet was sick. On the Friday and Saturday, Simpson came to work as normal, but his mind was elsewhere: with his baby. Blincoe took charge of the routine jobs in the smithy, leaving Simpson to mope around. Martha remained at Leisure house, and her dad was left to fend for himself at home. Blincoe wanted to say something; he wanted to say something kind to Simpson *and* send a message to Martha, but fearful of saying the wrong words, he said nothing.

After work on the Saturday afternoon and still with no words, Blincoe set off to Leisure house. The quickest way was up Slack hill and then across two fields. On the way, he tried out loud words he might use, but he was not happy with them. He stopped and wondered if he should carry on and found himself picking flowers. He tied the flowers at the bottom with some grasses and wondered if he should have written a note, but it was too late for that. He carried on.

At the door, he was met by a very pale and ill looking girl. He recognised her; she was one of the Irish girls. They called her Lotty when they were playing.

'Can you give these to Martha?' Blincoe asked. He thrust forward his flowers. 'She'll know who they're from.'

Lotty slowly hobbled out of the kitchen into the house. Blincoe gently shut the door and left.

On the Sunday night, Elias Lingard, the carpenter and undertaker from Tideswell, was called to Leisure house to collect the bodies of Janet Simpson, aged four months and of Charlotte McNally, aged fourteen years. Janet had been too frail to fight the tuberculosis and died in Martha's arms with Nancy watching at a distance. A few hours later, Charlotte succumbed to blood poisoning from infection.

Twenty Eight

THURSDAY 11TH JULY 1799
LITTON MILL

It was exactly a week since baby Janet was buried; she was buried on the Thursday after she died. Simpson did not go to work that week, which came as no surprise to anyone, and Blincoe was again in charge of the smithy. Blincoe had not been to Janet's funeral as he had been warned of the consequences by Woodward. Woodward had visited him on both the previous Monday and Tuesday. On the Monday, Woodward found Blincoe sweeping up, and he told him of Janet's death and that Simpson wouldn't be in work for a while. On the Tuesday Woodward again came to the smithy and again found Blincoe looking busy.

'The Simpson's girl's funeral is this Thursday,' he began, 'but you will be here, all day. Do you understand?'

Blincoe nodded.

'We wouldn't want to see you swinging in the wind would we? You would be in the newspapers mind: Robert Blincoe, aged fourteen, hanged for arson.' Woodward laughed and then left.

Blincoe was now actually fifteen, but it was of no importance; he had no plans to hang, fourteen or fifteen. However, he *had* planned to go to the funeral; it was all worked out. He was going to take the horse and cart to Baslow for coal, and he had planned the journey so that he would be passing through Tideswell at the time of the funeral. But Woodward was one step ahead this time, and fearful for his life, Blincoe stayed away. On Wednesday, Blincoe developed a new plan, one that Woodward could not argue with, not that he was about to share it with him. On the day of the funeral, he would write a note and deliver it to Littonslack in his dinnertime. Simpson and Martha would be at the funeral, and he would leave it for their return. Paper wasn't a problem as Simpson had a drawer full of odds and ends, books and old journals; it was the words that were the difficulty, in particular what were the right words? He didn't want to be too jovial, but then he thought he shouldn't be too miserable either; not too brief, but not long winded; not too religious, but then something religious should be there. He wondered why words were so difficult for him, and he promised himself to pay more attention in his Sunday writing lessons. After spending most of Wednesday on the problem, he arrived at his words: *I am thinking of you all. My prayers are for you. God bless. Robert Blincoe.* He was pleased with that, especially *you all*, which could include baby Janet, if anyone wanted it to. On Thursday, he ran up the hill to Littonslack and left the note on their doorstep, weighed down by a stone. He ran down again thinking about the funeral and imagining the pathetic number of people that would be there. Probably the same as at Martha's mam's funeral he thought, less Robert Blincoe. In fact, there were more at baby Janet's funeral; three of Martha's work colleagues from Cressbrook mill were there, as was Nancy, who had been able to slip out, there being no very poorly children in her charge. Blincoe arrived back at the mill, his absence noticed by no one and still in time for some dinner.

The same week saw the funeral of Charlotte McNally at Taddington. Not a single mourner attended. The only people there were there in a professional capacity, helping carry the coffin, saying the prayers and finally the man with the spade, who had the last words, as he covered her over.

'Poor little wretch.'

All this was a week ago, and Blincoe now sat in the smithy trying to work out how he could escape this evil place; a place that now stank of punishment and death, more than it ever had. All anyone did here was sleep and work, and accompanying that, they suffered punishments and inedible food. If this was life, he thought, he might as well be in the cold ground with Lotty, Phoebe and all the others. Perhaps they were the lucky ones: they had after all escaped.

So, what about his plan; where was he with his plan to escape? Well he was back in the smithy, and that gave him more time to think and the opportunity to think about this cotton waste business that Herbert from Manchester was so keen on. So, in a roundabout way, baby Janet's death did have something good to come from it: time to think. Of course, he was sad that she had died, and he really did feel for Martha and her dad, but it didn't change the facts: things had changed in his favour, just a little.

The following day Herbert came to the mill.

'Morning Blinkie,' said Herbert.

'Morning Berty,' Blincoe replied. Blincoe had already decided to try to annoy Herbert and call him Berty.

'Gaffer off again?'

'Yes, his baby daughter died.'

'Oh. Oh dear. He's never here is he? He must be hard up, with no wage half the time.'

'He's alright for money I think,' Blincoe said.

Blincoe was correct. Money was not one of Simpson's problems; he had plenty. Blincoe didn't know it, but Simpson too had a tin, although it was much bigger than Blincoe's washer tin and contained much more money, in fact most of the money from his *other* work had been saved in there. He kept it hidden under the hearthstone in the bedroom.

'Anyway,' said Herbert, 'I have some very exciting news for you, so as soon as your kettle has boiled, I'll tell you all about it!'

Blincoe had no illusions about Herbert. He was over confident, loud and probably some of what he said was best taken with a pinch of salt, but at least he had some life in him, some hope and some ideas for the future. Blincoe admired that, as everyone else around him had long lost any of those qualities; they were all beaten, literally in many cases, into a life where survival itself was the best they might hope for.

'Tell me your news then,' Blincoe said, after he had brewed and poured the tea.

'I, or maybe we, depending if you are joining me in this venture, let's say *we* for now. *We* are the proud owners of a cart.'

Blincoe looked unimpressed.

'As in a horse and cart,' Herbert went on to say.

'Blincoe raised his eyebrows, he had been thinking of a hand cart.

'So how come I am part owner of this cart?' Blincoe asked.

'A gentlemen owed me a favour, and we agreed that I would have the cart. It needs a bit of work to sort it out, but I thought, I know just the person who could fix that up!'

Blincoe sat down and sighed. 'I'm still not sure if I can join you,' he said.

'Well, you need to decide soon. Listen, I've also got the chance of renting an old stable block. It would be perfect. We need somewhere to store and sort the cotton waste and somewhere to stable a horse, although we'd have to hire a horse at first as horses are upwards of twelve pounds to buy. There's lots of space there for everything, and I'm told that the rent is eight shillings a week.'

'I've still got to find a way out of this place,' Blincoe said. He was thinking as he spoke to Herbert, but he was still up against the difficulty of his indentures. He had told himself that he would see if Needham would free him from these indentures, although so far he had not pursued it.

'When are you here next?' Blincoe asked.

'Not sure whether I am Blinkie; my gaffer is talking of putting me on the York and Tadcaster run. Look, I'll give you my address, and then if you want me you can come and find me.'

Herbert wrote down his address, and after he had gone, Blincoe put it safe in his washer tin.

That afternoon, Blincoe nervously climbed the stone stairs to Needham's office. He knocked on the door, and it was opened by Woodward.

'Blincoe! What can we do for you?' Woodward returned to Needham's chair.

'I came to see Mr Needham.'

'Well he's not here today, so can I help?'

Blincoe thought that he might as well ask Woodward. Woodward had worked here a long time, and if this release from his indentures was possible, or if anyone had done the same before, he would probably know.

'I wondered,' Blincoe said, 'if it would be possible for me to be released from my indentures?'

Woodward remained calm; he didn't laugh, and he didn't look as though he was going to shout.

'The two usual ways are these,' Woodward said, 'you either reach twenty-one, or you die. I know of no other ways, and as you are not anywhere near twenty-one, that just leaves you one option: dying!'

Woodward then burst into laughter. He was both taken-aback and amused that someone should ask such a question. He laughed for so long that Middleton, the counting house clerk, came up from the office below to see what was going on. Woodward took a minute to calm down and then explained to Middleton.

'This little fellow wants to know if he can be released from his indentures!'

Middleton smiled, although he failed to fall into the fits of laughter that Woodward had.

'Interesting,' Middleton said. 'That's certainly a new one!'

'I have some money sir,' Blincoe said. He directed his plea now to Middleton as he understood him to be the money man.

'I could pay up to five pounds sir.' Blincoe pleaded.

'Five pounds Mr Middleton,' Woodward said. 'Is that an offer we should consider?

'Pass me that scrap of paper, Middleton said. 'Now, young man, how old are you?'

'Just fifteen sir.'

'We'll say fifteen, so you have six years remaining. So around three hundred weeks. Is he a useful worker Mr Woodward?'

'He is.' Woodward admitted.

Middleton knew that a *useful* apprentice was worth somewhere around four shillings a week to the mill. This took into account that the mill paid for their lodgings, food and clothing.

'If you had a sum in your pocket of around sixty pounds,' Middleton said, 'then we might be able to do something. I would suggest you go back to work and stop dreaming!'

'Go on then!' Woodward was now shouting. 'Back to your work.'

Blincoe, now well practised at running down the stone stairs from Needham's office, did as he was told.

'Any news?' Woodward asked Middleton after Blincoe had gone.

'Nothing,' said Middleton. 'If things stay as they are, I can't see how we're going to be able to pay anyone's wages after next week.'

Twenty Nine

SUNDAY 14TH JULY 1799
CRESSBROOK MILL

The party at Cressbrook mill was largely a copy of the Easter Monday party at Litton mill. The idea was similar in that it provided an occasion for the workers to enjoy a feast at the mill owner's expense. It also provided an opportunity for Newton to put on a better party than Needham had, and as a result, there were differences between this and the Litton mill party. One of those differences was that this event had a title, and a title that was visible to all on the posters that were put up around the locality: *The Cressbrook mill Sunday School Anniversary.* At Litton mill, the children had only been required to attend the afternoon service; at Cressbrook mill, the children were an integral part of the service and were to sing, give readings and say prayers. Parson Brown had nothing to do with the Sunday school at Cressbrook mill; this was all looked after by a local Methodist preacher and farmer: James Warhurst.

'It doesn't matter that it is not the anniversary of the formation of the Sunday school,' Warhurst said. 'It can still be a celebration of the Sunday School's achievements over the last year.'

Warhurst knew they had to start somewhere, and he was sharp enough to realise that when they reached next year's anniversary, the debate would be over anyway, as that would be the anniversary of the previous one!

The event may have been advertised as a Sunday school anniversary and party for the workers, but it was also about showing off the wealth of the mill and how generously the workers were treated. As with the Litton mill party, public figures and business men from the locality were also invited. Newton wanted as many people as possible; the more people to witness this, the better.

Newton had declined to attend the Litton mill party and Needham might have done the same when he received his invitation to Cressbrook, had it not been for one thing: Ellen Baker. Opportunities for Needham to meet Ellen alone had proved impossible: this would be his opportunity.

On Sunday the fourteenth, Cressbrook mill was a very busy place. It bustled with the workers, their families, friends, local dignitaries and people of note, like Needham. Apart from the apprentices at Litton mill, who had been confined to their own mill for the day, almost every local person was there. Needham arrived and joined the bustle, but there was only one person he wanted to see, and he couldn't find her. He did find Parson Brown, who also hadn't seen her, but wanted to talk to him about difficulties he was having with Taddington parish, over the move of the apprentice house. Taddington had finally realised their responsibility should Needham's mill fail, but Needham wanted none of this today and told Brown so, brushing him aside and continuing the search for his future wife.

'Good luck,' Brown shouted after him.

Needham still could not find Ellen, and he would not find her for another hour as she was in Newton's office.

'Please, sit down,' Newton said.

'Thank you,' Ellen said, 'I love surprises! What is it you have to show me?'

'Well it's here,' Newton pulled from his drawer a tiny scroll, sealed with a ribbon, 'but before I give it you, I need to be honest with you regarding my motives.' Newton took a deep breath and closed his eyes, partly for effect, partly to shield himself from her reaction and partly to remember his lines. 'Ellen, I will be brief, and I will come directly to the point. I have watched you closely over these last few months, and you must have noticed how passionately I admire and love you. As you know I am wealthy, someone who is at the core of commerce and the community, and I can provide for your every want. Ellen, I ask that you pass through life at my side and that we might soon be married.' He opened his eyes; the world was still there.

'I will give you my decision within the week,' she said, trying to feign surprise. She could see that Newton was nervous, and she deduced that this would be the moment: the moment she had been expecting for some time.

Newton took her hands, held them for a moment and then passed her the scroll.

'Why thank you,' Ellen said. 'Should I open it now?'

'If you wish.'

She undid the ribbon, unfurled the scroll. She saw that it was just a short poem, and so she read aloud.

'I tremble when a thought of thee comes o'er my lonely soul;
To find in memories of thee my helpless passions roll;
I shudder if I chance to dream thy heart with mine may beat,
And feel that to possess thy love would make my ills complete.'

She then took his hands. 'That is beautiful,' she said.

'I was hoping I might see you today,' Needham said, with his face slightly red and his forehead perspiring. He had been frantically searching for Ellen for over an hour, and although she had left William Newton's office sometime ago, Needham had still spent some time before he found her in the crowds.

'Would you walk with me?' he asked, 'perhaps by the river?'

'Of course,' Ellen replied. Again, there was no doubt in her mind; this was going to be a proposal.

They walked downstream away from the crowds. Needham made some small talk until he was at a safe distance, and seeing a large stone that they could both sit on, he decided the time was now. He produced a single flower that he had picked along the way.

'Ellen, I will be brief, and I will come directly to the point. I have watched you closely over these last few months, and you must have noticed how passionately I admire and love you. As you know I am wealthy, someone who is at the core of local commerce and the community.'

Ellen recognised the speech. She had been looking ahead at the river, but turned to look at Needham, frowning as she did so.

'Are you alright?' he asked, interrupting himself.

'Oh, yes. Please go on.'

'I can also provide for your every want. Ellen, I ask that you pass through life by my side and that we might soon be married.'

'Why thank you Mr Needham.'

'Call me Ellis, please.'

'Ellis, I will give you my decision very soon.'

They walked back to the party, Ellen playing with her flower and wondering if there was some sort of gentlemen's book of etiquette they had each consulted, perhaps containing a sample marriage proposal that they had each copied. She wondered if she could go home tonight with three mementos, and three proposals, but it was Ellen who had to seek out Parson Brown.

'Thomas!' she called, when she finally located him.

'Ellen, how are you? It's very busy here.'

'I'm very well. I hoped I might see you here,' she said.

'Listen,' Brown said, 'can we go somewhere a little quieter?'

'Perhaps by the river?' Ellen suggested.

They walked by the river with Ellen now more nervous than she had been all day. She thought he seemed excited, and that was surely a good sign, but very slowly she realised that again there was to be no proposal from the parson; there was no talk of passion and admiration and no offer to go through life at her side. He again talked about slavery and again thanked her for her help, but the excitement in his voice was about his future involvement with *The Clapham Sect*, and not his future involvement with a wife called Ellen. He explained that he now knew that his work in Clapham would begin on the first Monday in September. Ellen was further infuriated when he said how lonely he would find it in Clapham, not knowing anyone there. Eventually though, and resigned to going home with just two proposals of marriage, she did discuss abolition matters with the parson. They were agreed that owning slaves and trading in slaves was wrong. That was the easy part. The difficult part, and the one Brown was about to immerse himself in, was how to bring about change, when much of the commerce, trade and success of the country would be affected by that change.

'Shall we go back to the party?' Brown said. 'I fear my conversation is getting a little serious.'

Before the walk with Ellen, Brown had already enjoyed a quart of ale, and in a weak moment, he had thought he would propose to her. As they began to walk, he immediately sensed that had he proposed to Ellen, such a proposal would have been greeted favourably, and perhaps, he later surmised, this was what brought him to his senses. His talk of abolition, and then finally his move back to the party had been purely to keep his mouth from saying what his heart really felt.

Back in the Red Lion Inn that evening, Molly and Ellen again sat in Ellen's bedroom discussing the excitement of the day. Molly had some idea of what had been going on, but only an idea.

'Well?' Molly asked. 'What have you got to tell me then?

Ellen told Molly about the two proposals and how, and when, they occurred, and she showed her the mementos.

'If I am honest,' Ellen said, 'I was hoping Parson Brown might propose to me.'

'I think two proposals is a fair day's work,' Molly said. 'In any case, Parson Brown seems rather busy at the moment, so maybe he wouldn't make such a good husband.'

'So what are you going to do?' Molly asked, 'and don't ask me for my opinion!'

'It's difficult to choose between them,' Ellen said. 'I'll make my mind up by the weekend.'

Thirty

FRIDAY 19TH JULY 1799
CRESSBROOK MILL

There was certainly nothing to choose between their speeches, and as far as their mementos were concerned, Newton had certainly put in a lot more effort, but then Needham's single flower was more spontaneous. Newton was probably wealthier, although how much of it was his own, and how much of it belonged to his father was impossible to know, whereas Needham's wealth was his own, although with Needham there were always rumours around the precarious nature of his mill business. As for their looks, there again there was little to choose, both were good looking men. Newton was also her cousin, and whereas she knew the family well, she did have a desire to marry outside of her family, and she didn't really want to marry a man whose father was involved with slavery, a matter which following her discussions with Parson Brown she was now firmly against. Ellen had weighed all the arguments for and against each of her suitors during the week. She liked both of them equally, and had there been just the one offer, she would have been happy and settled. But she had two offers, and with Parson Brown seemingly uninterested, and with no other likely suitors in the neighbourhood, then that number was unlikely to change. In the end, she decided that it came down to a decision of safety or risk; Newton being the safer option and Needham the riskier, and whereas Ellen, now a confident young woman, was not averse to risk taking, in the end Needham just seemed too big a risk. Her mind was made up.

Ellen discussed all this with Molly over breakfast, and although Molly had said Ellen should make up her own mind, she did hope that it was Newton she chose. In the past, Molly had thought differently, but with Needham's future now less certain than it had been, she was of the same mind as Ellen.

It was a clear summer's day, and Ellen decided that she would walk to Cressbrook mill and give William Newton her decision. She hadn't decided how or when to give Ellis Needham the same news, but that could wait; she didn't want to spoil today.

It was just after breakfast and today was certain to be another hot day; already the sun was beating down. But undeterred by the heat and full of hope and excitement, Ellen set out on the mile and a half walk to the mill. There was little shade on the way, and so she sensibly took frequent rests; there was no hurry. After leaving the village of Litton, the road took her past Leisure house and then started to drop down to the river level and towards the mill. Not far after Leisure house, she took a rest under the shade of a tree enjoying the quiet and watching the birds playing beneath the tree. After a minute, the quiet was disturbed, as out of the track that led to Leisure house, trundled a horse and cart. As it passed her, the man waved, and she waved back. She knew the man, as he was a regular drinker in the Red Lion; it was Elias Lingard, the carpenter from Tideswell. A few yards after he had passed her, his horse stopped, and he turned around.

'Can I give you a ride miss?' he shouted.

Ellen hesitated, but then decided that a little less walking might mean that she would arrive at the mill in better condition.

'Thank you Mr Lingard. I'm going as far as Cressbrook mill.'

'I can drop you at the door miss,' he said as he helped her up. 'I'm going there too, more's the pity.'

'More's the pity?' Ellen asked.

'Well, I say more's the pity, but I suppose I shouldn't complain. It used to be that about a tenth of our work was making coffins and all the fetching and carrying, but now it's over half. It's the mills, and I'll tell you this: there's farmers around here that treat their beasts better than these mills treat their people.' He turned to look at her. 'I'm not joking,' he added.

During his rant, he had rattled the reigns and the horse was moving slowly towards Cressbrook mill. Ellen knew Lingard a little, she had come across him in the Red Lion; he always had plenty to say, and she began to regret accepting the lift, but the mill was close, and the remainder of the journey would be quite short.

'Take this little lad,' he said, pointing his thumb to the back of the cart. 'The cause of death is *infection* according to this certificate,' he waved a piece of paper in the air that he took from his top pocket. 'What it doesn't say is that a week ago he was half beaten to death by two overlookers, that's why he's in my cart.'

'Which mill was he from,' Ellen asked.

'Cressbrook, but he's been in Leisure house for the last week. Cressbrook mill is where I'm going now to pick up another one. That's why I've got two boxes on.' He again pointed his thumb behind him. 'The girl I'm fetching from there fell into some machinery last night. God knows what they'll write on her certificate, *broken wrist* perhaps? Whatever's on there it won't be the truth.

'Who fills in the certificate?' Ellen asked. 'Doesn't it have to be a doctor?'

'Anyone can fill 'em in. You, me, anybody. That means you can put on there just what you like! In reality, it'll probably say *accident* on this one, but it's no accident when children who are working over ninety hours a week fall asleep and then fall into some machinery.'

Lingard turned through the mill gates, into the yard and pulled up near some out buildings.

'Well this is where I need to be. I better stop going on and be all polite now I'm here! Are you alright from here miss?'

'Yes. Thank you for the ride,' Ellen said, and she looked around as to where she might need to be. She was shocked by what she had heard; she had little idea of the working conditions at these places. She had heard stories and rumours before, but sitting on a cart alongside a dead child was making it all too real. She felt quite dizzy taking it all in, but she climbed down from the cart, composed herself and strode confidently towards a man hammering away, who she presumed could help her.

'Could you direct me to Mr Newton,' Ellen said.

'He's not at the mill,' the man said. 'More than likely he's still at the hall.' The man put his hammer down and stood up, straightening his back. He squinted through the sunlight at Ellen and then shaded his eyes to see her better. He noticed she was rocking a little.

'Are you alright miss? You look a little pale.'

'It's just the heat.'

'Why don't you sit down here for a minute miss,' he said and dusted down a stool. 'Have a minute to catch your breath.'

Ellen took him up on his offer and even accepted a drink of water. It was then that she realised that she was sitting outside the blacksmith's shop.

'It's too hot to work inside in this weather,' he explained. So, when we can, we work out here, away from the furnace.' He then held up the piece of metal he had been hammering, holding it up to his eyes to check it was true.

'What is that?' asked Ellen. She asked, but she thought she knew what it was, and she was alarmed yet again.

'It's my new design,' he said. 'I've been thinking about it for a while. It's my new design for adjustable leg irons. You see, with the old ones, we have to have different sizes, to match different ankles, and as you can imagine with youngsters here now as young as five, we need every size imaginable. If these new irons work, it will make life so much easier for everyone.'

Ellen knew what leg irons were; she had seen them in Jamaica. There were many different designs, some were connected by chains, some by a stiff bar, some had extra chains for tethering people together, but they all did the same job.

Ellen had learned a lot today; her eyes had been opened. She was now aware of cruelty and disregard for people's lives equal to anything she had seen in Jamaica. In fact, she thought that overall, the working conditions here, were probably worse. She had seen no five-year-old children working as slaves in Jamaica, and on Newton's plantations the slaves went home at dusk. Sitting down with the smith had not calmed her down at all. In those ten minutes she had spent with him, everything became so clear, and one matter that was very clear, was that she could not marry William Newton or Ellis Needham; she could not be joined with anyone who treated people like this. A further problem bothered her, and that was if young apprentices were bought, sold, abused, tortured and imprisoned in England, why was there such an emphasis on the Negro slaves living on the other side of the world?

Ellen thanked the smith and walked out of the yard muttering to herself, 'shouldn't we sort our own problems out first?'

At the same time that Ellen was leaving the yard, so was Elias Lingard, and he again offered her a lift, and she again accepted. She didn't relish the long hot walk, but as she climbed onto the cart, she wasn't sure where she would go. Should she go and see Newton and tell him what she thought of him? Should she go home and write to both Newton and Needham? She decided on none of these: Instead, it was Brown she would see, and she would ask him to explain how he could be so sympathetic towards the Negroes whilst overlooking the white slaves under his own nose; the white slaves that were owned by his friends.

'Are you going back to Tideswell?' Ellen asked.

'I am.'

The sun shone from a clear blue sky, and on any other day it would have been a beautiful journey, but Ellen was not in the mood for looking at scenery or flora or fauna. With two dead children rattling on the cart behind her, she became even more angry, and when she finally got to Parson Brown, who she found digging his garden, her tirade began.

It ended some three quarters of an hour later. By this time, they had moved to the side of a garden shed for some shade, but Brown had barely spoken; Ellen had not given him the opportunity.

When Ellen had finally exhausted herself, Brown spoke.

'I cannot argue with anything you have said,' he said, 'although, just because we have problems in England, doesn't mean we should ignore English problems abroad, but you are absolutely correct, and I have been slowly becoming more uncomfortable with the way the mills are operating. Of course, if you talk to the mill owners, or the workhouse people in London, they will tell you that if the children stay in the workhouses, they are likely to end up as thieves, beggars, or prostitutes. I used to believe that, but now I am beginning to think they might be better off as thieves, beggars or prostitutes!'

'So what are you going to do about it?' Ellen asked.

'Do you mean what are *we* going to do about it? I can't solve the problems of the country single handed. Someone else might need to lend a hand!'

Ellen smiled.

'What I thought,' Brown continued, 'was that I would see what the Clapham Sect has to say on the subject of white slavery. I believe they are a powerful body and hopefully they will be interested in becoming involved, that is if they are not already.'

Ellen and Brown moved to the vicarage parlour, and Kezia brought a tray of tea. They continued to talk for another hour, but much more calmly. When Ellen left, Brown kissed her on the cheek. It was an impulse, but he didn't regret it.

That evening, Ellen wrote letters to both William Newton and Ellis Needham, rejecting their offers of marriage. The letters were identical.

Thirty One

FRIDAY 19TH JULY 1799
TIDESDWELL VICARAGE

With Ellen gone, Brown was again left confused. He felt distant from his immediate world and a little nauseous. Ellen affected him very badly. He tried to bring himself back to his world and attempted something normal by carrying the dirty pots through to the kitchen for Kezia, but the idea failed, and he nearly tripped over on the way when he found himself gazing at Ellen's still half full tea cup.

'Here you are,' Brown said.

Kezia turned around, wiped her hands and took the tray from him. Even that was difficult; Brown was not paying attention and handing over a tray of pots from one useless pair of hands to Kezia's capable hands, nearly ended in disaster. Kezia looked at him; she was fairly sure that Brown didn't know what was going on and so she thought it was time to tell him.

'You know that Miss Baker is fond of you don't you?' and she added. 'Very fond of you I think.'

Brown looked at Kezia and then pulled a chair from under the table and sat down.

'I know she is fond of me,' he said, 'and I am fond of her. I wish I was free to pursue her, but I am not, and God cannot change that which is past.'

That was one of his bishop's favourite sayings, and Brown liked it. He believed that people spent too much time dwelling on the past, on events that couldn't be changed, but Kezia did not follow Brown's thoughts, or understand what he meant about changing the past.

'But surely you are free to pursue and court her?' she asked.

Brown closed his eyes. He was now trying not to become angry.

'Yes, I am free to court her, but then what? Kizzie, my son lives here, and the mother of my son lives here. How could I bring a wife into this house? It is impossible. When Ellen marries either Needham or Newton, which she surely will, then that will be an end to it and I will remain calm and understanding.' Brown paused and took a deep breath. 'At least then any temptation to do anything foolish will be removed.'

'I'm sorry,' Kezia said, 'and I feel for you, not being able to be with the one you truly love.' She looked wistful for a moment, but then not knowing what more to say, turned back to her work.

Brown tried not to think about his situation and the hidden burden that he carried, but there were times, and times that had occurred much more frequently following the arrival of Ellen, when he wished he had never asked Kezia to come back to Tideswell.

'I'm going out,' Brown announced. 'I'm not sure when I'll be back.'

Kezia watched him as he left the room, and when she heard the front door close, she sat down and she cried. Kezia too carried a burden, the burden of guilt. She was one of two people in the whole world who knew who Samuel's real father was, and it was not Parson Brown. Her guilt though came from allowing Brown to believe that he was the father, although that had never been her intention.

Initially her understanding of why Brown wanted her to leave Tideswell was that it would cause him considerable embarrassment if he had an unmarried woman and her bastard child living in the vicarage. She also thought that the people of Tideswell might assume Brown to be the father. She thought she understood Brown's position.

It was only when Brown walked with her at Whaley Bridge that she realised that he had misunderstood her position, and her his. Although she had never said Brown was the father, she realised then that he must have assumed their liaison, on that drunken Tuesday night in the school house, had resulted in her being with child.

Sam Slater was Samuel's father, and Kezia knew she was already with child when she lay with Brown. When Brown asked her to come back to Tideswell, she had made the decision for her son, for herself and for the child's father. She had said to herself that pleasing three people at the expense of one must be the right thing to do, and on balance, the result was more happiness in the world. It had only been a small lie, or maybe it wasn't a lie at all, just Brown's misunderstanding. Misunderstanding or lie, today for the first time she realised the consequences of her decision, and how it had blighted Brown's whole life.

Brown went to the church and prayed silently. For once, he prayed for himself and asked that he could be released from the burden of responsibility so that he was free to marry. It was not possible for Brown to untangle the mess he was in, and so he needed some help from the Almighty. He then prayed that he might be given a different position in the church; one that took him permanently from Tideswell. Perhaps he might be appointed to a lasting post within the Clapham sect, but that was a muddled prayer as he wasn't then sure what would happen to Kezia and Samuel, so he went back to his original more general plea - for release.'

The back door opened and Sam Slater stood there. He didn't see that Kezia was crying.

'I just saw the parson in the town. How long have we got?'

'I don't know,' she replied.

Sam then saw that she was crying, and he went over, knelt by her side and put his arms around her.

'What's wrong?' he asked. 'Is Samuel unwell?'

Kezia had never told Sam that Parson Brown thought that Samuel was his son, and she had never told Sam that she had lain with the parson; after all, she didn't want to be abandoned by everyone. When she came back to Tideswell, she asked Sam not to tell anyone that he was the father, as she didn't want anyone to know. Without questioning it, Sam had agreed.

'Tell me what's wrong?' he asked again.

Kezia couldn't now tell Sam why she was upset, and she had to explain her crying with another lie, but this time it was a lie containing a truth.

'I just want us to be together,' Kezia said. 'Together as a family, not living like this. We can't live like this for ever, with you sneaking in the back door to catch a glimpse of me and Samuel.'

'That's what I want too,' Sam said. 'I've thought about it, and I want to be with you both and be able to bring up Samuel properly. Where is the boy anyway?'

'He's asleep.'

'The real reason I came here today is because I'm going to see about a job tomorrow, a proper job that could last years.'

'Go on,' Kezia said. Her tears had now stopped.

'I've been told there's work for a company at Disley. They say they need men to build chimneys for the mills. Most of them are moving from water power to steam, and there's plenty of building work, especially for those who are not scared of heights. There's no funerals or digging tomorrow, so I'm headed there first thing.'

'When will you get back?' Kezia asked.

'Not sure, but if I get a job there, we could perhaps move over there and become a proper family.'

Kezia was about to say something, but Parson Brown was opening the front door. Sam and Kezia shared a snatched kiss, and Sam Slater slipped silently, as he had done many times before, out of the back door.

Thirty two

MONDAY 22ND JULY 1799
LITTON MILL

By the beginning of July, Litton mill was struggling more than ever. Needham did not have the cash to purchase raw cotton, and to keep the mill running, he had struck up a deal with a Manchester mill, *messrs Sharp and Twiss*, and he was processing cotton for them. They delivered the raw cotton to him, and they collected the finished yarn. The price he could get for such an arrangement was not enough; it did not cover his costs, but it kept the mill working and gave them some thinking time.

'Good morning everyone,' Needham said.

Present at Needham's Monday morning meeting were Robert Needham and all of the managers except Simpson. Simpson had not returned to work after baby Janet had died, and he now filled his days doing nothing at Littonslack; he just sat in the cottage all day. Martha went back to working at Cressbrook mill, although it wasn't for the money: she went back as she couldn't bear the long days at home without baby Janet to look after. With the mill finances as they were, Needham had settled for leaving Blincoe in charge of the smithy. As far as he could tell, Blincoe was reliable and a good worker, and if he needed help there was always Palfrey. Blincoe was still an apprentice though and as such had never been invited to the Monday morning meeting.

'I'll ask if anyone has anything useful to say in a minute,' Needham said, 'but first I want to explain a little about the likely future of the mill. I am sure there have been plenty of rumours around what is going on, but today I will tell you the truth, although it is for your ears only; I don't want to leave tonight to a riot.'

No one smiled at that, and no one was sure whether they should.

'In short, we have little money left and processing cotton for Sharp and Twiss is not making anything. The mill has been advertised for sale, but there has been no interest. Unless we can think of something different, we only have a week or two to go. I've sunk everything I have into this mill, and I have nothing left to give.'

No one was surprised by what Needham had to say; the rumours had been close enough. There had been a noticeable increase in people calling at the mill to collect, or attempt to collect, payment for what they were owed; tradesmen and deliverymen talked amongst themselves, and they talked to people at the mill, so Needham was only confirming what everyone feared. The men in the room in front of Needham had talked amongst themselves, and the consensus was that it would all end soon. Of course, the best, and probably most realistic, possibility was that someone would buy the mill, in which case the jobs would be safe, and with this in their minds, coupled with a dearth of jobs in the neighbourhood, no one had yet left the mill.

'Any questions?' Needham asked, but there was silence. 'Any other matters from anyone?' he asked, but again there was nothing.

Ellis Needham, Robert Needham and Middleton remained in the room. Needham sat back in his chair, arms behind his head.

'I'm not sure it was the right thing to do,' he said, 'but it's done, and my instinct was to let everyone including the workers know the predicament we are in. It will be less of a shock if things get worse.'

'But the workers don't know,' Middleton said.

'They will. There won't be anyone who hasn't heard by dinner, that's why I told them: I wanted it to be known. Now then, when I said we have a week or two, I am afraid that might have been a little optimistic. I am going to the bank tomorrow, and they may, or may not, let me draw on my account. If they don't then there will be no wages this week.'

'Something came to me last night,' Richard said. 'An idea as to how we could save the mill. I'm not sure if it will work though. We would need to take advice.'

'Go on then,' his brother said. 'Anything is worth a try.'

'Well, if you can't sell the mill, and assuming there are no other miracles, then you as sole owner of the mill will have your loans called in and your assets, including the mill seized. Is that correct?'

'It is.'

'So, if you were to sell the mill and its machinery to me before this event, then they would not be able to take the mill, and I could continue running the mill, as could you of course; you would only be bankrupt in name.'

'But you have no money to buy this place,' Ellis said.

'It would be a notional sum, say ten pounds. With the loans written off, the mill would then be profitable. I have discussed this very briefly with Mr Middleton.' Middleton nodded cautiously, before confirming what Robert had said.

'If the mill was freed from the burden of the interest payments on all the loans, then it would be profitable; even spinning Sharp and Twiss's cotton, it would be profitable.'

'Is what you are proposing legal?' Ellis asked of his brother.

'I'm not sure. Obviously we would need an attorney to transfer the deeds, I presume we would use William Cheek as normal; he could advise us on the legality.'

'We will need to see Cheek, but whatever happens with this idea, I still need the wages for this week, and so I will ride to Chesterfield first thing tomorrow to see the bank. I will then see you in Bakewell at noon. We can meet in The White Horse, and we will see Cheek after that.

Needham had a hard time with the young assistant manager of *Heywoods Bank* in Chesterfield. The manager was out, and Mr Pendleton, as the sign said on his desk, spent the first half an hour going through all Needham's loans. Needham was considerably behind with his repayments, and although it was not the purpose of Needham's visit, he let Pendleton have his way. Pendleton then checked all the securities for the loans, making sure nothing had changed. Finally, he moved to Needham's request and asked him about some new assets he might put forward to secure the new loan, but there was nothing that Needham could offer.

'You are considerably in arrears on your loan repayments,' Pendleton said. 'If we are going to lend you this money, I have to put it against something.'

Eventually Pendleton adjusted the value, slightly, of Needham's home at Wormhill and went to fetch the cash. When he returned, he had with him another man, the manager.

'Mr Needham, good morning. I won't keep you further, but I have had a short conversation Mr Pendelton, and we think it best if we send our people across to you early next week. Perhaps they will be able to help you with your business.'

The rest of the day went exactly according to plan. The Needhams met in The White Horse, and in the afternoon, they saw Cheek.

'Are there any loans secured against anything you are selling? Cheek asked.

'No,' Ellis replied. This was a lie, but the Needhams needed this transfer to take place. It was their only hope.

'Are you selling anything that is unpaid for, stock or machinery; anything like that?'

'No.' This was another lie, although next to Heywoods', the other creditors were insignificant.

'Then I can see no reason why we cannot transfer the title deed to Robert.'

Not one, not two, but three men arrived at Litton mill on the following Monday morning. They were straight into Needham's office and joined Needham, his brother and Middleton.

The tallest of the three men spoke, 'Mr Ellis Needham?'

'Yes,' Needham said. Needham had expected his local manger; he knew none of these men.

'You may want to dismiss your colleagues. This is a rather delicate matter.'

'They can stay,' Needham grunted,

'Very well,' the tall man said. 'My name is Fletcher of Heywoods Bank. I am here to seek a settlement in the loans that are outstanding. I have to ask you Mr Needham if you are in a position to repay all of your loans today?'

'I cannot.'

'Mr Needham, the loan repayments are significantly in arrears. In law, if there is default on any loan then it is lawful, to enter and take possession of all or any part of the assigned interests. In summary we are here to take possession of your house and of this mill including some land and ten cottages.'

'Very well,' Needham said, 'but the mill is not owned by myself anymore, and I have papers to show this.'

'Can you show me the papers?' Fletcher asked.

Needham passed Fletcher the papers, and he immediately passed them to the second of the three visitors. The second man shook his head before speaking.

'I am Mr Jason by the way.' Jason held out is hand to Needham, but Needham did not move. Jason withdrew his hand. 'Mr Needham, this is a very recent disposition of the mill property for …' Jason moved through the document until he found what he was looking for. 'Oh ten pounds!' Jason put the document on the desk and looked at Needham. 'This is not a legal transaction Mr Needham. I can give you two reasons why this is so, although I dare say I could find more! First, this transaction undoubtedly would make you insolvent, and it therefore made in contemplation of bankruptcy and consequently is held to be void by the bankruptcy laws. Second, the bank has this property as security for the loan, and such a transaction is contrary to the contract you have signed. A very feeble attempt Mr Needham, very feeble. I'm surprised you found an attorney willing to go along with this.'

Fletcher took over again. 'Well that's cleared up that little misunderstanding, but shall we sit down gentlemen? We may be here for a while yet.'

Everyone sat down. Needham was still behind his desk, although he feared, not for long. Fletcher remained standing.

'The bank will take possession of your house, of the mill including the associated land and of the ten cottages known as Littonslack. Possession of the house is straightforward, and you will be allowed to live there for three months or until it is sold, whichever is the sooner. You will keep the place in good repair during that time, and my colleague here, Mr Jason, has a document for you to sign agreeing to that. Mr Jason is our attorney by the way.'

Needham signed the document and Fletcher continued.

'The Littonslack cottages will be put up for sale. The mill, however, is a little more complicated. If we are to recoup our money and act responsibly, then we really need to sell it as a going concern. Now if there is a queue of creditors in addition to ourselves, then keeping the business running tends to be very difficult, and in situations like that we have a responsibility to act correctly, which usually means beginning bankruptcy proceedings. Now we will be looking at all your books over the next few days, but perhaps, Mr Needham, you could give us an idea as to what we might find?

'There are no other creditors,' Needham said. 'None to speak of anyway.'

'Thank you. Of course, I must point out that when everything is sold, if there is a surplus of money, then after the bank have taken off their costs, any balance would be yours, although I'm afraid this tends to be a rare event.'

Everyone, including Needham, was very calm and business like. There was no shouting, no visible emotion.

'Finally before Mr Jarvis, takes over the running of the mill, I need to formally escort Mr Ellis Needham, any business partners and any family of theirs, from the premises. In this case, you will be seen out of the gates.'

'There's just me and Robert,' Needham said, pointing to Robert.

After Fletcher's attorney had formally showed the Needhams to the gates, shook hands with them and wished them well, Needham reflected on what had happened in the last half hour. He had taken in a great deal and was shocked how quickly everything in his life had changed; he was also annoyed at the way the bank people had tricked themselves into the meeting, and he wondered if he should have seen what was coming. His world had fallen apart, and yet at the same time there was a growing glimmer of relief, a growing realisation that although he was soon to be homeless and had no income, he now had no responsibility for the mill. It was no longer his worry.

Ellis and Robert stood at the mill gates, their horses taken from them by Fletcher. They agreed to meet the next day, although neither were sure why. Robert walked home along the river, but Needham sauntered up Slack hill. He needed a drink, and a slow walk to Litton would see The Red Lion open.

Needham arrived at the Red Lion as Ellen was opening the door. He had not seen her since the Cressbrook mill party, and there had been no communication other than Ellen's letter rejecting his proposal. The meeting was a little difficult, but Needham said nothing about the letter and sat alone drinking his ale. He drank three quarts very quickly, and by the time Ellen brought his fourth quart, the events of the day, and of his life, were becoming very clear.

'Sit down a minute,' he said. 'I wanted to thank you for your letter, and I understand your view on the way the cotton mills work and so on.'

Ellen wasn't sure where this was leading, but she had no other customers or any excuse to leave. He was a little drunk, but nothing she hadn't seen before.

'I want you to know that I now have no involvement whatsoever in the cotton business, absolutely nothing. I am not anymore the owner of a cotton mill, or the owner of any apprentices. Therefore, as I am not involved with the practices that take place in cotton mills, of which you disapprove, then those particular criticisms cannot be delivered to me. Now it maybe that I am now a poor man, but if you married me, I would love you and care for you as no one else ever could. That, my dear Ellen is my proposal.

'I'm sorry,' she said.

Thirty Three

SUNDAY 4TH AUGUST 1799
TIDESWELL VICARAGE

It was just two o'clock. Kezia was getting ready to go to her grandmothers for the weekend, and Parson Brown was putting the finishing touches to his Sunday sermon. Kezia still went to her grandmother's for twenty-four hours at the weekend, and whereas Kezia used to be looked after by her grandmother, it was now Kezia who was doing the looking after. Kezia's grandmother was in her eighties, and her legs prevented her getting around as well as she once did. Now Kezia's time away from her work at the vicarage brought even harder work, looking after both her grandmother and baby Samuel.

Parson Brown had been grappling with the structure of his sermon since eleven o'clock, but he was now happy with it; he just needed to decide whether the five main questions at the end of the sermon, which were each quite short, should be numbered for the congregation, or not. He wasn't sure, but he decided he would read it aloud after Kezia had gone. It was at that point that he noticed Kezia standing in the open parlour doorway with Samuel in her arms.

'Kizzie. Are you away to your grandmother's now?'

'Yes, but I wanted to speak with you first.'

'Of course,' Brown said. 'Come on in. Do you want to sit down?'

Kezia didn't answer the last question. She remained standing.

'It's about the future, sort of,' she said.

'Ah yes,' Brown said, he turned around on his chair to face her better. 'I meant to talk to you about that. I was thinking that while I'm away, you could carry on as before and keep this place tidy. There will be a lot less work for you with me away.'

'It wasn't that,' Kezia said, and then she did sit down. 'It's that I'm leaving here. I'm getting married.'

This was a shock to Brown. He had no idea this was coming. Then he immediately started to worry about what would happen to Samuel. Was she leaving him with the baby? He had visions of sitting at his first meeting in Clapham with a baby on his knee!

'So who is the lucky man?' Brown asked. He would ask about Samuel next.

'Sam. Sam Slater. He's got a job now, so we can afford to get married.'

'Good,' Brown said, 'but where are you going to live?

'To start with we're going to lodge with my aunt at Whaley Bridge. It's close to Sam's work at Disley. He's got a job building chimneys for the mills. Apparently they are all converting to steam, and they need builders for the chimney stacks.'

'And Samuel, will he go with you?'

'Yes. Although there's something you should know about Samuel.'

Brown put his pen down, now giving Kezia his full attention. Kezia looked down at the baby, not wanting to look at Brown during her next announcement.

'Samuel isn't yours,' she said. He's Sam's. I've wanted to tell you for a long time.' Kezia then looked up at Brown. 'Let me explain, although it's not easy. When I first moved away from Tideswell, when we agreed that was the best thing to do, I had no idea that you thought the child was yours. I thought it was that I couldn't be seen to be living in the vicarage. It wasn't until our meeting in Whaley Bridge that I realised that you thought it was your child I was carrying. I had a choice to make then. One option was to come back to Tideswell where I could bring up Samuel properly in the vicarage and be near Sam, Sam Slater I mean. The other choice … well what was the other choice? Probably abandoned in Whaley Bridge with my money cut off.'

Kezia's explanation tailed off, and she stopped speaking without really finishing, but she had explained enough. Brown was taking all this in. On the one hand, he had been badly misled, but on the other hand, he was now totally free and absolved of any wrong-doing.

'This has come as a total surprise to me,' he said, 'all of it.'

'I am very sorry,' Kezia said. 'It was the best I could do for me and Sam and his father. We three have gained, but I realise now how much you have suffered.'

Brown decided very quickly that there was no point in being angry, Kezia would be leaving whether he was angry or not, and he was well aware that God can never change that which is past. The joy of his freedom was already a much more powerful emotion than any anger, and he realised that he was in a much improved position compared to where he had been five minutes before.

'Kizzie, tell your grandmother that I will call and see her later this week. And give my congratulations to Sam and ask him who is going to dig my graves when he is married and living in Whaley Bridge!'

Brown was smiling; he stood and then moved over to Kezia and Samuel.

'I offer my congratulations, and as a wedding gift, I am happy to marry you in the church here.'

Kezia quickly put the baby on the floor; she wrapped her arms around Brown and kissed him on the neck. She picked up the baby, thanked the parson again and ran out.

Brown felt quite lightheaded, and as if the whole situation wasn't confusing enough, the smell of Kezia so close to him, took him back and confused him even more. Brown spent a difficult afternoon trying to work everything out. His life had suddenly changed, yet through no effort on his part; even his history had changed, with events in the past now rewritten. It was a strange world.

He tried to move his thoughts to other matters; he tried to think about his sermon, but he couldn't concentrate. He turned to thinking about Needham. The word has travelled fast about Needham's misfortune, and how he was turned out of the mill, and although Brown had made two journeys to Wormhill this week to see him, Needham had been out on both occasions. Needham's world had changed in a few brief moments, and then Brown was back thinking about how his own world had done the same.

Just as Brown settled himself down at his desk, this time determined to look again at his sermon, he saw Needham walking towards the Vicarage. He looked at the clock on the mantle shelf, and with only an hour to the service, it seemed his sermon preparation was finished after all.

Needham had been drinking in the New George; he was in a dreadful state, drunk, unshaven and dirty. Brown sat him down in the kitchen.

'I've lost everything,' Needham said, focussing on the patch of floor just in front of his feet. 'Everything. You try to do some good in this world, and all that happens is you are punished - and punished severely. I have no home, no employment, nowhere to go. I have no wife because the bloody Baker girl won't have me. Mind you,' he looked up from the floor at Brown, 'she won't have Newton either!'

Needham's head wobbled, and he broke out into an evil laugh. He was struggling to find anything cheerful in his life, so Newton's misery was something he could lean on.

'It's been some week,' Needham continued. 'can you imagine what it's like for your life to change so quickly?' He tried to click his thumb and finger, but there was no noise, and he looked at his hand as though it was at fault.

'I do understand,' Brown said.

‘Anyway, I shall attend church this evening,’ Needham said. ‘Perhaps your preaching will show me the way?’

‘I doubt it,’ Brown said. ‘I think you would be better going home and getting cleaned up. A good wash and shave would be a start.’

‘You cannot tell me,’ Needham protested, ‘that the Lord will judge me on whether I am unshaven, or shaven. Christ had a beard anyway!’

There was no sense in Brown arguing with him. If he chose to come to church, he could; it was after all open to everyone. Brown knew that Needham’s drunken presence would be a nuisance and definitely wouldn’t help his sermon flow easily, but he would manage.

‘Just don’t get too close to anyone else,’ Brown said, and he opened a window, which he thought might clear the room after they had left.

The congregation gathered in the church, with Needham sat on his own, three rows from the back. Brown was delighted to see Ellen in church; she was three rows from the front. She had positioned herself deliberately near the front so that Brown would see her.

Brown had written his sermon hoping she would be there, although he hadn’t written it with Needham’s presence in mind. Needham, if he was awake, was going to find the sermon very difficult.

‘As you may know, I will soon be leaving this parish, to a temporary post assisting with the anti-slavery movement. This Church and the associated duties will be looked after by our neighbouring parishes, but I will give more information on that in due course. Today’s short sermon therefore is appropriately on the subject of slavery.’

Brown began his partially practised sermon. It began with some background information; some social and theological contexts, and finally he led the congregation to his conclusion.

‘Revelation thirteen verse ten tells us that, “He that leadeth into captivity shall go into captivity,” that is that we must condemn those who lead others into captivity, or condemn those involved in slavery. I have five questions for you to consider, and I ask that you answer these as a Christian, as a member of the Church and as a member of your own family. They all concern the treatment of slaves.'

Brown cleared his throat and paused before beginning his now unnumbered list.

'Is it rational that one human being should be taken against his will from one place to another? - like we might a farm animal? Is it rational that one human being should be sold from one person to another? - like we might sell a farm animal? Is it rational that one human being should be claimed by another as his property? - like we might claim a farm animal? Is it rational that a human being should be kept in shackles and chains and thus be herded and kept secure, like a farm animal? Is it rational to work human beings so hard that many of them die through exhaustion or accidents,' Brown paused for effect. 'Surely this is something we wouldn't do to farm animals!'

There wasn't laughter, but some coughing and smiles from the congregation. Brown thought it was going well, and he was going to enjoy the next part.

'I put it to you that we are treating our fellow human beings the same, or even worse, than we would a farm animal. Can this be right? Surely as Christians, this evil behaviour must be challenged and fought. I hope you are alongside me in this straightforward argument. But let me take the arguments to another place, to a place closer to home. Very close to home. Allow me time to repeat those same five points, but now, rather than the negro, consider the young apprentices working in the factories and mills of England. I am sure that you wouldn't want to treat a child less favourably than a negro? So, is it rational that a child should be taken against his will from one place to another? Is it rational that a child should be sold from one person to another? Is it rational that a child can be claimed by someone as their property? Is it rational that a child can be kept in shackles and chains? Is it rational to work children so hard that many of them die through exhaustion or accidents?'

By this point Brown has reached a crescendo, shouting into the church, spittle shooting from his mouth. He paused and allowed himself time to calm down.

'It cannot be rational, and I have already spent too much of my time conducting funerals of children from this parish. I am sure that, like me, you have come to the only conclusion possible, and that is that this practice is evil!'

Needham was squirming at the back of the church, his head in his hands. No one heard him muttering to himself, 'Kick a man when he is down.'

'But is that it?' Brown continued. 'Listening to a sermon on a Sunday? Will that change anything? The black slaves cannot plead their own cause, and the children cannot plead their cause. So I beg of you, if you can find a way to contribute towards the end of this evil practice, then do so, and do so with enthusiasm and with a pride that you are doing so in the name of God.'

Brown looked at Ellen who was smiling and, as always, looking beautiful. 'Let us pray.'

Ellen was delighted with the sermon. Clearly, the discussion with Brown about the relative importance of white slavery had been worthwhile. At the end of the service, Needham slipped away. No one saw him leave. Brown as usual, stood in the porch, shaking hands and speaking to the congregation, mainly about the weather. Ellen held back; she wanted a longer conversation with Brown.

'I am full of admiration for the sentiments you expressed in your sermon,' she said.

'It is because of you, that I now see more clearly,' Brown replied.

Nathan Booker shuffled past them and muttered, 'Goodnight.'

'Do you consider that we might somehow find a way of working together towards these causes?' Ellen asked.

Brown took hold of her hands and looked into her eyes, 'As husband and wife perhaps? Ellen, would you come to Clapham with me, as my wife?'

Ellen had given up waiting for Brown's proposal, and when it came, it took her by surprise, but her answer was simple, short and clear.

'Yes.'

Brown looked around him, and still holding her hands, he kicked the outside porch door shut.

Thirty Four

TUESDAY 27TH AUGUST 1799
LITTON MILL

It was four weeks since Ellis Needham had last been at Litton mill. Since then, Jarvis had been running the mill assisted by a fourth man from the bank. The fourth man was Mr Silkstone, who had been brought in to make sense of the accounts. In the spinning rooms, the first rumour was that Jarvis had bought the mill from Needham, but that rumour didn't last long, and by the end of the second day, the truth was out: Needham had been turned out of the mill, and the bank was in charge. The mill managers were gathered together at the end of the third day, and Jarvis explained to them what was happening.

'If we can sell the mill, then we will safeguard not only the bank's investment, but also your jobs. What we don't want to happen is for people to leave the mill in numbers and put us in a position where we do not have a business to sell. As a business, it is worth something, but as a stone building, it is worth very little. We must stamp out immediately any rumours that may lead to a panic. Is that clear?'

By the end of the second week, a new advertisement appeared in the *Derby Mercury*, and then everyone understood. In the event, there was no panic, and no one resigned. The business had never been especially secure, and it was little different now. Had there been any other employment to go to, people would have already left; they wouldn't have waited for Needham to go.

Blincoe had been privy to some of this information before anyone else. On the very first day that the bank had moved in, Blincoe, as the only fit apprentice not involved with production, had been asked to move some papers around. He had to move all of the papers and books from Middleton's counting house, up one floor into Needham's office, and later on the same day, he was asked to provide and fit a hasp on Needham's office door. At the time, most of the mill workers knew nothing of the events of that morning and although Blincoe was involved, he initially had no idea what was happening; all he knew was that there were very strange goings on. By the time Blincoe came back from the smithy with the hasp, Jarvis had his name on the door, *Mr Jarvis, Heywoods Bank.* But although the words were clear enough, Blincoe still failed to understand. Blincoe fixed the hasp, and he and Jarvis made sure that the lock passed through it so the bank's office could be secured.

The mill carried on, seemingly unaffected by the change. The long hours and tiredness continued, the beatings and suffering were just as frequent and the disgusting food was still disgusting. In fact, all of the misery that everyone had blamed on Needham remained the same after his departure. Even the Sunday school was the same, except on the most recent Sunday, Parson Brown had announced to the apprentices that this was his last Sunday school for a while. He explained that he was soon to be married, and then he was going to London to another job.

Jarvis had invited Needham to the mill to look at the list of creditors and debtors that over the last few weeks he had collated. An exercise like this was much easier to do over a three or four-week period, as any creditors usually made themselves known during that time. The debtors were a little more difficult, as this relied on good book keeping, or the help of the owner. Middleton's books had been well kept and appeared accurate, and for Jarvis and Silkstone, this had been a simple exercise.

'Thank you for coming Mr Needham,' Jarvis said. 'We have prepared what we believe is a list of creditors and debtors as of the twenty-ninth of July. We just need you to check over those and see if there are any errors or omissions.'

Silkstone passed him a single sheet of paper on which they were recorded. Needham studied the lists.

'It appears correct,' Needham said. But looking at the lists reminded Needham that there were some cash jobs for which he was still owed money; jobs that had never been recorded in the books. He needed to pursue those.

'Was there anything else?' Needham asked.

'Nothing else,' Jarvis said, 'although we haven't had any interest in selling the mill as yet. So that is a concern for us all.'

The same day at three o'clock in the afternoon, Jarvis and Silkstone gathered the entire workforce in the mill yard. They stood on a cart that Blincoe had moved specially for the occasion.

'Quiet please. Quiet please!' Jarvis shouted, and the murmur faded to nothing. 'As you may know, we are representatives of Heywoods Bank and we have now been running the mill for four weeks. It was our hope that we would find a buyer for the mill and all jobs would have then been safe. However, so far we have had no firm offers, and I have to tell you that unless we receive a firm offer in the next two weeks, this mill will close.'

The murmur grew again and Jarvis gave people a little while to have their say. They calmed down and he continued. 'We will continue to do our very best to sell the mill, but that prospect is looking less likely. We will pay wages for the next two weeks, but I urge you now, that if you can find other employment, then it may be to your advantage to pursue that. If there is any change, I will let you know. Are there any questions?'

Blincoe had one burning question, and as he was almost out of work anyway, he had nothing to lose by asking it, so he raised his hand. Jarvis pointed to him to speak.

'Yes?' Jarvis said.

'Apprentices are tied by their indentures and aren't free to look for other work. Has that changed sir?'

Jarvis and Silkstone whispered to each other, and then Jarvis spoke.

'As from today, that restriction is lifted.'

Blincoe returned to the smithy now free to do as he pleased. He planned a cup of tea and a good think, but when he returned to the smithy, Simpson was in there. It was quite a surprise as Simpson hadn't been to the mill for weeks.

'I've taken what I want,' Simpson said. 'This place is finished, so if there's anything any use to you, you should grab it while you can. People will be in here soon enough, *and* without being invited, so you might as well have first, well second, pick at it all.' He looked around again. 'That needs moving too,' he said, and nodded in the direction of Blincoe's washer tin.

'What are you going to do?' Blincoe asked.

'I'm thinking of going back to Scotland. I have family up there. I'll maybe wait until the bank throws us out of the cottage. What about you?'

'I've got the chance of a job in Manchester, so I'm going to see about that.'

That evening Blincoe sorted through what was in the smithy, and he made two journeys, laden down with heavy bags, to the cave where Martha had first taken him. He took what he could carry and what might be useful. Simpson had taken most of the tools, but he took those that were left, and he hid them in the darkness of the cave. No one would find them there.

The following morning, with his money spread amongst his pockets he set off for Manchester. His goal was to find Herbert and see if he was still looking for a partner for his new business. He read the address he had kept safe all these weeks in his washer tin. *Herbert Beard, 2 Little Sea Lane, off Plymouth Grove, Chorlton, Manchester*. Blincoe's plan was to get a free ride on a wagon going to Manchester. This he did, although he soon found that it was the custom to pay the driver a halfpenny. This he was happy to do as it was still much less than the coach. He did the journey with three rides: Tideswell to Buxton; Buxton to Chapel en le Frith and Chapel to somewhere near where he wanted to be, or at least that's what the driver had told him. He wandered around asking people and soon found Plymouth Grove. After that it was straightforward, he found Little Sea Lane, and before he knew it, he was drinking a cup of tea with Herbert's mum.

'He should be back from work in the next hour or so,' she said. 'You put your feet up. It sounds like you've come a long way.'

'Blinkie!' shouted Herbert on coming in to the house. It was just past five.

'Berty,' said Blincoe, and they shook hands like long lost brothers.

'Are you here for the reason I think you're here?' asked Herbert.

'I am,' said Blincoe. 'Well I think I am.'

'We're going out mam,' Herbert shouted to his mam who had disappeared into the kitchen. She came bustling out.

'What about your tea, and what about your friend? I bet he hasn't eaten all day.'

'Can you do us something later? Herbert asked, 'and can Blinkie sleep here tonight. You'll be alright on the floor down here won't you?'

Blincoe nodded.

The plan was still on for the new business partnership. Herbert had done some more work and had a list of mills where they could buy cotton and the price the mills would charge them for it. The price was often just a nominal figure, but even when it was higher, Herbert explained how it still left room to make good profits. They soon arrived at the stable block, which was just at the far end of Little Sea Lane; Blincoe found out that Herbert had known the owner all his life. The stable block was left over from a working farm that the owner, a man named Ferguson used to farm. Ferguson was now in his late seventies and with no children and unable to manage the farm, he had sold off all of the land to builders. He was left with the farmhouse, where he lived, the adjacent empty stable block and a pot of money.

'I made more money in one day,' Ferguson said, 'selling all the farm land, than I made in a lifetime of farming!'

The stable block was as Herbert had described. There were buildings on three sides of a large yard, with the fourth side being the end of Ferguson's house. Inside the stables were dozens of rooms, of different shapes and sizes, although many were still full of the paraphernalia left over from a lifetime of farming.

'If you want to take the place, I'll clear it all out,' Ferguson said. 'I'll leave you to look around on your own, I'm going back to the house now; come over there when you've done.'

This had been a very big farm, and evidence of that came when they found a room that must have been where the farm workers ate. The room had a table, chairs; in one corner a stove and in another corner an inside pump. This was quite different from most of the rooms that were built for animals.

'Look how many chairs!' Herbert said. 'He must have employed a fair few people.'

Blincoe wasn't looking at the chairs, he was looking for somewhere to live, and this room would be perfect; he just needed to be sure that Herbert was happy with his plan.

'I'm going to need somewhere to live when I move up here,' Blincoe said. 'Would you mind if I took this room?'

'A smart idea!' Herbert said. 'It will keep the place safer too.'

After exploring every room, they went over to the farmhouse, agreed the rent and shook hands with Ferguson. Blincoe and Beard each handed over sixteen shillings, which was their share of four weeks' rent.

‘I’ll let you have five weeks’ for that,’ Ferguson said, ‘on account of the tidying up they you’re going to have to do.’

The loss of sixteen shillings from Blincoe’s pockets reduced the ridiculous weight he had been carrying around, but only very slightly. He was still left with pockets full of coppers and sixpences, and Ferguson saw how he was struggling.

‘Do you want me to change that for you lad?’ Ferguson asked. ‘Tip it on the table here and count it out.’

They counted out the remainder of Blincoe’s savings: five pounds seventeen shillings and seven pence.

‘Wait here,’ Ferguson said, and reappeared a few minutes later with five gold guineas, which he exchanged for the same value in small coins.

‘I think that’s everything for now,’ Ferguson said. ‘I’ll get anything I need out of the buildings over the coming weekend, and then it’s yours from Monday.’

The two youngsters looked at each other, both smiling. The new partnership of *Beard and Blincoe* was formed.

Thirty Five

FRIDAY 30TH AUGUST 1799
LITTON MILL

The morning bell rang at the usual time. But in the apprentice house, the urgency to get out of bed and go to work was no longer there. The mill was almost certain to close, and the apprentices knew they would then be thrown out. They were generally confused, as any reason to carry on working had all but vanished. If they did work, they might receive just one more penny, but there was now no hope of the promised apprenticeship, or the prosperous future that they were told it would bring. Surprisingly though, many of the apprentices continued to work in the mill; they told themselves that the mill might yet be saved, but the truth was that they knew nothing else, and familiarity, as bad as it was, was somehow comforting. The confusion for the apprentices was only surpassed by that of the over-lookers. For the last few years, they had ruled and motivated the apprentices by generating a climate of fear, but that fear was now fading, and as the days passed, and the end came closer, even the most compliant of the apprentices knew they could, at any time, walk away. To keep the mill running, the over-lookers found themselves practising new skills of negotiation and kindness, skills that did not come easily.

Blincoe had no concerns about what he would do today, and it wasn't working for the mill. He had been missing in Manchester the last two days, and when asked by Milner where he had been, he had simply told the truth.

'I went to see about a job in Manchester, 'he said, 'and I'm starting work there next week.'

'Well done lad,' was all Milner said. There was not even a hint of any punishment.

The day before, Blincoe had left Manchester. Herbert thought he might have stayed there, but Blincoe said that he needed to go back to Derbyshire to say some goodbyes, which was true, although there was another reason too.

Despite having no plans to work at the mill that day, Blincoe was up with the bell, and five minutes later, he was having a good wash under the pump. The Manchester dirt washed off much easier than mill grime, and before either Litton or Cressbrook mills were in power, Blincoe was away, running along the river edge towards Cressbrook. At Cressbrook mill, he stopped running, but then turned and walked quickly up the track away from the mill. Halfway up the hill, just as he was at the entrance to Cressbrook hall, he saw her. He hid in the entrance gates and waited. His heart was now beating quickly, and when he heard her footsteps closing on him, he judged that it was the right time to jump out.

'I am the ghost of Cressbrook hall,' he shouted.

'No you're not you're Robert Blincoe,' Martha said. 'What on earth are you doing here at this time?' She was more confused than frightened.

'I'm here to see you,' Blincoe said.

'Aye, well you've seen me now,' Martha said. 'Now I need to be at work, or I'll be fined a penny for being late!'

'I don't want you to go to work,' Blincoe said, 'not today.'

'If I don't go at all, I'll lose eight pence!'

Blincoe thrust his hands in both his pockets and produced a shilling. 'Here,' he said, 'take this.'

Martha laughed at him. 'I don't think you're right in the head!'

Still in the entrance of Cressbrook hall, Blincoe then went on both knees.

'Martha,' he said looking up at her. 'Please listen to me. Needham has gone from the mill, and I have been told I am free from my indentures. I'm leaving for Manchester after the weekend where I have a job to go to. I also have somewhere to live, my own place. Martha, I want you to come with me, and I want to marry you.'

Martha pulled him up from his knees, and hugged him. When they broke from the hug, Blincoe saw tears in her eyes, and yet she was smiling at the same time. He didn't have to wonder for long, what those emotions might mean.

'Aye,' Martha began, 'alright then! But we'll have to see dad and make sure it's alright with him.'

Martha kissed him. 'You're not a knight and you have no armour, but you'll have to do I suppose!' And she kissed him again. 'Mind, I'm keeping this shilling, in case this is all talk!'

They walked back to Littonslack and on the way Blincoe told her about *Beard and Blincoe* and about where they would live.

'Oh it's you,' Simpson said, in a matter of fact way, on seeing Blincoe hovering in the doorway. 'And you!' he said, a little more surprised to see Martha back so soon. Simpson was no fool and before they had said anymore, he had fathomed why they were there. Simpson was sitting in his chair; Blincoe and Martha remained standing, now just inside the door.

'I want to marry Martha,' Blincoe blurted out.

'I see,' said Simpson calmly. 'Does Martha want to marry you though?'

'She does,' said Blincoe.

'I do,' said Martha. Martha was now holding Blincoe's hand.

'Are you able to look after her?' Simpson asked, and again Blincoe gave his explanation of what *Beard and Blincoe* would be doing, and where he and Martha would live.

'Well you have my approval,' Simpson said. 'It's not as though you are a stranger, I know you well enough. But, mind you look after her!'

'Oh I will,' Blincoe said. 'What will you do? I mean what will you do without Martha?'

'I'll go back up to Scotland; there's work up there and I can lodge with my brother. It seems as though it's time for us all to move on.'

Simpson hadn't worked for a while now, and whereas initially it had been due to his grieving, it was now more to do with laziness. He didn't need the money, and even before the demise of Litton mill, he had been thinking of moving on.

'So when is the day? The day when you take my daughter from me?' Simpson asked jovially.

'I was thinking, tomorrow,' Blincoe said.

'Tomorrow!' Martha and Simpson exclaimed together.

'Well, I need to be in Manchester on Monday,' Blincoe explained, 'and I thought if we had the wedding here, we could invite people we knew.'

No one there in the cottage at Littonslack knew whether getting married the next day was possible. Martha and Blincoe knew nothing at all, and Simpson knew only a little; he had some vague idea that *banns* had to be read out in church, but he wasn't sure and he suggested they go and see Parson Brown, especially as they would need him to conduct the ceremony.

The young couple found Parson Brown in the church at Tideswell.

'I think it's a wedding,' whispered Martha. 'We should watch; we might learn what goes on.'

Brown stood at the front with a couple facing him, and behind them was a huddle of people sat on the immediate pews. Martha and Blincoe sat on the back row, but they were so far away, they struggled to hear what the parson was saying.

'I require and charge you both, as ye will answer at the dreadful day of judgement, when the secrets of all hearts shall be disclosed, that if either of you know of any impediment, why ye may not be lawfully joined together in matrimony, ye do now confess it.'

'I can barely hear,' Martha whispered. 'Let's move forward.'

They moved forward, to about halfway down the church, and quietly sat down again.

'Samuel Isaac Slater. Wilt thou have this woman to thy wedded wife, to live together after God's ordinance, in the holy estate of matrimony? Wilt thou love her, comfort her, honour and keep her in sickness and in health; and forsaking all others, keep thee only unto her, so long as ye both shall live?'

Sam answered very confidently, 'I will.'

Martha and Blincoe were holding hands, and Blincoe whispered to Martha, 'I will.'

Martha squeezed his hand and whispered in his ear, 'I will too.' She then bit his ear, and they spent the next few minutes trying not to giggle.

Blincoe and Martha had no idea who the parson was marrying today and consequently no idea of the relationships, past and present, of all those involved. At that moment, their only interest was for each other, and exactly who Samuel Isaac Slater, and Kezia Abigail Roebotham were, was of no concern.

Blincoe and Martha followed the wedding out of the church, but always at a safe distance. There was a lot of handshaking and talking as they waited. Eventually an older woman handed over a baby to the now married Kezia, and the crowd slowly disappeared. Parson Brown made his way back towards the church and Blincoe with little time to play with, approached him.

'Sir, we want to get married,' Blincoe said.

'And we're not quite sure what we need to do,' Martha added.

'Come into the church, Brown said. 'We can sit in there and talk. Robert and Martha isn't it?'

Blincoe and Martha told their story and explained how, and why, they hoped to be married this weekend. He liked Blincoe, and when he heard the end of Blincoe's story, which included how he hoped he would be a much better employer than Needham had been, Brown warmed to him more.

'Getting married tomorrow is not straightforward; there are a few problems, Brown began. 'I'm not sure whether it will be possible, but let us see. How old are you both?'

'Fifteen,' Blincoe said.

'Fifteen,' Martha said.

'At fifteen, I need the consent of a parent or guardian. I presume, Martha, that your father is happy about this?'

'Yes he is.'

'Now, Robert? You have no parents I believe?'

'No sir.'

'And your guardian for the last few years, Mr Needham, is no longer your guardian.'

'Martha's dad, Mr Simpson, he's been my boss for the last few years,' Blincoe said.

'And do you think he would consent to your marrying Martha?' Brown asked.

'Of course. Yes,' Blincoe said. Blincoe was a little lost as to why the question was being asked; if Simpson was happy to let Martha marry him, he wasn't likely to object to him marrying Martha!

'The second problem is the most difficult one. Now, it is normal to have the banns read in church on the three Sundays before the marriage. The purpose of the banns is to give anyone the opportunity to raise any legal objection; this helps prevent marriages taking place that are not legal. Now there is an alternative to the banns, and this is to obtain a licence, which, as it happens, I can sanction, but there is a bond to be signed, and I'm afraid to say, a fee of twenty-five shillings.'

Brown assumed that the cost of the bond would put an end to the entire plan, but Blincoe stood up, emptied one of his pockets and counted out the money. Brown felt guilty taking this amount from the youngsters, and wouldn't have taken it, but it was the law, and the money did not go to him.

'The final obstacle, is that I am getting married myself tomorrow at two o'clock in the afternoon, and so if I was to marry you, it would need to be in the morning, say half past ten. Would that suit?'

Martha and Blincoe looked at each other and nodded.

'Do I have to pay you for the wedding sir?' Blincoe asked.

'No, that won't be necessary,' Brown replied.

On the way back to the vicarage to sign the papers, another thought occurred to Brown.

'We're having a little celebration on the vicarage lawn after our wedding,' Brown said. 'If you want to celebrate your marriage at the same time, you would be most welcome!'

Thirty Six

SATURDAY 31ST AUGUST 1799
TIDESWELL

For the last time Blincoe woke up to the Litton mill bell. He didn't need to be up this early, but lying in bed was not really an option as most other apprentices were getting up to go to their work, and in any case he was too excited to stay there. Blincoe would leave the mill this morning for his wedding at half-past ten, and he had no plans to return. He had little in the way of possessions to take with him: he had no money to collect, as he had never trusted the mill with it; he had no wage to collect this week, as he had hardly been there, apart from sleeping and the occasional meal and he had no indenture to collect as at fifteen, he was still almost six years away from completing his apprenticeship. All he had were clothes. He had his best clothes, which today he would wear, as on this occasion there was no doubt about which set to put on, and that just left some other odds and ends of work clothes, and although these were almost rags, they were all he had. He washed under the pump for the last time, dressed in his Sunday best and stuffed his remaining clothes into a sack. That was it. He was done with the place. He didn't bother with breakfast, and he didn't say goodbye to anyone; he just walked confidently through the mill gates.

The day before though, he has said a few goodbyes. After Blincoe and Martha had obtained their marriage licence, and after they had quickly gone through what would happen in the service with Parson Brown, they returned to Littonslack where Simpson immediately gave then two pounds as a wedding present.

'I want you to use this and stay in a hotel in Buxton on your wedding night,' he said. 'I hear *The Hall* is very good. I'm going to sort out a horse and cart to get you there too. What's left you can put towards whatever you need to get you started in your new home.'

His gift was both kind and thoughtful, as at Buxton, they were on the Manchester Road and from there, they could easily get to Manchester by Monday. Blincoe went back to the mill to say goodbyes and invite friends to the wedding; Martha went to Cressbrook mill to do the same and Simpson went down the row of cottages to invite neighbours.

Blincoe invited Moss and Durant, his closest friends and a few other apprentices. He only invited apprentices, as there were no adults, other than Simpson, that he got on with. Mr Palfrey, the carpenter, had treated him fairly, but as a neighbour of Simpson's, he was getting an invite anyway. Martha did the same at Cressbrook mill, inviting her friends Jane, Charlotte, Mary and Alice. Simpson knocked on all the doors at Littonslack, except for the Woodwards'.

But when Martha returned from the mill at Cressbrook, she found her father in tears.

'What is it?' she asked.

He was sitting in his chair and she knelt down and held his hands.

'I'm just getting upset for nothing,' he said.

It sounded like an explanation, but made no sense to Martha. People didn't cry for nothing. It was a while before anyone spoke.

'Have a look in your bedroom,' Simpson said.

Martha ran upstairs and laid out on her bed was her mam's ivory wedding dress. She recognised the dress, as she had once been given a very painful thrashing when, as a very young girl, she had been found trying it on. But this time the dressing up would be real. She then understood, and then she too started crying. Back downstairs, the two of them held each other and cried together.

'We better stop this,' Simpson gasped between tears. 'Tomorrow is going to be the best day of your life.'

Eventually they calmed down and managed to talk about the wedding.

'Mrs Palfrey is coming later,' Simpson said, 'to make sure the dress fits right and make any changes, but I'm going out now as I need to see a man about a horse and cart.'

Simpson left, knowing that he could call in a favour. He was determined that Martha would arrive at the church and leave for her wedding night in grand style.

Blincoe walked up the hill with his sack of clothes on his shoulder and the mill behind him. After walking for just a minute or so, he turned and took one last look at the mill, but there were no fond feelings for the place, or any emotion of any sort; he was now only looking to his future. Apart from a couple of friends, there was nothing good about the place. In any case, the mill was finished, and he was sure that in a few days' time, the gates would be locked for good. In fact, it would be the following Monday afternoon when the workforce were gathered in the mill yard and sent home; by then Blincoe and Martha would be absorbed in their new lives in Manchester, and Ellen and Parson Brown would be on their way to Clapham.

At Littonslack, Simpson was up early and busy telling himself that whatever happened today, he must not break down.

'It will be a happy day,' he muttered to himself, but his emotions were all mixed up, and he was finding this day very difficult. Martha came down an hour later. It was still early, but by then Simpson had talked himself into a better frame of mind.

‘I’ve been thinking,’ he said. ‘If I’m going to go back to Perth to lodge with my brother, then I have no need of most of what is in this house, and it doesn’t make any sense for me to be throwing away the very same things you will need to buy! So after the wedding, I’m going to pack up everything here. I’ll borrow a horse and cart, and drop everything off with you in Manchester. If you can just get by until mid-week, then I can bring you everything then, even the best china!

Blincoe was also early. He was in Tideswell many hours before his wedding was due to take place, and after hiding his sack of clothes behind an overgrown gravestone, he wandered around Tideswell exploring little lanes and alleys that he had never seen before. Just before ten o’clock, Moss and Durant arrived, and he chatted nervously to them. Shortly after that, Parson Brown arrived and Blincoe went in to the church, only to become even more nervous. The guests slowly trickled in. There was Mrs Palfrey and another neighbour from Littonslack. One of Martha’s friends, Alice, came; the others could not get out of work, and two other boys arrived from Litton mill and joined Moss and Durant, making up what Parson Brown later called ‘the noisy pew.’

Blincoe’s wedding service might have passed unnoticed, with the local Tideswell people missing it altogether, but there were advantages being married on the same day as Parson Brown. Not only were Blincoe’s party invited to the vicarage, but Brown had arranged for the church bells to be rung, and from ten o’clock they rang out across the town bringing a late flurry of people from Tideswell, mainly those who never missed a wedding! Under the din of the bells, Blincoe was relieved to see that there were no grown-ups from the mill; the last thing he wanted to see today was Woodward’s face, or any reminder of his bad times there.

Unseen by Blincoe, Martha arrived in a cart, which Simpson and some neighbours had dressed. There were flowers on the front and back and even some on the horses head; the wooden bench seats were draped in white sheets, and pink bows had been tied here and there. As soon as Martha came in the church, Blincoe's nervousness vanished. It wasn't that he feared she wouldn't come, but when he saw her, looking so beautiful in that ivory dress, he just relaxed, and when she moved up the church to stand by his side, he could not have been happier.

Blincoe and Martha sniggered a little during the service, especially when Blincoe gave a very stern look and nodded in agreement when Brown said, 'Wilt thou obey him?' But trying to maintain a serious expression became worse when Parson Brown produced the rings. The couple had discussed this matter the day before with Simpson.

'Leave it to me,' Simpson said, 'but don't expect gold or silver. I'll get something that will do for the service though.'

The priest offered the rings that Simpson had given to him, but they were just iron rings. Blincoe recognised them immediately as the washers, under which he had hid his money since coming to the mill. Blincoe began to smile, and he glanced at Simpson, and then they were both smiling. Before long, Blincoe was struggling not to laugh out loud, and as he looked at Martha's ring and tried to repeat, *With this ring I thee wed,* his replies to the parson came out a good octave higher than normal!

Rice and wheat were thrown on the couple, and Simpson, who was still smiling and actually coping with today much better than he had feared, told their guests that they were all welcome for a drink on him at the New George. Parson Brown politely declined, explaining that he ought to be clear-headed for his own wedding, but again invited everyone to the vicarage party later.

At the same time as Martha was standing in the church and becoming Mrs Blincoe, the preparation for the later wedding was taking place. At the Red Lion, Molly was keeping busy by worrying, fussing, and harassing anyone in her vicinity; she was rushing about, organising everyone, checking everything, losing things and forgetting things, but most importantly enjoying every minute of it!

The scene at the vicarage could not have been more different; everything was much calmer. Brown was dressed, and although he was nervous, there was no outward show of this. The man with the honour, as he later said it was, of marrying Brown, was the parson from the neighbouring parish of Eyam, Charles Hargrave. Hargrave would be taking over some of Brown's duties so it seemed appropriate for him to be there today. Brown had no other close friends there, although until the last month or so, he would have had Needham at his side, but the combination of Litton mill's problems and that Brown was marrying the woman Needham wanted, made this all impossible, and Needham sat at home. In fact, neither Needham nor Newton, both of whom had been invited, showed at the church or the party. Newton was Ellen's cousin, and was expected to be there, but he had not been seen for the last fortnight. When he had left, he claimed he was going on a business trip to York, but the rumour was that he was heartbroken following his rejection by Ellen and unable to concentrate on the cotton business, he had gone to Lichfield to seek some comfort with his literary friends. Lydia though, Newton's sister, was there; she was there as Ellen's bridesmaid.

Brown looked at Ellen in the church, and he had no doubt he was marrying the most beautiful woman he had ever seen and intellectually she was his equal. He was very happy and as expected, he delivered his lines perfectly.

After the weddings, the two wedding parties merged on the vicarage lawn, with Molly rushing around, now in charge of serving ale and wine. The talk was initially of weddings, dresses, cotton mills, and those missing from the scene.

'It's a shame Mr Needham and Mr Newton couldn't come,' Ellen said. 'They are strange people though.' She looked at her husband. 'Did I ever tell you, their proposition speeches were identical? Word for word the same!'

Brown took a step back and raised his voice slightly, 'Ellen, I have watched you closely over these last few months, and you must have noticed how passionately I admire and love you.'

Ellen recognised the words. She had last heard them spoken by Needham and Newton.

'I don't understand,' Ellen said.

Brown paused to give her time to work it out, but she didn't.

'I wrote their speeches!' Brown said and laughed.

'Of course,' he went on, 'I didn't want to make the speeches, too convincing!'

Until Kezia had revealed the truth about Samuel's father, Brown was resolute that he would not pursue Ellen. But Brown had been forced to watch as Needham and Newton worked out their strategies for courting her. The mill owners behaved in their usual ruthless, selfish and single-minded ways on this matter, and to further insult Brown, they each asked him for help with their marriage proposals. It occurred to him that the proposals might sound much the same; they both claimed to be wealthy, both were land owners, both would claim to be pillars of the community, they were of similar age, and so on. It was at the point when he was wondering how he could make the proposals different, without favouring one or the other, when the idea came to him: they would be the same. Exactly the same! He wrote the proposals with little care, except the care taken to make sure that the two copies were identical. Brown considered they had brought it on themselves, and after all, it was only an elaborate joke, although perhaps there was a hint of revenge. Fate then played further into his hands as he found out that Needham and Newton were both planning to propose the very same day at Cressbrook mill.

'I hardly think that was the action of a true friend,' Ellen said. 'It appears to me that you didn't want them to succeed.' She then feared that she was getting a little too serious, and so slapped him in a playful way; he spilt some of his drink, and then they both laughed. They then returned to talk to their guests, but Brown's ears pricked up when he heard Martha's father talking about Ellis.

'I'll bring Ellis with me too; you can have him as an extra wedding present,' Simpson said. 'I don't know how I forgot him.'

Brown looked at his drink as though it might have been drugged.

'It sounds like you've got plenty of room for him,' Simpson continued, 'and he'll need slaughtering in November. Robert will be alright doing that, won't you?'

Blincoe didn't answer; he had seen the Parson's confusion and as Simpson became more excited about Ellis, Blincoe quickly explained to the parson that Ellis was a pig.

'So all Ellises will be gone from my life by November,' Blincoe said. 'I'll raise a glass to that and I hope Needham rots in Hell!'

'I think that's a wee harsh on the man,' Simpson said, and I don't want to spoil this occasion, but when you've been left here a while, have a think about Needham. Think about how he behaved, how he ran his business, the decisions he must have had to make and whereas the fellow will never be my friend, I think he probably did his best. He was committed to that mill and whatever he did, he always tried to keep the mill going, and he lost all his money doing that.'

This time Blincoe was the one to prevent the conversation becoming too serious as he quickly ended the Needham conversation.

'I'll think about that, sometime,' Blincoe said, 'but not today!'

The two wedding parties then began to mingle properly.

'Did you two meet in the mill?' Ellen asked, of Blincoe and Martha.

'Aye we're both mill workers,' Martha said, avoiding explaining that they were each at different mills, 'it's been a bit up and down at times, but it had its fun moments. Once,

Robbie was imprisoned in the coal-shed at the mill, and I delivered some pie with a love note attached.'

She smiled at Blincoe, but Blincoe looked surprised. 'I enjoyed the pie,' he said. 'I remember that very well, but it was pitch black in that coal-shed, and I never saw any note! What did it say?'

'I can't remember now, just something nice.'

'The things I never knew!' Blincoe said.

The talk moved away from the past and present, away from Needham, Newton and cotton mills and to the future. The talk, especially amongst the two new couples was of change, what they could give and what the future might look like. The Browns wanted to legislate, to ban and eradicate the practices of the past, and the Blincoe's were all set to embrace those changes. Certainly, there was an air of optimism and slowly, very slowly, the tide was turning. There was a growing understanding that there must be a better way to treat workers, whether they are slaves in a different country, or child slaves in the factories of Britain. Blincoe, Martha, Parson Brown and Ellen stood together in the Vicarage garden and raised their glasses to a better and fairer future.

Also by Stuart Courtman

Robert Blincoe and the Cotton Trade
Author: Stuart Courtman
ISBN: 9781907219283
Format: Paperback

A Memoir of Robert Blincoe' published in 1832 was influential in improving the working conditions of children in factories. It is also believed that Charles Dickens based his character Oliver Twist on Robert Blincoe. This book contains the original full 1828 text of the memoir by John Brown and historical notes by the author, Stuart Courtman. The historical notes give information on the influences that led to the development of mechanised cotton production and notes on the political and economic changes that shaped the industry; some detail on how children were treated in the workhouses and mills; and background on the anti-slavery movements.

Other Peak Platform Titles

Gandhi: From Monu to Mahatma
Author: Bolwar Mahamad Kunhi
ISBN: 9781907219511
Format: Paperback

This is a story of a great visionary and freedom fighter of India, Mahatma Gandhi. The narration of the evolution of Gandhi is simple, straight-forward, unembellished but never simplistic. It is written for children but when an adult reads it the child in him is alive again. The Mahatma also had kept the child Monu alive in himself until he died as a martyr. This is a unique biography of a great visionary of our times. English translation of Kendriya Sahitya Academy Award winning Kannada title: 'Papu Gandhi Bapu Gandhi Aada Kathe'.

About Bolwar Mahamad Kunhi

Bolwar Mahamad Kunhi (born 1951) resides in Karnataka in India. He writes in Kannada, the official language of the State, with a literary tradition going back a thousand years. A postgraduate with a gold medal in Kannada literature, he has written eight collections of short stories, a novel, two stage plays and six children's books.

Goodbye Old Chap: a life at sea in peace and war
Author: Philip Algar
ISBN: 9781907219047
Format: Paperback

This is the story of Philip Algar's father, Stanley, a Merchant Navy Captain, and his life at sea which spanned two world wars and a long period of imprisonment in Germany. Philip has added much social, economic, military and political research to provide the background to his father's diaries and the book contains fascinating details of a dramatic century which is already fleeing into history.

About Philip Algar

Philip Algar, B.Sc. (Econ.) F.I.J., has written five previous books. For many years, as a freelance editor and writer, he contributed regularly to UK and overseas publications on energy, economics and crisis management. He also wrote a regular and humorous column, on business topics, for a national newspaper and for a business magazine, but is now concentrating on writing books.

Red, White and Khaki: The Story of the Only Wartime FA Cup Final
Author: Matthew Bell
ISBN: 9781907219177
Format: Paperback

When, on April 24th 1915, Sheffield United captain George Utley lifted the FA Cup, it brought to a close one of the most controversial football seasons in history. The same day, thousands of allied troops were killed or injured in a German poison gas attack near Ypres. The two contrasting scenes underlined the fierce debate that had endured for many months about the continuation of professional football whilst innumerable young men were being sacrificed in the name of freedom and democracy.

Matthew Bell is a mechanical engineer by trade but spends every spare moment writing about Sheffield United. He has edited the United fanzine, 'Flashing Blade' for over twenty years and has written a weekly column in the Green 'Un since 1993. He was co-editor of 'Blades Tales' and 'Blades Tales 2'

Sonny: The Truth Between the Lines
Author: Gordon Wallace
ISBN: 9781907219290
Format: Paperback

Non-fiction and based on the life (and death) of a First World War soldier, 'Sonny' Boothroyd, a volunteer soldier who was killed in a trench raid on Boxing Day 1917. It includes extracts from the letters he wrote to his mother from the battlefields. Some of these deal with issues not likely to be found in any books about the First War, usually focusing on the machinations of senior politicians and military commanders.

About Gordon Wallace

A freelance writer for over 30 years. A radio documentary 'Just A Few Lines' based on the letters of a First War soldier was scripted by him and broadcast by BBC Radio. His short story 'Picture in a Junk Shop' has also been broadcast by BBC Radio 4. He is a Churchill Fellow. and married to the artist, Mary Louise Coulouris. They live in Linlithgow near Edinburgh, but spend much of the year on the Greek island of Hydra.

344 - Inspired by the Diaries of Elizabeth Gore 1844-1923: Pretoria Pit Disaster Lancashire
Author: Andrea Jane Finney
ISBN:
Format: Paperback

Andrea's story, with the help of her great, great grandmother's diary, covers three generations of the Gore family in Lancashire, England from the late 19th to the early 20th century. It covers the tragic loss of Elizabeth's son in the Pretoria Pit disaster of 1910, when 344 men and boys lost their lives and tells of the hardships faced by the family, of tragedy and loss to people already struggling with life. Further research took Andrea into the archives of the 'Bolton News' and reports of the disaster form the second part of the book. Andrea has captured the taste of the time, and we have the privilege of tasting it too, Jack bait and all.

About Andrea Jane Finney

Andrea Jane Finney (nee Shaw) was born in 1966 in the village of Westhoughton, Bolton, Lancashire. She attended Westhoughton High School and then Bolton College. Andrea is married to Nigel and has one son, Alex and a black labrador called Holly.